Tyrant of
the Mind

Also by Priscilla Royal

Wine of Violence
Sorrow Without End

Tyrant of
the Mind

Priscilla Royal

Poisoned Pen Press

Poisoned Pen Press
6962 E. First Ave., Ste. 103
Scottsdale, AZ 85251
www.poisonedpenpress.com
info@poisonedpenpress.com

Printed in the United States of America

"Thou tyrant, tyrant Jealousy,
Thou tyrant of the mind!"

John Dryden, *Love Triumphant:*
Act 3, Sc. 1, "Song of Jealousy", 1694.

To Henie Lentz
For so much but especially giving me focus

Acknowledgments

Every Other Thursday Night critique group: Bonnie DeClark, Liz Hartka, Anne Maczulak, Sheldon Siegel, and Meg Stiefvater. Whatever would I do without your friendship and honesty!

Peter Goodhugh for all you have done to make this wonderful experience possible.

Ed Kaufman, owner of "M Is for Mystery" in San Mateo, CA, for encouragement and for making my first book signing such a pleasant experience.

Barbara Peters for being the ideal editor, Robert Rosenwald for being the publisher writers dream of having, and to Monty Montee, Marilyn Pizzo, Jennifer Semon, and J.J. Smith-Moore for all you have done to make the publishing process a joy. I can never thank you all enough!

Elaine and Bill Petrocelli and the staff of Book Passage in Corte Madera, CA, for creating an independent bookstore which should go down in history for its innovative classes and conferences.

Bonnie DeClark, Esta Fischer, Carol Haskins, Jill Hollander, Shirley Humphrey, Mary Anne Johnson, Dianne Levy, Marianne Silva, Sharon Silva, Lyn and Michael Speakman, and Barbara Truax. Thank you for spreading the word, being supportive, and giving me photos and books. I appreciate you all so much!

Chapter One

Brother Thomas shattered the film of ice in the basin with the edge of his hand, then gingerly splashed the freezing water into his eyes, rubbing them clean of the gritty residue of his sleepless night. Father Anselm, the resident priest of Wynethorpe Castle, whose room he had been invited to share, must have already left to perform Mass, he thought, running his wet hands down his cheeks to soften the thick auburn stubble. He winced with the stinging cold. Although he had always been a fastidious man, today he hated the idea of scraping his flesh clean of beard. The morning had such a piercing chill.

"I am growing soft," the young monk muttered as he reached for a curved razor. Despite his loathing for the desolation of Tyndal, a priory on the North Sea coast where he had lived since last summer, he had never lacked for warm water there when it came time for his weekly shave. Faced with these more spartan conditions, he realized he had grown quite used to those previously unacknowledged comforts in recent months. With irony-tinged amusement, he found himself longing for Tyndal.

"Fuck!" he said, cutting himself. His penance for missing Mass, he decided, as he grabbed a thin shard of ice from the basin and held it against the wound until the numbing water ran clear of pink blood. With a wry twitch of his mouth, Thomas quietly thanked his Saxon friends from the village near the priory for teaching him some of their more colorful words. His own

Anglo-Norman tongue often lacked the hard sound that was so satisfying in such frustrating moments.

Bloodied but clean-shaven, Thomas left the comparative warmth of Father Anselm's room, walked down the torturously curved stone steps past the great hall, and emerged into the chaos of an early morning in the inner ward of a working castle. As a child, he had spent time in one of his father's castles, but this godforsaken pile of rock bore no resemblance to that. Wynethorpe was not only cramped for space, it also had the dubious distinction of lying in the wilds along the Welsh border. A primitive place for cert, but Thomas knew he had only himself to blame for being here.

Wynethorpe belonged to his prioress' father, the Baron Adam, and, when illness in the family demanded that Prioress Eleanor journey back to her secular home, Thomas had agreed to accompany her. At the time he had done so with great eagerness. His spirits had lifted at the thought of new sights, and he was willing to do almost anything to get away from the fogs and fish stench of the East Anglian coast. Had he known he would be exchanging one bleak landscape only for another, he might have hesitated. Then again, perhaps not. At least no scent of dying seaweed filled the air here. He smiled to himself. Perhaps the Wynethorpe family had some partiality for barbaric places like Wales and East Anglia, but he would always long for the more civilized delights of London.

He paused to look around. They had been here only a few days and he had had little time to accustom himself to the place. In such a small fortress, most suited to repelling wild Welshmen, only a fool stumbled around blindly unless he fancied being knocked to the ground by a harried servant or whacked on the head by a soldier swinging a pike. He looked around for a clear path through the turmoil.

Havoc reigned here indeed, he thought as he looked around for a safe path to the kitchen where he might find bread and ale to break his fast. To his left, fires already glowed from the blacksmith's forge and the clashing of hammers on red-hot iron would soon increase the dissonant and deafening din. Men were herding squealing swine toward the narrow gates and low wooden bridge that led to the woods and acorn forage. On his other side, women maneuvered around beasts and men alike. Some hurried with backs bent from huge armloads of laundry; others walked, fingers white from the cold as they struggled with heavy buckets of well water. A flock of geese, cackling in outraged protest, scattered from under their feet as the women rushed to get out of the cold.

Although snow white as the Virgin's linen had fallen in the night, the once lacy flakes had since melted into multicolored muck and were mixed with matter of such foul origin that Thomas did not care to think on it. As he stepped cautiously into the open ward, he felt his feet begin to grow numb. The ground was too cold for his thin-soled low shoes. If he did not take care, he would slip and find himself flying into barnyard filth. He would never make a countryman, he decided, as he had oft done since his involuntary exile far away from his beloved city. He shifted from one foot to another, stretched his muscles to bring back some feeling, and yearned for thick leather boots.

The watch shift was changing. Two short lines of common soldiers in quilted, stuffed tunics and kettle-shaped metal helmets passed each other without speaking. A grim-faced, chain mail-clad sergeant accompanied each group. Thomas noted that the men who had finished their shift walked more quickly than those who were heading for the icy walls. Aye, he thought with a smile, those lucky ones could look forward to a hot fire, warm bread to break their fast, and soft straw to lie in, with or without the comfort of some woman beside them. Thomas had never been a military man, but he had grown up with those whose lives were centered in war and thus could judge, with some knowledge and appreciation, how well Baron Adam of Wynethorpe had maintained the discipline of his soldiers.

Methinks my father would approve, he decided as he watched the precision with which the men kept to their lines despite the civilian disorder around them. Briefly he speculated on how well his father might know Baron Adam. With greater brevity he wondered if his father, an earl of some note, knew or even cared that his son was at Wynethorpe. With an abrupt shake of his head, Thomas banished the latter question with customary speed. Indeed, Baron Adam had done well in maintaining the castle as a working fortress. Apart from keeping the temporarily quiet Welsh in check—a breed most likely to do almost any thing at any time, he thought with a snort—civil strife in England still drew fresh blood. Although it was now 1271 and Simon de Montfort had been dead for over six years, pockets of rebellion still smoldered in secret, sometimes flaring into brief but scorching bonfires. At a time when King Henry III was in failing health and the Lord Edward was off on crusade, it was men like Baron Adam who kept the land calm, however fragile that peace might truly be along the Welsh borderlands or in the heart of England itself.

Thomas slid and struggled to keep upright. As he regained his precarious balance on the frozen ground, he heard loud shouts and the clatter of weapons. From the direction of the gate, where the last of the swine had just disappeared, a pack of barking hounds emerged in a churning pack. Horses massed just behind. A successful hunt, he concluded, catching his breath and watching as the men rode into the open ward, scattering fowl and tradesmen with equal abandon in the pale light of the morning.

Kitchen servants quickly ran to a huntsman who directed them to a skinned and roughly butchered boar as well as several smaller carcasses. As the kill was carried to the kitchen shed, black blood dripped here and there into the brindle slush, adding a pinkish hue.

"You have risen early, brother," one thick-robed hunter called out as he rode up behind his fellows.

"If you followed the Offices of prayer as I must, Robert, you'd have been awake far earlier." Thomas grinned as the man slid from his mount.

"On the contrary, good monk. At Matins, I prayed for a fat deer despite the winter snows. By Terce, God had answered me with a boar and several hare."

Thomas laughed. "Matins, you say? Then you have prayed on horseback while your hounds sang the Office. To find such game when the sun has yet to climb fully above the horizon, you must have been out before dawn!" Although he'd had only brief acquaintance with him, Thomas had quite taken to his prioress' older brother. Like Prioress Eleanor, Robert was in his early twenties, of short stature, and had gray eyes that sparkled with intelligence and humor. Unlike Prioress Eleanor, he was wiry, muscular, and sported a curly black beard.

"God gave me keen sight in the dark hours. A curse, I am, to the hares in winter," Robert replied as he walked up to Thomas. Then all brightness faded from his eyes. "How fares my nephew?" he asked, his voice now hoarse with concern.

"All is well. Sister Anne says that God will spare the child. The crisis has passed, and the boy sleeps well."

Robert spun around. "Elwyn," he shouted to a portly man with the red face of one who spends much time sampling his own sauces. "Make sure the best portion of that boar is saved for my nephew." He gestured at Thomas. "Our good brother tells me Richard is recovering!" When Robert turned back to the monk, his smile was broad and joyous. "God be praised!"

"And Sister Anne. I've never known a more skilled hand in the healing arts." Thomas was about to say more when he noticed a servant tossing aside a branch that had been used to transport the boar. "I need that limb," he cried out, then turned back to Robert as the man brought him the bough. "Between the rich meat of a lusty boar and a stick sturdy enough for me to make your nephew a hobbyhorse for riding through the passageways at Wynethorpe, I do believe he will be both a healthy and a happy boy."

"You are a kind man to think of that." Robert slapped Thomas on the shoulder. "Although we may live to regret your gift. Richard will destroy any peace with his valiant joustings at such imaginary foes as his grandfather's shadow or my cloak. If you are so fortunate, he may even deem you a good replacement for the Welsh dragon. Your red hair might warrant such a conclusion." Robert's look was affectionate, but his gaze was distant. "Despite his youth, he has all the markings of his crusader father."

"Have you word of your elder brother?"

"Hugh may love his family with a whole heart, but he is not known for the diligence with which he sends us messages. We have heard that he is in good health, however, from those to whom he has given generously—returning soldiers, motley friars, and assorted beggars. We are most fortunate that they remember his kindness well and do bring us word of him. Nonetheless, he will not return home until the Lord Edward comes back to England."

Thomas wondered in silence about Robert's future when his elder brother did return. On the way from Tyndal, Prioress Eleanor told him that her father had put this second son in charge of the Wynethorpe lands in Hugh's absence. Robert had shown both inclination and even greater talent for the work, if a loving sister could be considered a fair judge. With the heir's return, however, Thomas knew well that a younger son must find another way to earn his meat.

As if he had read the monk's thoughts, Robert continued. "By the time he does come home, our lord father will have me married off to the Lady Juliana of Lavenham. She comes with enough lands to make me quite rich with her dowry, and those lands are close enough to my father's that I may continue to watch over his as well until Hugh is ready to choose his own steward." He clasped Thomas by the shoulder and shook him affectionately. "Fear not! I am not destined to become your new prior at Tyndal. I'd rather study Walter of Henley's *Husbandry* than the Venerable Bede's instructive writings on abbots and saints. Unlike you, neither Hugh nor I is inclined to a contemplative vocation, good monk. A sister already encloistered provides intercession with God and prayers enough on behalf of this family and its sins!"

Thomas smiled at Robert's assumption that he had entered a cloistered life prompted by any calling whatsoever, but there was no reason to shatter the man's illusion. "You are betrothed then?"

"Almost as we speak, or so I believe. The lady's father and Henry, her eldest brother, came to meet with my father on the contract not long after you, my sister, and her sub-infirmarian arrived to care for my nephew. The Lady Juliana accompanied them for a swift courtship and as companion to her father's wife. Have you not seen the family or passed them in the hall outside your quarters?"

Thomas shook his head.

"How could you not? Lady Juliana has been put in Hugh's empty chambers while her father and his wife have taken my quarters near the stairs. They are near enough to the room you share with our priest. Henry you might not have seen for he and I rest, if such is possible, in the barracks. There is no other accommodation for us over the dining hall."

"At the hours I have walked the halls, the wiser among the living are still in bed and the spirits of the dead have long since returned to Hell. Sister Anne, our prioress, and I have all been with Richard day and night, taking turns with his care until the fever broke. Even our meals were taken in his sick room. Most nights I have watched over the boy to allow the women to sleep."

Robert looked up at the position of the indistinct sun hiding in the graying sky, then motioned toward the great hall. "You will finally meet your fellow guests at today's dinner, for it appears to be within a couple of hours of noon."

Thomas nodded. Then, with a less than monkish grin, he returned to his previous subject: "Is she pleasing to you, your lady?"

Robert shrugged. "She will probably please me as much as I do her. She was an agreeable enough child, as I remember from years ago, but I have seen little of her in recent times." He hesitated. His eyes narrowed. "I know her two brothers better.

I believe she favors her younger brother, in which case we will suit each other well enough. The eldest is a sour, petty-minded man. Henry has done nothing but quarrel with my father over which family shall give what to this happy union." Thomas blinked at the barely concealed resentment in Robert's voice. Before he could question further, both men heard the clatter of more horses' hooves coming across the wooden bridge and turned toward the dark archway of the entrance gate.

"I do believe that the Lavenham family has just returned from their morning ride," Robert said, raising his hand in greeting to the lead horseman. Then his countenance hardened. "Yet I fear their ride was not a pleasant one." His voice dropped to a harsh whisper as he gestured toward the arriving party. "That horse bears a corpse."

Chapter Two

The guttering candle flame competed half-heartedly with dull morning light to chase the shadows from the room. A small, young nun sat on a stool near a large bed, rubbed her hand across her eyes, and began another story.

"Once upon a time, in a sweet land not much different from our own, there lived a happy people, strong-limbed and handsome, who were ruled by a brave and noble king. This king was blessed with a beautiful, loyal wife, and the couple had a son whose name was Richard. Richard was a fine lad, fair-haired and blue-eyed, and he longed to prove he had the courage to become a knight. He had begged his father to take him on crusade to the Holy Land, but his father insisted he was still too young for battle and must stay at home with his mother, the queen. 'You must protect her and her ladies from any and all dangers,' he told the boy. Indeed, the king believed that no peril would threaten his beloved land while he was reclaiming Jerusalem, but he had no sooner ridden away with his army than there appeared at the castle gate, a man dressed in black armor..."

Eleanor Wynethorpe, prioress of Tyndal in the woman-ruled Order of Fontevraud, stopped in mid-tale. The flame from a deeply furrowed candle flickered more weakly now as shadows retreated into the crevices of the rough stone walls in the gray dawn. She looked toward the tall, older nun standing on the other side of the bed and frowned with worry. Only her eyes asked a frightened question in the silence of the room.

Sister Anne bent over the bed where a young boy lay very, very still. As she gently tugged a fur cover up around the child's neck and tucked it loosely around him, she turned to her prioress and smiled.

"Fear not, my lady. Richard's fever has not returned. His sleep may be deep, but it is a healing one. When he awakens, I think he will have good appetite and want more fables from his doting aunt."

Eleanor sighed with relief, then rose from her stool to put some wood into the smoldering hearth to chase the chill out of the air. The smoke from the dying candle, impaled on the iron tripod stand near the boy's bed, had stung her aching eyes, but the tears that started down her cheeks were from joy, not pain.

"I don't know what my family would have done if you had not come with me to Wynethorpe Castle, Anne. Your skill has saved my brother's son. Had Richard died, we all would have grieved deeply, but the news would have killed Hugh more surely than any Saracen arrow. He loves this boy more than his own life."

Sister Anne reached down and wiped a thin film of moisture from the child's forehead with a gentle caress. He smiled in his sleep. "Out of friendship even more than duty, I would go with you no matter where you wished, Eleanor, but I needed no urging when you told me that your nephew was gravely ill and your father had asked for my insignificant skills." Her expression softened as she looked at the boy. "Indeed, your brother has been blessed with a sweet child."

Eleanor walked to the nun's side and put her arm around her waist. Anne, who was much taller than her prioress, put her arm around her shoulders and the women hugged. As Eleanor well knew, the saving of this young life had special meaning to her friend, whose own son had died despite her best efforts. They stood in silence for a long moment and watched as the boy continued to breathe easily in the huge bed.

"Your expertise is not insignificant, Anne. My aunt at Amesbury told me that your reputation has reached the court. As proof, my father has certainly heard of your talent. How ever shall I thank you for saving my nephew's life?" Eleanor whispered. "Richard may be my brother's by-blow, but Hugh adores this child as much as if he had been born of a lawful wife. As do we all. My lord father even gave up his own bed and room when the boy sickened." She chuckled. "He softens like silk whenever the boy throws his arms around his legs. In a year or two, when Richard is old enough for such training, I swear he will beg the king to take him as a page at court so he will not suffer any separation from the boy."

"What will happen to Richard when your eldest brother returns from the Holy Land and must marry?" Sister Anne's eyes turned sad with the question as she looked down at the lad.

"Hugh knows his duty to beget legitimate heirs, but he will tarry to the fulfilling of it. In truth, he is such a chaste Sir Galahad we were amazed when he presented us with this boy as his own babe. Even our father couldn't believe that he took enough time away from warrior sports to sire a son." Eleanor smiled. "Neither of my brothers has been in a hurry to wed. Even Robert's greatest love has been taking care of the estates. The land has always been his wife and he has shown no more inclination to be false to her than Hugh has to his knighthood. Our parents did breed a monkish brood, although my brothers, both, would deny it."

"What of Richard's mother? Is she dead then?"

"So we understood. My brother said little about the mother but much about how he doted on this boy of his. You'd think none but he had ever fathered a child before. But marry he must, and Hugh will do well by Richard even when he has legitimate heirs. His wife will have to love the child too. He has our father's stubbornness and will have naught to do with any woman who would not treat Richard as a child of her own body."

Anne nodded. "Then God has blessed the boy with a good and loving family. It is not always so. Still it would be hard not to love the child. He shows such a sweet disposition and more grave courtesy than one would expect of such youth. Even at the height of his fever, he was never peevish. He wins hearts quickly."

She laughed softly. "Indeed, when I told Brother Thomas of Richard's recovery, he smiled with such joy I knew he was quite taken with the boy as well. He was always eager to relieve you on the storytelling." She lowered her voice. "Although I thought you told the better ones. You must tell me later what happened after the man in black armor arrived."

"I don't know myself! I have exhausted all the tales I heard as a child and was beginning to invent them. Not having the talent of Marie de France, I was most grateful Brother Thomas knew stories I had never heard."

"He once told me he came from London. Perhaps they have tales there we have yet to hear?"

Eleanor shook her head. "We are not so removed from the latest songs and stories at Tyndal, methinks, and my father has but recently been with the king in Westminster. Surely he would have heard the latest. But come, we must tell him the happy news about his grandson."

As they pushed open the thick wooden door, it creaked loudly. A round woman, lying in a warm pile of clean straw just outside the door, started awake. She struggled awkwardly to her feet, brushing broken bits of yellow from her robes.

"My lady?"

Eleanor smiled. "He will live, good nurse."

The woman wiped a plump hand across her reddened eyes. "May God be thanked!" she said, raising her eyes to the wooden ceiling. Then turning to Sister Anne, "And for the skills He gave you, sister. May I tend the lad now? Is there anything I should watch for? Is he sleeping? Can he eat?" Her words, spoken in one breath of air, collided, one on top of the other.

"You may watch for a ravenously hungry boy when he awakens," Anne laughed. "Give him what he wants but in small amounts and only after he takes the medicine I left in the footless mazer cup by his bed. It has a bitter taste. He will hate it. Later he may have some sugar for his chest but may not have both the bitter and sweet too close together."

The nurse frowned. Little pink worry lines puckered the white skin between her brows. "Just tell him that Sir Gawain would have taken the draught without complaint," Eleanor said. "Should he question the word of a mere aunt, tell him that I will send Brother Thomas to confirm what I have said."

"Aye, my lady, that should help him with the bitterness. He has grown quite fond of Brother Thomas and brightens when the good priest comes to care for him. A fine storyteller, he is, the kind brother! Indeed," she continued with a healthy blush and a fluttering hand to her ample breast, "he became like a mighty warrior himself when he told his tales of knightly deeds."

Eleanor smiled in sympathy at the betrayal of color in the nurse's face. Indeed, her own heart still beat with too much enthusiasm at the sight of the tall, broad-shouldered monk. When he had first come to Tyndal, just after her own arrival, an unchaste heat had quite suffused her loins and lingered there far longer than was seemly for a woman dedicated to chastity. Although she had tried to cool her passions with abstinence from meat as well as prayer while lying face down on the stones in Tyndal's church, she had not succeeded in quelling the lusty fires with the finality she had implored. She had met with more success on the icy floor of this castle chapel but even that had failed to banish her desire entirely.

She would certainly have preferred that some other monk accompany her and Sister Anne to Wynethorpe Castle, but her prior at Tyndal was in poor health and the man she might have chosen instead was the one best suited to remaining as sub-prior. Then Sister Anne had suggested that Thomas would be a good choice to help care for the boy. Based on his work with her in Tyndal's hospital, she knew of his talents with the young. When Eleanor at last mentioned the possibility to him, she saw his keenness for the trip. She could only acquiesce, having no good reason to refuse him. None, at least, that she dared explain.

Now she was glad he had been with them. Richard had so taken to the monk that she was willing to suffer the all too frequent torture, however sweet a torment it might be, of lusty dreams in return for her nephew's faster healing. When she returned to Tyndal, her confessor would be much burdened to come up with sufficient atonement for her sins of the flesh, but he was a kind and wise man. The penance he ordered might be hard, but it would be both just and humane.

The sound of running feet burst through Eleanor's musings. A young page raced breathlessly through the entrance to the circular stairwell at the end of the passageway and skidded to a stop just in front of her.

"Breathe, lad," she exclaimed. "Is all well with my father and brother?"

"Your lord father did not say otherwise, my lady," the boy replied as he tried to force his soft features into a more mature expression of solemnity, "but he does ask that you attend him in the great hall forthwith."

Chapter Three

A shrill cry pierced the icy air. One serving woman dropped her armload of laundry and rushed to the horse bearing the dead man. As she grasped the head of the corpse, it twisted around at an unnatural angle. The eyes that now stared up at her were blank, unknowing.

Falling to her knees in the melting mud, she began to rhythmically beat her breast with one clenched fist as her animal wailing spiraled heavenward. Although many quickly whispered prayers to God, those for whom the sharp keening echoed in their souls knew that only time or death would bring this woman peace.

From behind him, Thomas heard a deeper pitched moan of pain. He spun around and saw a young horseman, round-faced and clean-shaven, kicking out at a gray-haired servant who was offering to help him dismount. The man's booted foot struck the elder so hard in the shoulder that the servant staggered backward, falling into yellowed slush. Shouting with ill-concealed impatience for a groomsman to take his horse, the rider swung out of the saddle, then stomped past the old servant who was struggling to his knees.

"That is Henry," Robert said.

"Such cruelty to a helpless old man is inconsistent with his knighthood vow to be honorable in his dealings with the weak."

Robert's laugh was without humor. "Knight? Nay, he may be heir to the title and lands of Lavenham, but he will never earn his own knighthood. Henry lacks the stomach for courage, unless his adversary's back is turned, and you see how he treats those of lesser birth."

Thomas clenched his fists, wishing he could forget his vocation and give the Lord Henry a direct lesson in the nature of pain.

"But forgive and excuse me, good monk. I must speak with Sir Geoffrey. That corpse is a man whom my father long valued for his good service. I am owed an explanation of how Hywel came so soon to his mortal fate."

"For cert," Thomas replied, forcing his hands into the sleeves of his robe.

With a nod, Robert strode off toward the riders, his boots crunching loudly against the ice-encrusted ground and his hot breath whitening the air with a muttered oath.

Thomas started forward as well, then thought the better of it. He was, after all, a guest and a stranger at Wynethorpe Castle. If he were needed, he would be summoned.

As Robert drew near the party, Thomas saw a second horseman nod a greeting. This man was of middle years, Thomas noted, his beard gray and tinted with only a light remembrance of brown. Tanned even in winter, his lean and hawkish face was deeply lined. He waved the servant offering a hand aside with some grace, then shouted to Henry to come to him. As he bent forward, he hooked his elbow and forearm around the pommel of his saddle and swung awkwardly to the ground, landing slightly off balance. He righted himself with dignity. There was only empty space where his right hand should have been.

Henry approached with reluctance, his face quite flushed as he pointed to the corpse. "I had naught to do with that," he yelled, directing his words to one of the two women in the party. Then glaring at Robert, he continued. "The man got in my way on the path. I slapped his steed to move him back and the beast threw him. Indeed, I might have been the one injured had I not done so! I cannot be blamed for the man's incompetence with a horse."

Robert pointedly ignored Henry. "Sir Geoffrey," he said with a bow to the elder. The latter put his handless arm around the younger man's shoulders, turned his back on the red-faced Henry, and gestured toward the corpse-carrying horse. As he did so, he bent to speak privately into Robert's ear.

Thomas could not hear what was said, but Henry most certainly did. "You lie!" the Lavenham heir shouted, shifting from foot to foot in evident frustration. The young man's shuffling reminded the monk of a little boy who needed to relieve himself. Anger over Henry's treatment of the old servant returned, and Thomas tightly closed his eyes to keep his temper cool.

When he opened them, he turned his attention away from the Lavenham party and back to the sobbing woman. Her grief now burrowed deeply into his heart and, however inadequate his words might be, Thomas longed to offer some comfort. Before he could do so, he saw an old woman pushing through the crowd of clustered fellow servants. He watched as she reached down and picked the young woman up. With the gentleness of a mother with a hurt child, she folded the wailing woman into her arms, then began crooning words in a soft tongue Thomas assumed was Welsh. Silently, the crowd of servants parted and the old woman led the younger away.

Perhaps it was best, Thomas thought, that he, a stranger and an Englishman, stand aside. At such a time, the woman would surely want the comfort of a priest she knew.

"Brother Thomas!"

Robert was gesturing him forward. "Brother Thomas accompanied my sister, Sir Geoffrey. He is a priest in the Order of Fontevraud," he explained to the man beside him.

The older man ran his eyes over Thomas with the quick assessment of a commander determining a soldier's competence for a required task. "That man died unshriven, brother. We returned immediately, but I fear for his soul."

"His soul may still be within hearing, my lord," Thomas said. As he turned toward the dead man and his hovering spirit, he overheard Sir Geoffrey say to Henry: "If this man's soul has fled, his woman will not be alone in praying that your soul will one day share his sufferings in Hell for your actions this day."

Chapter Four

Baron Adam of Wynethorpe drank from his cup of steaming, mulled cider and stared into the dancing flames of the hearth. He was a tall man whose lean and muscular frame suggested he was too young to have three surviving children, all grown into their third decade of life; yet gray had begun to dull his fair hair and a battle injury had stamped his walk with a pronounced limp. Such were the limits of observable human frailty.

He was not known for weakness. Like most military men, he had little patience with inactivity, but the austerity with which he chose to ignore the pains of his old wounds exceeded that of almost all his fellows. He rode daily when he could and paced nervously when he could not. After he was no longer able to swing a sword in battle, he had turned to the games of the king's court and played them with equally cold precision and unemotional practicality in the service of his liege lord. Indeed, many might have said that strength was a virtue he sometimes took to obstinate excess. Few could remember the last time the baron had laughed with abandon. No man could claim he had ever seen him weep.

Weaknesses he had, of course, albeit ones known best to God and to his own soul. Had those in his circle of acquaintance been asked what chinks the baron might have in his armor, some would have pointed to his code of honor, which he would not bend for solely personal gain. Others might have suggested it was his passionate loyalty to king, friends, and family. Had this been brought to his notice, he would have smiled and shaken his head. To him, his greatest vulnerability was love.

Since the death of his adored wife almost fifteen years ago, he had lost all tolerance for stabs to the heart. Physical pain from a sword or mace was naught compared to the pain of her loss or to the possibility of betrayal because of love. As a consequence, he guarded against expressing the emotion with the ferocity of Cerberus, the three-headed dog standing at the gates of Hell.

There were exceptions. His grandson knew he loved him. After all, a six-year-old boy could do little to hurt him, except die, and Adam had reacted quickly when the lad had sickened, demanding a healer whose reputation was rooted in fact, not rumor. On occasion, Adam had shown his boys how dear they were to him, for he was lucky in his sons. As children, Hugh and Robert had always been both obedient and loyal to their father. They had also grown into good men.

Eleanor was different. He had adored her above all his other children from the moment of her birth, but, since the death of his wife when Eleanor was six, he had been unable to look at the daughter without seeing his beloved Margaret. Whatever joy he felt when Eleanor stood beside him was instantly balanced by the ever-fresh pain of his wife's death in childbirth. Thus the love he bore his daughter had become the one emotion he feared most, his greatest weakness, and the one he kept most carefully hidden. Especially from Eleanor.

ᗧᚋᑽ ᗧᚋᑽ ᗧᚋᑽ

"My lord father."

Eleanor walked into the dining hall, accompanied by Sister Anne. As the baron bowed out of respect for her vocation and she curtsied in acknowledgment of his rank, she felt herself tremble. She still felt reduced to the status of a child in her father's stern presence despite her taking office as the head of a sizable priory.

"How fares my grandson?" he asked, emotion roughening his voice.

"Well, my lord." Eleanor gestured to the woman beside her. "Sister Anne has brought her fine skills to bear. Richard has passed the crisis." Once again she folded her arms into the sleeves of her habit and grasped her arms to stop the shaking. Sister Beatrice, her aunt, had oft told her she was foolish to react so to her father, but his deep voice had always sounded so formidable to her young ears.

"As soon as I let him out of bed, Richard will play havoc with any calm here, my lord," Anne added. "You might find greater peace fighting the Welsh."

Eleanor watched her father smile, the relief painting his face with a glow she saw only when his grandson was the object. In truth, she felt no jealousy of her nephew. Still, her heart did ache on occasion when she saw her father smile at Richard, and she wondered if the memory of the baron looking on her in such a fashion in the years before her mother's death was only a fancy born of longing.

After her aunt had taken Eleanor to Amesbury to raise, he had visited her, but she soon began to wonder why he bothered. Whenever she had run to him, arms open as had been her wont in a happier life, he would step back and greet her with formal severity, his dark eyebrows coming together like armies engaging in battle. Although he did hug her at the end of these short visits, the gesture was abrupt, and he would quickly depart, leaving only the scent of leather and horses in her empty arms.

The baron's voice broke into her musings. "I am deeply in your debt, sister," he was saying to Sister Anne. "Ask what you will, and I will give it to you if it is within my power to do so."

These words brought back the one memory that Eleanor kept close to her heart for those times she most doubted her father's love. It had been the winter after her mother's death. She had been not much older than Richard, and, like her nephew, had had a dangerously high fever. She thought she was having a vision when she looked up and saw her father bend over her bed, then lift her up into a fierce hug, his cool tears falling in great drops on her fevered neck. Later, when she told her aunt of this thing, Sister Beatrice said it had been no fevered imagining at all. When he had gotten the news of her illness, she told her, the baron had ridden without a stop from Winchester to Amesbury in a torrential rain to be at his daughter's bedside.

Why then, Eleanor had asked, did he never show her such love at other times? As her aunt took the thin little girl onto her lap, she had explained thus: "Because your mother took both your father's heart and the babe she died of with her to the tomb. You look so much like your dead mother that he can never see the daughter without seeing the ghost of the wife."

Sister Anne's voice brought Eleanor back to the present once again. "You should ask God for what He wishes, my lord," the tall nun was saying to the baron. "Your grandson's return to health is His doing, not mine. I am only the instrument of His grace."

"It seems that He and I must work out due recompense then." Adam smiled and nodded at his daughter. "Perhaps the Prioress of Tyndal will act as mediator."

Eleanor caught herself smiling back at her father with the eager pleasure of a child just given rare acknowledgment. Indeed, she had had nothing at all from him, either encouragement or family news, since she had left Amesbury to take her new position until Richard's illness. Yet Sister Beatrice had told her that tales of her cleverness in keeping Tyndal from debt after the events of last summer had reached the court. Surely, her father must have heard the stories. After all, how many prioresses had ever been faced with a priory full of resentful monks and nuns, a murdered monk in their cloister, a hard winter of reduced revenues, and all at the same time? Even if any other women had been so tested, how many had successfully surmounted each difficulty with skill and wit? If she had not brought wealth to her family by consenting to a good marriage as her father had wished, had she not at least brought honor?

Anne touched her arm. "If I may be excused, my lord," she was saying to the baron, "I will return to your grandson and leave you and my lady to speak in private."

"Good sister, you must take some refreshment first. Food and wine will be brought to you. I'm sure Richard's nurse can watch over him for a few more hours while you take your ease. She may be a fluttery woman, but she is competent enough in her care of the boy. You need the rest."

The tall nun bowed her thanks, smiled at Eleanor, then left father and daughter alone.

"She is clever, your nun," the baron said as he gestured for Eleanor to sit in one of the chairs at the high table. "Where did she come by her training?"

"Her father was a physician who shared much of his knowledge with her, I believe. She and her husband also had an apothecary shop before she came to Tyndal, although I have heard from a reliable source that their success at it was due most to her skill in the healing arts."

"A physician's lass then, and an apothecary's widow too? Death must have had a hard time wresting her husband from her with her fine skills. How did he manage to die on her?"

"She is not a widow, father. Her husband wished to become a monk and she followed him to Tyndal."

"Nor would I have thought her so compliant! I have heard tales at court about the rough treatment she deals out to any patient who fails to follow her direction." His lips twitched into his usual humorless smile, but she saw no mockery in his eyes. "Does she long for the world?"

"She is content." Eleanor bit her tongue from saying more. Sister Anne's past was her confessor's concern, not her father's. As a rule it was none of hers either, for whatever grief and secrets Anne kept close within her soul, the nun had proven to be a loyal friend as well as a talented healer. Like her father, Eleanor cared much for loyalty and honored the private places in the hearts of others, unless her instincts sensed a festering therein that must be lanced before contagion was spread to the innocent.

She glanced up. Her father had been silent while she reflected on Sister Anne's past. He was studying her.

"Well and good," he said at last, "but there are more important things than your nun's history. I have something to discuss with you, daughter."

Eleanor raised a questioning eyebrow. "I hope I may be of service to you, my lord." Her trembling returned and, again, she hid her hands in the sleeves of her robe.

"Well said," he replied, eyes sparkling with brief amusement before his eyebrows bent once more into their usual stern expression. "Since your arrival, you have been so busy caring for your nephew that I have not had the chance to tell you of my plans. I am arranging a marriage between your brother and the daughter of a friend and former comrade-in-arms."

"Hugh will not come back from the Holy Land for any marriage, father. I hope this happy alliance can wait."

"Robert, it is, not Hugh. I'll settle my eldest when he comes back, unless Prince Edward wants to marry him off to one of his close relatives." He grunted. "That was a jest, mind you. The prince knows too well that our loyalty is secure. He would never waste such a marriage on Hugh."

"Perhaps our good king would instead grant the hand of one of his queen's Savoyard relatives to Hugh?" Eleanor suggested, attempting to match humor with humor. Despite her father's eagerness to arrange advantageous matches for his children, he had adamantly refused his liege lord's offer of a similar match for himself. Not many men of his age would have rejected such a profitable alliance that brought with it the comforts of a warmer bed. Nor had she heard any rumors about any longtime leman, whether hidden in the nearby village or in the servant quarters. Not that she would have begrudged him that, but she was touched nonetheless by such fidelity to her dead mother.

Adam's brief smile faded rapidly. "Our good king is getting old, as are we all, my child, and has lost interest in his queen's relatives. Now his waking hours are spent dreaming about a shrine to his beloved St. Edward the Confessor." He lowered his voice. "I admit that I wish our king's son was not off fighting the

Saracens. The Lord Edward should be here to ease his father's burdens and give comfort to his people."

King Henry III was suffering from more than just a few inconvenient infirmities related to age and her father knew it well, Eleanor thought. What she had heard from her Amesbury aunt, a woman of extraordinarily good sources, was that the frail monarch was now showing signs of senility and was so ill that a letter had been sent to the Lord Edward begging his immediate return. Many at court were worried about the still unsettled peace in England. Should the king die, civil war could well break out again unless the heir was home to take firm control of the throne. The land could ill afford another such rebellion. It was still bleeding from the last one.

"You mentioned the arranging of a marriage for Robert, my lord. Have you spoken with him about this?"

"I am not without concern for my son's future happiness, Eleanor," the baron snapped. "As you would do well to remember, I allowed you to take the veil much against my own wishes."

Indeed he had, but then few had ever won an argument with his elder sister, Beatrice, she thought. "I remember with gratitude, my lord. Who is the woman and what does she bring to this marriage?"

"Do you remember Sir Geoffrey of Lavenham?"

The name was familiar, but the man she knew was a poor one. Was she mistaking him for his elder brother? She shook her head.

"Perhaps not. I think it was your fifteenth summer when you last saw him. He and I were pages together, and we fought de Montfort at Lewes and Evesham."

"I was not aware that he had lands to give a daughter."

"Indeed he was a landless knight at the time you knew him, but his elder brother died of tertian fever some years later and Geoffrey inherited all Lavenham lands and title. His elder brother was a good enough man, but I must say his death was timely, soon after Geoffrey suffered the jousting... Did I not write you of Geoffrey's accident?"

"Robert did, father. He lost his hand, if I recall, and I do remember him well. He had two sons and a daughter. George is my age…"

"…and would have made you a fine husband, if you had but listened…"

"…and the other two were, indeed I may hope that they still are, a few years older? Yes, that year I lived at Wynethorpe before I took my vows, we all spent much time together." Eleanor smiled. "There was a young ward, I think, and I also remember Sir Geoffrey's sweet wife. He was so devoted…"

"The mother of his children is dead. He has since remarried. To the Lady Isabelle."

Eleanor blinked at the harshness of his retort but chose to ignore it. "The only Isabelle I remember was his ward, his daughter Juliana's good friend."

Adam's face reddened, then he turned away and walked toward the huge stone hearth cut deep into the wall just behind the high table. His limp was marked, made worse with the cold, Eleanor thought, and it pained her to watch him struggle not to grimace. For a long time, he stood in silence, his back to her as he heated a poker. When he thrust the glowing iron into a nearby pitcher of cider, the hiss was like that of a trebuchet flinging a stone at a castle wall, but the cold air soon grew warm with the pungent scent of spices. Eleanor watched and waited for him to speak. As he passed her a steaming cup, she noticed that his hands were shaking ever so slightly.

Adam sipped at his own hot drink in silence. "Geoffrey was besotted with her," he said at last. "I swear his good wife was barely in the ground before he had the whore in his bed." The baron looked up, his face a mottled red. "I beg forgiveness for my crude language. That is not something I should have said to a daughter, let alone a woman dedicated to God."

"You may say what you will, father. I am no longer a child and, thanks to your sister, I am neither ignorant nor disapproving of the carnal pleasures between men and women."

The corners of Adam's lips twitched upward. "A spirited enough response and direct enough to match my blunt words. I see the fine hand of Beatrice in that as well. She always was one for plain speech. Her desire to forsake the world for the convent after her husband's death made as little sense to me as your desire for the same." He coughed. "That aside, I need a woman's help and have no other to turn to."

Anger in her heart swelled with her father's ever-dismissive attitude toward her wish to enter the convent over his desire to put her into an arranged marriage. Eleanor said nothing but only nodded in response, for she did not trust herself to speak with civility.

"To better answer your question, the Isabelle you mentioned is the one Geoffrey married. Perhaps you did not know that their arrival was not long after yours? Aye, I thought not. From my less than discreet words, you must also realize that I cannot abide the woman. I have had more than I can bear of her voice and company. Now that you have more leisure with Richard's return to health, I would be most pleased if you kept her out of my sight and well-entertained while Geoffrey and I finish the details of what Robert can offer as a dower and what Juliana should bring as her marriage portion."

"Who else accompanied…"

"The Lady Juliana, of course, and Henry came as Geoffrey's heir and interested party to the agreement. His inclusion was intended only as a courtesy, but he has thrown up such earthworks to a reasonable decision that both his father and I are now questioning our wisdom in asking his attendance. I do believe Henry is so niggardly that he resents every pittance removed from his own inheritance. It is Robert's task to entertain him, however, whether he fancies the responsibility or not."

Eleanor nodded. At least she did not have to see the younger son, George. Had he been here, it would have been painful for them both. Not only had he had been her father's choice for her husband, George had been eager for the marriage himself. She had been fond of him, a feeling perhaps rather different than what a sister would feel for a brother if she were honest with herself, but she had never felt sufficient lust to turn her heart from the convent. That passion, she thought ruefully, had not conquered her until she had met Brother Thomas.

Eleanor took a sip of cider to hide the blush she felt rising at the thought of the finely formed priest. "If Juliana is your choice to be Robert's wife, it is a good one," she said at last. "I remember her as a witty and lively girl, one who did not lack in certain feminine attributes which my brother might view with more favor than the fine mind I enjoyed."

Her father grunted with amusement, then his expression turned solemn. "Juliana has changed, child. Her mother's death and her father's over-quick marriage to her childhood friend have made her into a somber girl. Despite the bewitchment of his whore, Geoffrey still has wits enough to grieve over the change. He thinks a husband and children of her own will chase melancholy from Juliana's soul." Adam glanced away from his daughter and stared fixedly into the hearth.

As her father remained silent, Eleanor tapped her foot with impatience. "There is more to this story, is there not?"

"I hesitate to say that grief has unsettled Juliana's mind entirely, yet I have heard tales of most curious behavior. Her father does not believe she is bewitched, rather that her womanly humors have been unbalanced of late. If so, we must act quickly in the matter of this marriage to restore her to full health."

"Behavior such as…?"

"One morning she came to break her fast in a robe. A monk's habit. It seems she had slipped into their priest's room and stolen his summer robe."

"It would not be unlike Juliana to play such a mischievous trick, but I can only hope their confessor is more pleasant of scent than ours. Father Anselm has never exuded a sweet odor of sanctity. Unless I were performing a severe penance, I would not steal a robe from him." Eleanor wrinkled her nose.

"You will make me laugh, child, and this is a serious matter. There is yet more to the story."

"Forgive me, father. What else?"

"Before their arrival here, Juliana cut her hair, then shaved her head."

Eleanor frowned. "My jest was indeed out of place. That act is far beyond the innocent mischief-making of the girl I knew." She fell silent for a moment, then continued. "Juliana and her new stepmother were once friends, yet you suggest they may now be estranged. How has their behavior together altered? Do they no longer speak civilly with one another?"

"They have been seen to speak together, civilly enough I've been told, but Juliana is often in tears afterward. Were I Geoffrey's daughter, I, too, would be in tears. This marriage was not a happy pairing."

"Except, it seems, to Sir Geoffrey. If you will, father, what has so turned you against his second wife? Finding a good husband is the duty of most women of rank, and surely it is not her youth. She can bear children to bring him joy in his later years. Nor can you fault the dowry she brings, for I do recall that she had lands from which the Lavenhams took revenue whilst she was their ward."

Her father's face flushed a deep purple. "I would not fault the lands, but the son should have been the match, not the father. Henry both expected and has wanted the woman as wife for years. He resents that his father took her from him. In that he has the right of it. Nor do I understand why she chased after the father rather than the son, who would have been the better, as well as the expected, match for her. Yet I could have put all that aside had she been a more dutiful wife to her new lord once he took her bait and she had pulled him to the marriage vows." The baron banged his fist on the table.

"You have called her *whore*. Has she taken lovers? Is that your objection?"

Adam glared as he fell heavily into the chair facing his daughter. "This is something you know nothing about and have no reason to as prioress to women and womanish monks. When a man reaches his middle years, things often happen to him, which require a wife to be kind and resourceful in the marriage bed. I cannot speak of this to a…"

The sound of a pewter cup flung against the stone wall reverberated like the clank of a cracked church bell.

Adam stared at his daughter, his face paling as if he had just seen a ghost. "My child," he gasped, "I have not seen a woman do that since your mother died!"

"Did she have as just a cause with you as I have, my lord?" Eleanor's face was also white but with frustration overlying rage. "She did tell me that I sometimes gave her less than her due in comprehension."

For just a moment, father and daughter stared at each other, he in amazement and memory, she in fading anger but with stubborn determination.

The father lowered his eyes first, although a smile teased at his lips. "Very well. I see I may no longer regard you as an innocent child. In court circles, many have said that my daughter is gaining reputation in her Order as a resourceful woman with wisdom beyond her years. It seems only just that I treat her as such."

Eleanor bowed her head. She could feel the flush of pleasure the hard won words of praise brought. "As my mother would have wished as well, my lord, or so I would presume." She made her tone conciliatory.

Adam smiled at his daughter with both sadness and pleasure, and his hand moved ever so slightly toward hers. Then he quickly pulled it back, empty of any touch of her. "Aye, lass," he said, his voice catching almost imperceptibly. "That she would have."

Chapter Five

"How did he die?" Thomas asked as he watched two men lead the horse bearing the corpse of Hywel, the retainer, away.

Robert said nothing for a moment, then he turned his head away so his expression was unreadable. "The death seems to have been an accident. Sir Geoffrey said the horse bolted. Threw Hywel. His neck was broken in an instant." He swallowed. "He was riding as attendant to Henry at the time. However thoughtless Henry may have been in slapping the steed, the horse should not have reared like that." Then Robert ran one hand over his eyes and added, his voice sharp with anger, "Hywel will be sorely missed."

An accident seemed a reasonable enough explanation, Thomas thought. Nonetheless, Sir Geoffrey's overheard remark about Henry's soul finding a place in Hell suggested that there might be more to the tale, perhaps something omitted that would explain why this particular horse had bolted. Indeed, from Robert's manner of telling the story, Thomas suspected that he did not believe the servant's death had been an accident at all.

"The Lord Henry seemed uneasy lest others think he was in some part to blame for what happened," he said, curious to see how Robert would answer.

"The Lord Henry believes that he, not God's created earth, should be the center of the universe. Whether the matter be good or ill, he cannot bear to have attention focused away from himself."

An interesting reply, Thomas thought. It carefully evaded addressing whether carelessness, accident, or even a deliberate act had caused the death of the servant. "And the woman who so grieved over Hywel? Is she sister or wife?"

"Widow. In a fortress full of soldiers, she will not remain long without a man, but they did have young children together. Henry may not have dropped one coin into her hand, but his father has a more generous spirit. Nor would we let them starve. Nonetheless, even the promise of food in their bellies and a warm enough hearth will not chase the bitter chill of their father's death from the hearts of those little ones this winter season."

Thomas nodded in silence as he turned to look at Robert's future brother-in-law. Henry was standing with the two women who had been part of the tragic morning ride. At this distance, the color of his face seemed to have cooled, but he was waving his hands with animation. Thomas bent his head in the direction of the Lavenham heir. "Not even a coin? Has he always been such a brutish man?"

"Since childhood," Robert snapped, then he shook his head. "Forgive me, Thomas. My anger over this cruel death has unbalanced my humors and chased all impartiality away. A good man, Hywel was, and one of my brother's companions as well as a loyal servant. Indeed, they often jested about their shared names, despite the difference in their station and ancestry. I dread sending this news to my brother while he is in the midst of a war. Hugh will grieve deeply, as do we all." Robert hastily rubbed his eyes as if dirt had flown into them, but Thomas knew the cause was tears, not dust.

"It is true," Robert continued. "Henry and I have never gotten on, even when we were but children together. He has always had too much choler yet he would never face anyone in a fair fight. When men are faced with differences, I do believe they must live with those they can and exchange honest blows when they cannot. Yet, had Henry been a monk who must turn the other cheek, I would have acknowledged his courage. Instead, he attacks in deceitful ways..." Robert fell silent, then added,

"Perhaps it is enough to say that I have never liked Henry. Had his younger brother, George, been on this ride today instead, I do believe Hywel's wife would be kissing her husband's warm lips now, not bathing his dead face with her tears." There was no mistaking the bitterness in his tone.

"Pity the latter is the second son, then."

Robert nodded, but he seemed distracted.

"And Sir Geoffrey?" Thomas had been watching the older man stroke his horse's neck with the rounded stump of his arm, then bend to give instructions to a groomsman for the stabling of the animal. As the horse was led away, the knight put his left glove into his mouth and yanked it off with clumsy impatience. The leather glove fell to the ground. The knight muttered an oath as he bent down, swept the glove out of the muck, and jammed it under his belt. An unexpectedly angry gesture for such a minor mishap, Thomas thought. Was the loss of his hand recent?

"He is the father of the Lady Juliana and her two brothers. A fine knight. Far more a man than Lord Henry will ever be. You see he has lost his sword hand. A sad thing."

"In the de Montfort rebellion?"

"Not in battle. It was the result of a strange accident at a tournament," Robert explained. "He was waiting his turn in the tiltyard when a bee apparently stung his mount. The horse threw him, then reared. The edge of the front hoof came down on Sir Geoffrey's wrist and the bones of his hand were crushed. There was no question that it must be cut off."

"Thus his soldiering days were ended as well."

"For cert. But, as a man of faith might say, God smiled on him. He was a younger son who had made his living jousting when he was not fighting in the service of his king. As he lay recovering, his elder brother died of a fever and left him the Lavenham lands and title. He is now a rich man."

Thomas watched the knight walk over to a huntsman and begin a lively discussion about Robert's morning kill. The loss of his hand would explain why Sir Geoffrey had not joined in the early hunt. Perhaps he could still enjoy some falconry but hunting with spear or bow and arrow was out of the question. Chasing a boar or stag was far too dangerous with only one hand. Indeed, Thomas realized, there would be little pleasure left in the sport.

He thought of the angry frustration shown over the removal of a glove. Here was a rich man whose happiest days might well have been spent besting others in combat, not indoors polishing his plate and counting his coin. Sir Geoffrey was no merchant. The chance accession to the Lavenham estates may have guaranteed security and wealth for his family, Thomas decided, but he doubted it satisfied the fire in the man's belly for the thrill of challenge and rivalry. No amount of silver plate could ever pay for the loss of a sword hand.

Although there was good reason why Sir Geoffrey had not joined in the hunt, Thomas did wonder why Henry had not gone out with Robert that morning, a rare failure for a man raised to sport against beasts as well as his own kind. Perhaps he did not care for the company of his soon-to-be brother-in-law, a man who quite clearly disliked him. Or was it the lack of courage that Robert had suggested? Indeed, boar hunting was fraught with danger, but the hunters had been lucky to find one for the table. Boars were as rare as deer. Hares were the more usual game at this time of the year. Surely Henry could have coped with the hunting of hares.

Thomas watched Sir Geoffrey, lost in tales of past hunts with the huntsman, a distant look in his eye and a more youthful grin on his lips than the gray in his beard would grant. Nay, he thought, the more likely reason was surely Henry's sense of duty. Even a brutish son would know he must attend his father lest the elder man suffer an accident with his one-handed riding. Thomas shook his head as Sir Geoffrey and the huntsman roared with laughter over some story. 'Twas a sad state for a proud man to have fallen into, especially as he entered the waning years of his manhood.

A sharp burst of high-pitched mirth caught Thomas' attention and he glanced back to where Henry stood with the two women.

The monk had paid no heed to the women who had ridden in behind Sir Geoffrey and his son. Indeed, in the days before he had been forced to take vows, he would never have looked twice at the woman whose back was now to him. Although she was dressed well and warmly enough, her woolen cloak was without trimming and drab in color. Whether her face was as plain as her dress, he could not tell, nor did her cloak offer any hint that the body within was ample enough to give a man special joy when he rode her. He decided that she must be the maid.

The other woman, however, was buxom enough to put curves into any mantle, and her laughter once again rang through the cold morning air. Although the sound of pleasing voices was a passion of his, and the novice choir at Tyndal often dragged Thomas out of his more melancholy moods, this woman's voice, now sweet as chapel bells, inexplicably saddened him.

Thomas shook off the feeling with an abrupt toss of his head. "May I guess that Sir Geoffrey's better fortune includes a handsome wife as well," he said to Robert, nodding in the direction of the lady in question. "Although why she would have such a dull maid is beyond me." He waved his hand with a dismissive gesture toward the other woman in the more dreary dress. "Surely a woman blessed with such lush and welcoming curves would have no reason to fear competition for her lord's affections."

Robert chuckled. "That dull maid, good monk, is my intended bride."

Thomas felt the heat in his cheeks burning with mortal embarrassment. "'S blood, good Robert, forgive my churlish tongue! She would have charms, but the modest cloak she wears hides them from the common gaze. You are fortunate she saves her beauty for her intended husband instead of displaying them to the crude stares of such rude men as I."

Robert grinned at Thomas, then threw his head back with uncontrolled laughter. "Not long in the monastery are you, brother? Your words sing of both the court and the world, however hoarse your voice may be from lack of practice." He gave Thomas a friendly jab in the ribs. "Perhaps you will favor me with tales of your conversion to the contemplative life over a goblet or two of good wine someday?" He laughed again. "You owe me that as penance for insulting the woman who will soon be my betrothed, assuming the families can ever come to agreement."

"You have a generous heart to forgive this boorish monk, Robert. The wine and your company I'll happily accept, but let us talk of things more interesting than my entry to the priesthood. It is but a dull story and the telling is not worth wasting a fine Gascony red just off the boat."

Thomas glanced up through the increasing mist as the clouds that now effaced the sky began to envelop the earth. Dull the story was not, but he had no wish to recount his days in prison to this or to any man. Nor did he want to discuss the price he had paid for an act of sodomy, an act and a love he could never regret.

Robert tugged at the sleeve of his new friend's habit as the monk remained silent, his eyes turned to the heavens. "Have you left this world, Thomas, or have you just had a vision?"

"Neither. I was just thinking that we might be in for quite the storm. Those clouds will surely bring more snow. But let me return to my question. Am I right that the woman with the Lady Juliana is Sir Geoffrey's wife?"

The lady in question was now walking toward the main hall. His lusty jesting aside, Thomas did wonder why a happily wedded wife would look around with such suggestive boldness and walk with hips swinging so that men of any station could watch, then imagine how wildly those hips might shake the winnowing basket in the marital bed. In contrast, Robert's soon-to-be-betrothed followed with great modesty, head bowed, some steps behind the wife.

"You assume correctly. That is the Lady Isabelle, Sir Geoffrey's much younger second wife. As you would surely conclude from seeing the Lady Juliana and the Lord Henry, all his children are from his prior marriage."

"Not long wed, I would guess."

"More than a year."

"Then I am surprised the new mare has not yet bred."

"Aye, she has, but it came long before term. Or so she said."

Thomas raised an eyebrow. "I hear the hint of a tale there."

Robert's face flushed. "My father has always said I was too plainspoken."

"And I might say your speech is frank, as suits an honest man." Thomas smiled. "Tell me the story. I would know more of this family, for what you've told already is a sad but most compelling tale."

Robert shrugged. "I'll not pretend I believe all is thriving in this second marriage. You see, Sir Geoffrey's first wife was a woman well known for her sweet nature and godly heart. I remember her from the days when the lady and her family visited us, and the memory is a fond one." Robert's eyes glazed with sadness. "My own mother was still alive then and was good friends with the lady. Alas, Sir Geoffrey's wife sickened with a festering of the womb. I heard tell that he took a vow of chastity during her illness, hoping that God would restore his dear wife to health and his bed. God did not keep His part of the bargain, it seems, for the illness grew worse until she died in great pain. In quick succession after her death, Sir Geoffrey lost his hand, his brother died, and he returned to take over the estates." The wistful look disappeared from Robert's eyes, a brittle disdain replacing it. "Waiting for him was his young ward, the Lady Isabelle. In the time it took her to lean back and lift her robes so he could mount, she had bred a child. Out of honor, and some have said love, he married her. Then she lost the babe. She has not quickened since, and, as I have heard told, she no longer cares for his left-handed caresses. Perhaps they were sweet only before the vows and the dower she gained thereby."

"She was a landless ward?"

"Nay, she had lands enough to tempt a husband, but there is no denying she gained far more than she was able to give from this marriage. Still, it angers me that she drew the good Sir Geoffrey into her bed with false eagerness, only to turn her back on him after the vows. A London whore would have been more honest about what she'd give for the price of her favors."

Thomas saw the animosity flash in his friend's eyes and decided it would be wise to shift the subject. "Methinks you will be happy with the lord's daughter, however. She bears herself in a more seemly manner than her stepmother. Perhaps she takes after the mother who bore her?"

The anger in Robert's eyes faded, but in the murky light of the coming storm, Thomas could not identify the new emotion that took residence there. "The Lady Juliana was a gay child, as I recall. Even Henry laughed on occasion at her precocious wit and playful spirit. That aside, George has told me she has grown cheerless since her mother's death and her father's all too hasty marriage. He fears that the wedded state is one she no longer desires."

"Surely you will change her mind about the joys of marriage, Robert, if any man can."

As Thomas turned to clout his new friend on the shoulder with encouraging affection, the expression on the man's face stayed his hand. Robert's glance was shifting back and forth between the two women as they walked across the open ward toward the dining hall. His gaze had turned melancholy, causing Thomas to wonder if Robert's unhappiness was caused by Lady Juliana's sorrow or by some other reason altogether.

Suddenly, an angry voice called out, shattering Thomas' reflection, and he looked up to see Henry striding after his stepmother and sister.

Sir Geoffrey once again called to his son to stop, but the young man only quickened his step.

A cold shudder of premonition passed through Thomas' body. Had Henry not heard his father's command?

Reaching the two women, Henry grabbed Lady Isabelle by the arm, then glanced over his shoulder with a wild look of defiance at his father.

Sir Geoffrey called out again, this time ordering his son to leave the women be.

Henry did not release his stepmother. Instead, he pulled her to him in an awkward embrace. As he continued to stare at his father, a glow of triumph reddened his fair-skinned face even more than the biting wind had done. Then he quickly bent his head toward the struggling woman. She turned her face away from him.

Frozen in horror, Thomas wondered if he was trying to kiss or bite her.

Robert started forward.

Lady Juliana reached out, grabbing at her brother's robe.

Sir Geoffrey roared in outrage. With greater speed than Thomas would have credited a man with so much gray in his beard, the father leapt toward his son like a predator after prey. In an instant, he was at his son's side. Seizing him by the shoulder with his left hand, Sir Geoffrey spun his son around, then backhanded him across the face.

The Lady Isabelle, flung free by the violent assault, tumbled back into Juliana's arms.

Henry fell into the snow, blood from his nose running in a rivulet down to his chin and dripping into the urine-streaked slush.

Picking his heir up by the cloak with one hand, Sir Geoffrey spat in his face and tossed him back into the muck. Then, with a quick jab of his foot to Henry's groin, he turned and left his son writhing on the foul and freezing earth.

Thomas winced, then stepped toward the squirming figure on the ground. Henry may have richly deserved some punishment for his crass behavior, but Sir Geoffrey's assault was brutal. Suddenly Thomas felt a hand on his sleeve, gently but firmly pulling him back.

"Let him be," Robert said, his tone mocking and his gaze hard as iron. "He got no more than he deserved."

Chapter Six

Thomas hastened down the stone walkway toward Richard's chambers, shivering as he went. Even inside the walls, warmth was a relative thing. A bitter wind invaded the castle corridors through wood-shuttered windows and arrow-loops with far greater success than any human enemy ever could, and neither the spiced wine he had just drunk nor his thick woolen robe were of significant help in banishing the chill. When he had left the open ward, his feet had been numb from the ice-cold slush. Now, as feeling returned, they burned. He grumbled to himself, hugging his body with his arms and shaking uncontrollably. Without a doubt, Thomas felt utterly wretched.

However desolate Tyndal and East Anglia might be, its people surly with the damp and morose from the heavy gray clouds that weighed down a man's soul, there was nothing quite like this bone-snapping cold for misery. Sister Anne had warned him about it just before their journey here. If a man weren't careful, she had said, it could turn his flesh as black as charcoal and he would rot to death of it. Thomas shook his head as he stumbled with the pain in his burning feet. He did not want to see what color they might have turned.

Perhaps this northern cold also blackened souls like it did flesh? That might explain the scene between Henry and Sir Geoffrey. Yes, the son had been churlish, but the father's response had been malicious in the extreme. Although Thomas' own father had been remiss in displays of affection and easily distracted from his children, he had never been vicious. Yell he might have done on occasion, but never once, to Thomas' knowledge, had the earl struck any of his offspring whatever their legitimacy. On the other hand, neither he nor his half-brothers had ever tried to assault one of his father's wives.

Why had Henry attacked his stepmother? Thomas' first thought was that the Lady Isabelle might have played some part in the death of the Welshman. Henry had, after all, claimed the death was not his fault, that the attendant's horse had moved in front of his. Perhaps she had caused the Welshman's horse to charge forward, then allowed blame to be cast at her stepson's feet when he reacted by striking the beast. Could he have done nothing else? Was he innocent of thoughtlessness and unable to prove it?

Or had the lady perhaps taunted him during the ride, mocking his manhood because he had chosen feminine company instead of going out hunting with Robert? From what Robert had suggested and Thomas had witnessed himself, the lady enjoyed enticing hunters in an amorous chase. Perchance she had taken such a game too far with her stepson this morning?

Then there was the father's reaction. Thomas' first impression of Sir Geoffrey had been that of a temperate man with a gentle voice to the groom and a soft caress for his horse. Yet this moderate knight had quickly shown another side, one dark with rank malice. He recalled Sir Geoffrey's remark expressing a wish that his son would share a place in Hell with the Welshman. What father would wish such a thing on a son? Of course there might be details, like Hywel's friendship with the Wynethorpe heir, that Thomas knew nothing about. Perhaps Hywel had become a favored riding attendant over the years whenever Sir Geoffrey visited Wynethorpe Castle and that is why he had reacted with such fury. But to curse his son so, then kick him in the balls?

The monk shook his head. Even if the Welshman had been a special companion of the knight and his death had been caused by some petty act by Henry, surely that would not have been enough to generate such a curse nor such a strange scene between father and son. Nay, there must be some grave rift between Sir Geoffrey and Lord Henry, something that cut deeper than the understandable irritation felt by a father when an elder son showed defiance. Indeed, most fathers would not kick their sons in the balls just because the son was being churlish, any more than most sons would choose to assault their stepmothers to show their independence of a father.

Even the seemingly good Robert had countenanced Sir Geoffrey's act, however, and that disturbed Thomas. What about the raw display of animosity that Robert had shown toward Henry? What had the man done to Robert that he would smile so on his pain and humiliation? Of course, the dead Welshman had been a valued servant to the Baron Adam as well as a companion to Robert's elder brother. Had this been sufficient reason or was there a deeper cause? Surely, if this had been an accident, no matter how careless the act that produced it, it would have given birth to grief, but not such venom.

Nor did his prioress' brother seem the sort to take petty childhood quarrels into manhood. Indeed, he had expressed a desire to be fair about his dislike of Henry. Had something else occurred more recently between the two, or did Robert have reason to believe Hywel's death had not been an accident?

Thomas shook his head. "Nay," he muttered, "I am but a guest here and none of this is my concern." Although his curiosity was kindled, he decided that whatever lay behind the events of the morning was best left to those involved as he was not.

Thus he dismissed the incident as he approached the young Richard's sick room and turned his wandering thoughts back to happier things. He could hardly wait to tell the boy about the hobbyhorse he was going to make him. So eager was Thomas to the task that he did not notice the rising color on the cheeks of the nurse as he brushed past her at the door.

⌘⌘⌘

"Uncle Thomas!" Richard cried out in joy when the monk entered the room.

Thomas felt tears of relief sting his eyes as he looked down at the boy's broad smile, but he willed himself to frown with reasonable solemnity. "Not *Uncle*, but *Brother*," he corrected, sitting with care on the thick, feather-stuffed mattress and taking the small hand in his. Richard's face might be thin, but his cheeks had already regained a healthier shade of pink and his blue eyes sparkled with returning energy.

"You are not my brother, are you?" the boy asked with the most perplexed frown a six-year-old could muster.

"No, but..."

"Then *uncle* you are." Sister Anne put a hand on Thomas' shoulder and squeezed gently. He took the hint and fell silent. "When fathers are off to war," she continued, "uncles must set their nephews tests of bravery such as the drinking of bitter draughts. Brothers do not have the age or authority." She moved toward the bed and stroked Richard's dark blond hair, a gesture that made the boy blush with embarrassment.

"Aye, that we do," Thomas said, knowing that he was soon going to lose the battle to keep his expression stern. "Have you followed Sir Gawain's example and taken the bitter drink like a good and faithful knight?"

Richard nodded enthusiastically.

Thomas glanced sideways at Sister Anne, who nodded ever so slightly in concurrence. "Then you shall be rewarded," he said, pretending to then fall into deep thought for an appropriate length of time. "What would you say to having a noble hobbyhorse of your own? Might that be fitting recompense for your bravery, a hobbyhorse to ride through the corridors and on the ramparts when you are better and no longer need to take the foul draughts? Will that suit, do you think?"

The boy grabbed Thomas' hand in both of his and, with surprising strength, pulled himself into a sitting position. "When, Uncle? When? When?" Despite being weakened by the just broken fever, Richard began to bounce.

Thomas put his hands on the boy's shoulders and settled him down. "Patience! The steed must first be trained so he will be worthy of such a valiant knight as you. I promise you will have him soon."

"Will he be black as night?"

"I think that can be arranged."

"Will he have fiery red eyes?"

Thomas paused. "Well, now, would Sir Gawain have a horse with red eyes or great brown ones like your Uncle Robert's hunter?"

The boy thought for a moment. "Perhaps brown would be better."

"And white mane?"

"Yes! And leather…"

Anne put her hand on Richard's head. "Wouldn't you like to have some surprises left, my son? Surely this will be a fine horse, whatever his trappings, and well worth the waiting."

The boy wrinkled his forehead, trying as hard as he could to look older than his years. Failing that, he beamed with all the dazzling joy of youth. "I will wait, Uncle. It is right that I do so." He hesitated but a second. "Will you tell me a story now?"

Thomas rose and gestured to Anne to follow him. "That I will, but first I must discuss some very dull matters with this good sister which would be of no interest to such a knight as you. Will you rest a moment while we step outside?"

"I will, Uncle, but hurry. Please?"

As they closed the door to the boy's room, Thomas turned to Anne and grinned. "How am I doing as a new uncle?"

"Well, indeed!" Anne laughed. "I think our lady will be much surprised to find she has yet another brother, but she will approve of your new kinship." Her smile turned gentle as she laid a hand on his arm. "The boy brightens when you visit him, brother. He heals all the better for your presence."

"Then he continues to mend well?" Thomas asked.

"He grows stronger by the minute," she replied, then listened to some muffled sounds coming from the boy's room. "If you do not return soon with the story you promised, Richard will have bounced that bed to dust with his impatience!"

Chapter Seven

Eleanor rubbed her eyes. The verbal jousting with her father had left her exhausted, as had the long days of worried attendance on her nephew. When the news of Hywel's death came, her father had left her alone at the high table but not before ordering some food brought so she might break her fast.

The morning was now fully born, although the young light was a feeble thing and the huge dining hall where she sat facing a cup of watered wine, a manchet of white bread, and a small portion of salted fish in butter was more gray than bright. Fatigue flowed over her with greater force than the sun's light, and the exertion needed to slice bread or chew fish suddenly seemed overwhelming. She sipped at the wine and the warmth chased away some of that weariness. Perhaps a bit of that buttered fish might be worth the effort, she thought, and she reached out to retrieve a bite from the bowl.

"Alone, my lady?" There was a hint of supplication in the voice.

Eleanor looked up at sound of the once familiar voice. Juliana had entered the hall so quietly the prioress had heard no step. Her old friend was now standing, hesitantly, at the end of the long table, her thin face as colorless as the gray hood that framed it.

"Alone, indeed," Eleanor replied. "I fear I have just my company to offer."

"It is only your company that I seek."

"Will you join me in…?" Eleanor gestured at the food in front of her.

Juliana shook her head, then bowed it as if the weight was too much for her to hold upright. "You have heard the sad news about your father's retainer?"

"Aye, I have that," Eleanor said gently. "I will take whatever poor comfort my words may bring to the family." She hesitated. "It was an accident, I've been told, but I grieve for the wife and babes he left behind." She knew they would not starve, but even the security of knowing that would do little more than blunt one sharp edge of the pain they were suffering.

"As do I. My father swore he'd make provisions for them. He feels responsibility for Henry's ill-considered act that caused the horse to shy." She shuddered. "Nonetheless, his family will long rue this horrible day."

Where was that joy that once gave light to her friend's eyes and a flush to her cheeks, Eleanor wondered with a growing sadness. Juliana had always had a kind heart and suffered over the death of any of God's creatures, but her nature had been such that she had always quickly regained a delight in life, a joy that was contagious even to those who suffered the many sorrows of a mortal world. What was it, then, that had cast such a shadow on the spirit of her old playmate?

"Would you walk with me on the ramparts this morning, Juliana?" Eleanor asked. "The sight of a new day may help raise our spirits, and it has been many years since we last spoke. We have much to tell each other."

"I would be honored," Juliana replied, her voice almost a whisper.

"Come then and let us greet the sun. It is God's gift even in the dark seasons," Eleanor said and reached out to take her friend's hand. It felt so frail and dry, like that of an aged woman nearing death. She squeezed it with tenderness.

High on the castle wall, the air was biting sharp to the nostrils and brought pink to the cheeks of the two women standing quietly on the stone walkway. As they looked down over the dark-wooded valley, they could see mists swirling, hiding sights from view for a moment and exposing them with teasing brevity the next. White smoke from a few of the village houses, below the hill on which Wynethorpe rose, curled upward and disappeared into the growing haze. Wives were tending stews and baking breads to sustain their men and babes over the cold day. In the center of the village, surrounded by hovels, lay a small church. The women on the castle ramparts could see a cluster of diminutive figures, dull with the colors of poverty, coming for alms as well as for the fat-soaked trenchers and discarded scraps from the dinner the castle inhabitants had enjoyed the night before. Although they could not see them through the mists, Eleanor and Juliana knew that cattle wandered in the fields between the village and the forest in search of winter-faded grass beneath the snow. Dark-haired goats stood on their hind legs to nibble on low branches and brindled sheep huddled together for warmth. Indeed, they could hear their bleating cries through the frosty air. At such a distance and with the softening of the hazy light, it was an idyllic scene.

"I have a favor to beg of you, my lady," Juliana began, her breath turning into white curls like the outline of decorative letters in an illuminated manuscript.

Eleanor smiled at her. "My lady? Have you forgotten our youth together? We were Eleanor and Juliana once."

"Now you are head of Tyndal Priory. As prioress, I honor you."

"The honor is my father's. I wear it on his behalf."

For the first time, Juliana smiled. "From what we hear, you have earned enough on your own. George has told us how many at court sing of your wisdom and bravery." She reached over and touched Eleanor's arm. "He sends greetings and, aye, a brother's love as well."

"Were his greetings why you wished to speak to me alone?" Eleanor asked. She felt a knot of worry in her stomach. If George was sending a brother's love, she told herself, that was a good sign. Perhaps he had forgiven her? Perhaps he had even married by now?

"No, my lady, but he would not have you think he had forgotten you."

Eleanor smiled, but her friend's words were not exactly the news she had hoped to hear. "Then tell him I send him my greetings and affection as a sister would to her dear brother."

"He will be honored, my lady."

For a moment Eleanor let the silence hang between them. She watched her friend's eyes turn dark with sorrow. What little joy had briefly taken residence when she spoke of her brother now more quickly fled.

"May I speak from my heart." Juliana blinked as if to hold back tears. "I have no wish to offend. You must believe that."

"Speak, Juliana, and I will listen to your heart with my own."

"Then I must tell you that I have no desire to marry your brother." She stopped. Her face lost what color only the brisk air had brought to it.

Eleanor took her friend's hand. How thin Juliana had grown in the years since she had last seen her. Her gray woolen robe fell straight down from her shoulders to just above her shoe tops with no hint of a woman's curves underneath. She had always been a slender and lithesome lass, but now she looked as fragile as a dry twig. Had illness done this to her, madness perhaps, or was it the grief her father had suggested?

"You may say what you will. I promised I would listen out of the love and friendship between us," she said at last.

Juliana squeezed Eleanor's hand, the grip reassuringly strong. "Robert is a fine man, a man any woman would be honored to wed." She looked down, her voice fading to a whisper. "Please believe me when I say I know our marriage would not only give Robert the wealth he deserves but would provide me with a good husband as well. He would treat me with respect, even if he did not love me, and the alliance with your family would give honor to mine." With that, Juliana buried her face in her hands and began to weep, her sobs racking her delicate body.

Eleanor pulled the woman into her arms and rocked her like a child until the crying subsided. Then she drew back and wiped the tears from her friend's eyes. "Juliana, I am wed to Our Lord and have never been a wife in the earthly sense. Perhaps you need to talk to an older woman who has had joy in her husband..."

"You! It is you to whom I must speak!"

"Then I will listen," Eleanor said, as the deluge of hot tears began again and her friend buried her head into the prioress' shoulder.

"I do not wish to marry at all!" The voice was muffled, but there was no mistaking the determination in it.

"I know the dangers, if those cause you worry. My own mother died in childbed, and I would be false if I did not tell you that you would suffer pain in becoming any man's wife. Nonetheless, Robert is a kind man and will be gentle in taking your maidenhead. Pain is a part of our lives as children of sin, but God gives joy too. There is no reason not to believe He would give you both as much happiness as anyone can expect on earth. You and my brother are as well matched in your manners and wit as you are in your estate. I do believe you could be very happy together, and Robert would provide good stewardship of the land you brought to the marriage..."

"My lady, I do not dread bedding with a man nor is it childbirth that I fear." Juliana laughed, but the sound was brittle. "There is greater pain than the loss of a maidenhead or the hard labor of birthing an heir. Indeed I will confess to you that I am unwomanly and do not long for either a man or a babe in my arms, but that would be insufficient reason to refuse marriage with your brother. As you have said, he and I would be well-matched and deep affection would surely grow in our hearts for each other. We are both quite sensible about our prospects and responsibilities in this world, and we are each wise enough to be kind one to the other."

Eleanor stepped back and looked at the white-faced woman at arm's length, then she pushed back the cowl that had covered her friend's head and ran her hand across the rough stubble of blond hair. "Then tell me why you have cut your hair thus, Juliana?"

"As I said, my lady, there is greater pain than the loss of a maidenhead. I speak of what the soul feels, stinking with mortal frailties and standing at the fiery pit of Hell, longing to know, aye, even to *understand* the perfect and all-forgiving love of God."

"Are you telling me that you wish to enter a convent?"

"Not just any convent. I have a harsh calling." She quickly put a finger against Eleanor's lips as the prioress began to speak. "Nay, I care not for the degrees of strictness in enclosure between, say, a Benedictine house and one of the Cistercian Order. Such distinctions are but petty. My longing is for a life far harder than that. I desire a hermit's cell apart from other mortals where I may spend my life as an anchoress and ponder the complexity of God's love. Whatever wisdom He grants me, I will pass on to others who, like me, beg for such understanding."

Eleanor watched as Juliana's brown eyes turned almost black. She shivered, but knew the cause was something other than a gust of cutting wind. "How may I help, my child?"

Juliana threw herself on her knees and raised her hands in supplication. "I beg you to support my plea before the bishop. I want to be entombed as an anchoress. At Tyndal, Eleanor. Will you have me?"

Chapter Eight

Thomas had just finished gathering most of the items he needed to make the hobbyhorse. The tree limb for the body was straight and sturdy enough to survive almost anything an energetic boy would do to it. The rough cloth for the head would take a good dye for the requested dark color, and he could make the eyes and ears from small bits of cloth or leather. Surely someone would give him a few old but clean rags for stuffing the head.

One of the maids had gladly donated some ragged yarn for the mane, blushing quite prettily as she brushed her hand against his. His flesh had remained quiescent despite the feathery touch, and he had blessed her as thanks, knowing full well that she would have preferred his hand had done something else for her besides making the sign of the cross. He decided he'd ask Robert for those last bits he lacked. He had no wish to encourage the willing maid.

Now that the boy was on the mend and he had time to himself, Thomas felt a profound fatigue from his nights with little rest. Giving up sleep for the care of the little lad he had done with joy, but, when he did retreat to his bed, any deep slumber had been shattered by his all too frequent and terrifying dreams. In the months just after he had arrived at Tyndal, he had feared falling asleep because of them. When he did slip into unconsciousness, he'd soon find himself sitting bolt upright, sweating and whimpering like a child from the horrors they brought.

He did not remember feeling fear quite this strong when he was actually in prison and believed he might face death by burning because some zealous bishop had decided to make an example of him. Yet, in his dreams, the anticipation of the jailer's rape and the fires flicking out to lick at his feet were more than he could bear. Those dreams came less often now, but Giles would still appear in them, on occasion, to mock the love Thomas had borne him. In ways, those were the worst dreams of all.

He set his materials down on a stair and leaned against the stone wall. The cold felt good against his throbbing forehead. He knew he should go back to the room he shared with Father Anselm and sleep. No one needed his services and it would be good to rest, if he could. He sighed and looked out the narrow window of the stairwell into the inner ward. The sunlight was becoming weaker as the day went on. Snow was coming. Thomas wondered how soon it would be before this fragile light shattered into a myriad of white flakes.

Down in the ward, he noticed two women and a man walking. From her colorful clothes that stood out even in the misty light below, he knew one of the women was Sir Geoffrey's wife. She was walking at a discreet distance behind the couple. Thomas squinted to sharpen his sight. Surely the second woman was the Lady Juliana. Besides Lady Isabelle, she was the only woman of rank he knew to be in residence who did not wear a habit. If it was, then the man beside Juliana must be Robert.

Aye, he decided as he focused on him, that black hair and short stature would suggest that the man was his prioress' brother. As he watched Robert woo his lady, the monk chuckled with gentle amusement. A man of honor, Robert was. Even though they were out walking in public, he made sure they were properly attended.

Suddenly, the threesome stopped and looked back. Thomas was too far away to distinguish words, but he did hear shouting and watched the party below wait as another man ran up to them.

It was the Lord Henry, Thomas concluded, or at least the man had the same round face and was dressed as Henry had been after the hunt. Considering the encounter between stepson and stepmother earlier, this could not be a happy meeting. Perhaps the stepson now wished to beg pardon for his recent behavior? Thomas rather doubted it.

The monk watched Henry walk over to the Lady Isabelle, put his arm around her waist and, once again, pull her to him. As Thomas bent forward into the window opening, he saw Juliana quickly bend down to pick something up from the ground, then start toward them. Robert pulled her back, leaning over to say a word in her ear. Then he pointed at Henry, his voice raising enough for the monk to hear the anger if not his words.

Isabelle twisted in Henry's arms and pushed at him. Instead of releasing her, the young man rubbed his cheek against hers. She drew back and pushed again. He laughed, the sound of his harsh merriment rising easily in the cold air to the window where Thomas stood.

Robert abruptly left Juliana's side. Henry continued to laugh as Robert walked toward him, one hand on his dagger hilt.

Henry pushed his stepmother away and drew a knife. Robert pulled his dagger from its sheath, and the two men began to circle each other.

Juliana shouted as she ran to her stepmother's side, gesturing at something behind them. The men both stopped and looked where she was pointing.

As Thomas looked in the direction Juliana was indicating, he saw Baron Adam striding toward them as quickly as his bad leg would allow. In his hand was a sword and just behind him were several soldiers.

"Drop those weapons or I will have both of you put in chains," he shouted.

The baron was the only one whose words he could hear from that distance. Now that was a voice trained in battle, Thomas thought with admiration.

Both Robert and Henry sheathed their knives.

Henry bowed as he said something to the baron, then walked away.

When Robert turned to the Lady Isabelle, she reached out for his hand and pressed it to her breast. As he jerked his hand from her grasp, she laughed. The sound was so harsh that Thomas' ears ached more from that than from the cold.

Chapter Nine

Sir Geoffrey rammed his scarred stump into the palm of his left hand. "Juliana will marry and bed with Robert if I have to hold her down while he mounts her."

Eleanor winced.

"Surely such will not be necessary, Geoffrey." Adam shoved a pewter cup of wine within his friend's reach. "She will see that this marriage is both a wise and happy course. I remember her as a dutiful child, however high-spirited." He smiled.

Geoffrey did not.

"Has she never told you of her calling?" Eleanor asked her father's friend.

Geoffrey swung around and glared at her. Eleanor instinctively drew back, the ferocity in his brown eyes hitting her like a sharp slap on the cheek.

"Calling?" he snarled. "She has no vocation. She is doing this out of sheer spite."

"How so?" Eleanor asked. Her voice suggested greater calm than she felt.

"Because I married after her mother's death. You know the pettiness of women, my lady." His cheeks began to pale after the red flush of rage. "You are prioress over…how many is it now?" He sat back in his chair, the lines of his face sagging into the look of a very weary man.

"I, too, am a simple woman, my lord, and would benefit from your instruction." Eleanor cut to the chase. "Death does not often allow us the joy of having our own dear mother or father guide and protect us for the years we might wish, and we are thus accustomed to the remarriage of our parents. Please explain, therefore, why your daughter would wish to spite you so?"

Sir Geoffrey looked heavenward as if seeking guidance, then closed his eyes as if he did not care much for the response.

Eleanor waited. She found herself grieving over the change in her father's old comrade-in-arms. Once this man had been eager to bend his back and play horse to any child who wanted a ride. Once he had been a man who glowed like a young lover whenever his wife came into view. Now he was an old man, his eyes dull, hair lank, and his shoulders curved inward with whatever burdened him. Finally, with a soft voice, she continued. "In truth, the Juliana I remember from my youth was not malicious. Your daughter and now lady wife were as sisters. I would have expected Juliana to feel joy, both for her friend's happiness at a fine marriage and her own good fortune in having the Lady Isabelle a permanent member of the Lavenham family from whom she need not be long parted."

"Isabelle was her friend. That is true. Once they were like sisters, but when my beloved wife died…" Sir Geoffrey closed his mouth and turned his face away. His silence continued, stubborn and impenetrable.

Was there a connection between his wife's death and the current discord between the young women? Eleanor glanced at her father, but he refused to meet her eyes. Apparently, he had chosen to stand with Sir Geoffrey in protecting whatever secrets his friend wished to keep. She felt a short burst of anger. Had he forgotten all the fine words he had spoken earlier that morning? Had she so quickly and easily lost the ground she thought she had won with him? Or did all fathers forget that their daughters forfeited the innocence of Eden when they became wives, mothers, and, indeed, prioresses?

Whatever the cause, she decided there would be no way she could help resolve the situation if she honored such foolishness. With a deep breath, she turned back to Sir Geoffrey. "You were saying that something happened after your first wife died, my lord?"

He blinked as if surprised at her question, then coughed. "Let it suffice to say that a man must be married, Lady Eleanor. I had no wife, you see, and I was young enough to father more children. Marrying Isabelle would give me wife, babes, and the lands which our family had preserved for her until she married."

"A wise alliance," Adam added, this time giving Eleanor a look she interpreted as a clear warning not to pursue her questions. Given his own recently stated misgivings to her over his friend's new marriage, this remark was quite diplomatic. It was also a blatant lie. She chose to ignore his hint.

"Indeed. More good reasons for your daughter to celebrate your marriage," she said. "Perhaps the Lady Isabelle was shy about the wedding night? Many women are and that might have caused some concern to Juliana."

"Nay, the lass was willing, willing enough that she soon quickened with child. I knew it would be a good alliance with the lands, but, well, with the babe coming, I felt double joy. My daughter should have shared our happiness, but God gave me an unnatural child. Indeed she begged that I not marry her friend."

It was interesting, Eleanor thought, that he had avoided saying the child had been conceived before any contract to marry, then slipped in the final telling. A rare, albeit failed, subtlety for a man of otherwise blunt speech. "What reason did she give?" she asked, deliberately turning away from her father, whom she knew would try hard to gesture her into silence.

"What reason indeed? She had none. When I demanded she state her objections, she said first that Isabelle was too young for me." His laughter was biting. "Can you imagine? She thought me an old fool with a member limp from disuse!"

"Surely she did not mean that, Geoffrey." Adam filled his friend's cup once more with wine, then stood in front of Eleanor, offering her more refreshment as he glowered a silent demand that she cease her questioning.

Eleanor shook her head, refusing both, and gave her father a puckish smile. "You were saying, my lord?" she asked Sir Geoffrey.

"Indeed she backed away soon enough when I told her what I thought of that, but then she whined some female nonsense about her mother would not have wanted me to marry Isabelle. I told her that her mother had beseeched me to leave her be when she sickened, begged me to find some lusty young woman to warm my bed in recompense. You should have seen the shocked expression on Juliana's face when I told her that, the silly wench!" His face began to turn red and he threw his head back, swallowing the wine in one gulp.

Adam poured him more. Eleanor noticed, however, that her father had barely touched his own cup.

She turned back to look at Sir Geoffrey as he swirled his wine and stared at it with a determined focus. His last comment had been interesting, she thought, considering the vow of celibacy Robert had once told her Sir Geoffrey had taken during his wife's illness. Indeed, the man she remembered would never have forced an adored and ailing wife to bed with him. Had she not known that man, she would have believed that this man, now sitting in front of her, would have made a sick wife beg to be left alone. What had caused the change, she wondered: his lost hand, his waning virility, or something else entirely? "You did not believe her second reason to be the true one then?" she asked at last.

"She has no objection to my remarriage beyond jealousy. Jealousy is the sole reason, Lady Eleanor. Juliana is young, lusty as women are at that age, and long overdue for a husband and babes of her own. Isabelle was getting a husband first and Juliana was consumed with envy. She now pales with it. She has gone mad with it and does everything she can to cause me grief. Isabelle has tried to make peace with my daughter and has begged me not to send her off to a convent. I was willing to let her go to learn the barrenness of pride and jealousy, but my wife has a softer nature and I have chosen to honor her compassion. The ungrateful girl will marry Robert, gain a fine husband despite her undeserving nature, and thus stay close to a soul that loves her. Still, I do find it hard to forgive Juliana for playing so cruelly with my wife's good heart."

Adam poured another cup of wine for his friend. "This madness is surely temporary, Geoffrey," he said. "I remember far better days when your daughter delighted all of us with her quick wit and loving ways. Indeed, she shall marry Robert and, in good time, the foolish girl will make peace and be as a sister again with your wife. You speak the truth of it, I believe. A husband and babes of her own will, without doubt, put an end to such silly rivalry."

Eleanor bowed her head. Little was quite as everyone wished it to seem, she thought. Of course she had known there was far more behind Juliana's desire to enter Tyndal as an anchoress than she had expressed. Few women, even with genuine callings to the contemplative life, choose such a severe test of faith. Wisdom demanded that she look beyond a shaved head and eager words before accepting Juliana's sincerity about her calling, and she would. She would even take Sir Geoffrey's opinions into account with as little partiality as she was able, but she had also heard the ring of true coin in Juliana's plea, and that she would honor as well.

As to the other things she had just heard, she had been amused as her father so firmly expressed approval of the marriage between his friend and ward, an approval she knew he most certainly did not feel. Nor was Sir Geoffrey's current marriage the joyous one he tried to portray just now, at least according to the baron. Her father must have choked to hear the Lady Isabelle described as a woman of generous heart and softness, yet she had not seen even the barest flicker of an eyelid to betray his thoughts. From his days in the king's court, her father had indeed become quite skilled in diplomatic thrust and parry. She could learn much from him if he were willing to teach her.

Eleanor glanced up. Her father and Sir Geoffrey were now bending over the table, drawing imaginary maps with their fingers on the wood and lost in tales of old battles. Both seemed to have regained their youth in the telling, and the love born of much shared pain and joy over the years was so evident between them.

She looked at Sir Geoffrey and now saw remnants of the person she had known many years ago before his first wife died. She could not forget that he had once been a kinder man, one who would never speak with the harshness she had heard today. Nor would she ever forget that it was he who had saved her father's life after the Montfortians had pulled the baron, weakened from a deep thigh wound, from his horse. Had Sir Geoffrey not risked his own life to do so, she would be praying at her father's tomb this day, not arguing with him, a man she honored and loved, stubborn mule that he often was.

She took a deep breath and rose quietly to leave the old friends alone. Even if Juliana had convinced her beyond any doubt of the sincerity of her calling, Eleanor would win no arguments on her behalf this day.

Chapter Ten

Thomas' midday dining companions were less than congenial. On one side was the sulky and silent Lord Henry. On the other was Father Anselm, a priest of middling intellect but much higher odor. The company of a fellow religious was to be expected, of course. To be seated next to the Lavenham heir-apparent was intended as a compliment, and Thomas had mentally marked the honor with due gratitude. After five minutes between the two, however, Thomas was tempted to renounce both his vocation and the honor to seek a bench well below the salt.

"You eat meat, do you?" the good priest asked. His breath, heavily scented with a rotting sweetness from decomposed teeth, was even more fetid than the sour stench of his unwashed underlinen that enveloped flanking diners every time the priest shifted position.

Thomas looked at the dark slices of roasted boar meat on the platter in front of him. Due to Tyndal's reduced revenues during this first winter after his arrival, meat at any meal had been such a rarity that Thomas had almost lost the taste for it. Out of courtesy to his host, however, he had allowed the servant to put some ginger, wine, and garlic sauce on his trencher and had then accepted a small portion of the meat. What little desire he might have had for more had been destroyed by sitting next to the aromatic priest.

As he looked into the priest's tiny, close-set eyes, an irresistible impishness suddenly overtook Thomas. He reached out with his knife to stab a thick portion of the boar and, with an exaggerated grunt of pleasure, plopped the bloody slab onto his trencher, then turned and smiled at the priest.

The priest pursed his lips but was otherwise unfazed. "Heats the blood, you know," he said, nodding at the fragrant meat in front of Thomas.

Thomas was not to be outdone. He gestured at the goblet Father Anselm clutched to his narrow chest. "So does wine, I'm told."

The priest sniffed in contempt. "Our Lord drank wine."

Thomas coughed from the puff of bad breath. "Might have eaten venison for all we know. Boar, I'll concede, he did not."

"Our Lord ate only fish."

Thomas tried to remember what had been served at the marriage feast in Cana. Fatted calf came to mind as the popular choice in various scriptures he recalled. "How sad," he said. "Maybe there weren't any deer in Galilee. I'd wager Our Lord would have liked a good brisket." He hesitated and then let an almost beatific look transform his face. "What do you think? Perhaps God gave England so many deer so we'd know what a blessed land we occupied, that we were given what even His beloved son could not have." Thomas gave Father Anselm his most ingenuous look.

The priest blinked and Thomas could almost read what was going through the man's mind. To argue that God had not granted any abundance, no matter how it heated the blood, seemed rather blasphemous. To argue that England wasn't an especially blessed land to have it might cast doubt on his own loyalty to good King Henry and the Baron Adam who sustained him. Anselm resolved the entire dilemma by raising his cup in a vague toast to God and king, draining it thoroughly, and grabbing at the sleeve of a passing servant for a refill.

Having silenced one of his companions by driving him deep into a goblet of good wine, Thomas turned to Henry. The man was leaning over the table, a strange lapse in courteous behavior, and his hands were clasped so tightly his knuckles were white. His head was bowed as if in prayer. Thomas glanced at the man's empty trencher. Henry had eaten nothing. The poor would get little nourishment from his leavings. Thomas looked down the table at Juliana, then back at his silent companion. Brother and sister were much alike, he decided. Robert might be short like Prioress Eleanor, but he was also muscular. Henry, despite his round, fat face, was as slight in form as was his sister. A weakling son might not sit well with a battle-hardened father.

His curiosity still stirred over the morning events, and Thomas wondered if that was part of the trouble between them. Delicate or not, Henry had certainly shown no hesitancy in drawing a weapon against Robert earlier in the day. Was he trying to prove his manhood? Or did ill will truly exist between the future brothers-in-law?

A loud but pleasant laugh caught his attention and he looked down the high table once again. Next to Henry sat Sir Geoffrey and on the other side was the host, Baron Adam. Immediately to his left was the Lady Isabelle, who sat next to Robert, then the Prioress Eleanor and the Lady Juliana. Sister Anne had chosen to take her meal with the sick boy.

Then the Lady Isabelle laughed once more and Thomas saw her poking at some part of Robert below the table edge. The face of his prioress' brother turned a deep burgundy as he quickly rose and, after a brief word to his father, left the table.

Thomas couldn't hear what had been said but noted that his prioress was leaning over to say something to Sir Geoffrey's wife. Isabelle drew back her head, her teeth bared in a self-righteous smirk. As she did, Henry leaned back in his chair with an audible groan. His robe shifted and Thomas saw one excellent reason for his dining companion's distress. Henry was suffering from a rather impressive erection.

Seeing the direction of Thomas' glance, the man blushed and bunched his robes over the offending member.

From just a bit further up the table, however, other eyes had also seen the cause of Henry's discomfiture. Sir Geoffrey's face was pale as he slammed his goblet down.

During the course of the dinner, Eleanor had glanced down the table several times to look at Brother Thomas, a habit she had tried with no success to break. This once, however, she could blame the wandering gaze on amusement. Thomas was in conversation with the castle priest, his head bent back as far as possible from Father Anselm's mouth. She smiled. Indeed, her father's priest had breath so foul that Satan himself might flee from it. For the preservation of souls at Wynethorpe Castle, this might be a blessing; for poor Brother Thomas, it had most likely turned his stomach quite sour.

She shifted her attention back to her immediate companions and gestured to Robert to give her portion of the boar with its spicy sauce to the Lady Isabelle.

"How can your sister bear to forsake this meat?" Isabelle asked as she licked her lips in anticipation the moment that the extra portion hit her trencher. "Oh, I suppose you took some vow, Lady Eleanor," she continued, waving the concept away with the hand not occupied with her wine cup. "I would find such things very wearisome."

As Isabelle spoke, she leaned forward against the table. The gesture not only bespoke ill manners but also presented Robert, Eleanor, and the quiet Juliana with quite the view of her soft and ample breasts. The tightened cloth of her robe also accentuated, with a tantalizing shimmer, two erect nipples.

Eleanor blinked at the blatantly sexual display and hoped Sir Geoffrey had not seen any of it. Had Henry been sitting in Juliana's place, she thought, he would surely have been outraged at such an immodest display of what should have remained the private charms of his stepmother. Robert, on the other hand, had seen it all. Although he had drunk little wine during the meal, his face now flushed a blotched red.

Juliana shifted uneasily beside Eleanor. "Vows are not tiresome to those who take them, my lady," she said in a low voice.

"So you may say now, stepdaughter." Isabelle hesitated ever so slightly. "Vows are right and proper for one of the Lady Eleanor's vocation for cert." She slipped a palm under one breast, raising it as if offering a gift. "Still, you are not destined for the convent, are you? It is said that red meat heats the blood and makes one lusty for the marriage bed. You would do well to heed that and fortify yourself well in advance of the day." She smiled and leaned back into her chair. "Forgive me. I forget. You have never known a man, have you? Indeed, you would know nothing of such things, stepdaughter." She laughed. "Have no fear, Juliana, before you and Robert marry I will explain what a man and woman do on the night after they take their vows at the church door." Then she slipped her hand over Robert's thigh, and her laughter rang sharply over the noise of the diners. "I promise, my lord, that your wife will come well prepared to delight you in the thrust and parry of your marital bed." She winked in the direction of Eleanor and Juliana.

Robert brushed her hand away as gently as possible. His face turned a deeper scarlet as he rose and bowed to his father. "I beg pardon, my lord, but I must see that the oxen have sufficient hay now that the snows have come."

Adam nodded and went back to his discussion with Sir Geoffrey.

Robert turned with a perfunctory bow to the three women, muttered the standard courtesy, "much good do it ye," and left the hall as quickly as good manners allowed.

Although her father's expression had changed little, Eleanor knew from the movement of his eyes that he had noticed the reason for Robert's rapid exit from the dining hall. His opinion of Isabelle could not have improved.

She heard a soft groan and turned her head. When Robert left, Juliana had said nothing. Now one tear crested in the corner of her eye and slowly rolled down the woman's cheek. Her old playfellow may have been her elder by only a year or so, Eleanor thought, but she had the face of a much older woman with eyes sunken into darkness, cheeks gray and hollow with melancholy.

Juliana had once been such a sunny companion, always the first to think of innocent mischief. With a smile Eleanor remembered the day Juliana had climbed a tree and dropped a skirt full of rose petals on the woman who was now her stepmother. At the time, Isabelle had looked up at the impish girl and laughed with a simple joy, blowing at the pink petals drifting down on her as if they were fragile bubbles. The two had been as sisters then, Eleanor remembered. Now they seemed so sad together and much at odds.

Eleanor shook her head at the memory, then leaned over to Isabelle and said in a low voice, "This is neither the time nor place to jest over the marriage night, my lady. No agreement has yet been reached between our families. When it has, there will be much opportunity for such fond ribaldry."

Isabelle's fixed smile turned yet more brittle. "An admirable speech from a lady married to Our Lord," she said, then bent her head in a mockery of a bow. "So that I not offend your virgin ears further, lady, I shall indeed cease what you choose to call my *fond ribaldry*." With the petulance of a bored child, she slouched back into her chair and dipped her finger into the pewter cup in front of her and made waves in the wine. Then the brightness in her eyes dulled, she drained her cup in a trice, and her face flushed with the drink.

What a difference just a few years had made in both these women, Eleanor noted, as she chose to remain silent in the face of Isabelle's ill temper. Like Juliana, Isabelle was not the light-hearted girl she remembered either, a child who spontaneously hugged her friends and loved to crowd into the lap of her husband's first wife for the maternal affection that lady gave with as much abundance as if Isabelle had been her own child. As Eleanor recalled, the girl had been an orphan, not even distantly related to the Lavenhams. Sir Geoffrey's elder brother had received her wardship from the king and enjoyed the income from her lands while she was yet a child. Since he had never married, he had given Isabelle, with a small allowance for maintenance, to Sir Geoffrey and his wife to rear. There she had had a loving home. Until now, it seemed. In truth, despite her air of self-satisfied superiority, Isabelle looked no happier than her old friend. What had happened to cause such estrangement? Was it really jealousy? Could it be, as Sir Geoffrey had suggested, that Juliana resented his remarriage? And why had Isabelle married the father rather than the son? What…

Harsh masculine laughter shattered Eleanor's reflection. She looked up and saw Sir Geoffrey slam his goblet of wine down on the table. A burgundy stain spread across the white linen tablecloth.

Isabelle sat bolt upright, her face paled unevenly as she stared at her husband.

"Boy, you are a spineless whelp!" Sir Geoffrey snarled at his son.

"My lord…" Henry's round face was crimson.

"*My lord*," his father mimicked in a high-pitched voice. "*When you fathered me, you gave me balls, but I have since lost them.*" His voice dropped to a growling bass. "I cannot provide you with everything, boy. If you were a man, you'd get what you needed on your own." He looked down from the high table to the benches filled with men of lower status and his lips twisted into a thin smile. "But why should I think him a man? He has never given me reason to assume such." He nodded to his captive audience in the hall, then pointed to his son. "I fear his mother must have dreamed of Eve the night this one was conceived for she left me with a mincing cokenay instead of a son. Perhaps," he continued, turning to Henry, "you had best ask my wife for advice on the whitening she uses on her face and give your braies to a man, for a cokenay has no use for men's attire." He gazed around the hall and smiled at the sporadic laughter that greeted his angry wit. "Perhaps I'll see if I can find a man willing to be your husband amongst her many rejected admirers." Then the look in his eyes turned hard. He bent down for something under the table. As he rose, he tossed the raw testicles of the now roasted boar into Henry's lap. "Unless these can give you what you lack."

With his face turned as white as the table covering, Henry threw his goblet at his father, missing his head by inches, then stormed out of the hall.

Sir Geoffrey pursed his mouth and fluttered his hands. "Oh, but you frightened me so! What shall I do? *Cokenay*! You had best find Robert. Since you spurned the ones I offered, perhaps he can find balls to hang between your legs," he shouted with a mocking laugh at his son's retreating back, then lowering his voice, "although I doubt anyone could fill your lack."

Isabelle grabbed her goblet, now refilled with wine, and gulped it dry. A rivulet of red slipped down her chin and dripped like a bloody tear onto her robe.

Juliana sat with head bowed, motionless, silent, her hands gripped together against her waist so tightly they looked bloodless.

Eleanor watched her father reach up and grasp his old friend's arm, then gently pull him back into his chair and whisper in his ear.

Sir Geoffrey roared with laughter.

Chapter Eleven

Thomas could not sleep. Eating with Father Anselm was distasteful enough but sharing quarters with the man was more than Thomas could take, now that he need not spend his nights in Richard's chambers. Indeed, he had grown accustomed to some seclusion at Tyndal, where each monk had a small but separate place to sleep, but such lack of privacy here was the least of his problems. Father Anselm was not only foul-smelling, he snored, and, to make Thomas feel further cursed, the priest was a light sleeper.

"Going to the chapel to pray, brother?" Anselm's head popped up the instant Thomas' feet touched the rush-covered floor. "I'll join you."

Thomas rubbed his hand across his aching eyes in frustration. "Sleep on, good priest. My eyes will not close and I hoped to walk by myself in quiet contemplation until they became heavy again."

Anselm was already standing and adjusting the cowl of his robe around his neck. "Lonely contemplation for a meat-eating man is dangerous. It might lead to sinful thoughts and…" he gestured in the direction of Thomas' crotch, "solitary abuse. You need the discipline of company." The minor adjustment of his attire completed, he reached over and grabbed Thomas by the arm with greater strength than such a spare frame would suggest he possessed. "Together, let us go to the chapel and pray!"

Thomas was too tired to argue further nor did he care to explain to Anselm the reasons he rarely suffered from the sin of Onan. "Very well," he sighed and wearily headed for the door.

At least the priest chose not to speak on the way down the dimly lit passage to the stairs that led to the inner ward. Foul though it might be, only his breath whitened the darkness as they rounded the outside wall of the great hall to the chapel entrance. For this lack of talkativeness, Thomas raised his eyes heavenward in silent gratitude.

Later, after they had each slid to their knees, Thomas found himself admiring Anselm's ability to ignore the freezing stone floor. He might find the body of his companion thoroughly repellent, but, as the castle priest plunged into a prayer as lengthy and ardent as a lover's plea, he felt a brief twinge of jealousy. This man might actually have had a calling to his vocation. Thomas had not come willingly to the priesthood.

As he felt the chill of the floor seep through his woolen robe to numb his knees, he looked up at the carving of the twisted body of Jesus on the cross. The moving shadows from the flickering candles blackened the hollows between the jagged ribs but hid whatever expression the artist had carved upon the face. Thomas knew that there would be no individuality of features. They were irrelevant. The artist's sole focus would be the message of the Crucifixion. Indeed, Thomas did not need to see the face. Both agony and hope would be there. That he knew. The pain was understandable, the hope expected, but surely there would have been a hint of gratitude as well, indeed a joy that it would all soon be over? He thought so. After all, hadn't Thomas once looked upon death with some sense of eager anticipation?

He shivered, but the cause was not the icy floor. In a flash of memory, he was back in prison. He stifled a cry as he once again felt powerless, bound and naked, while the jailer, grunting like a pig in rut, clawed his buttocks apart and raped him on the rotting filth of that jail floor. Thomas bit into his lip to chase the image away, but the metallic taste only reminded him of the blood trickling between his legs after the jailer had left him.

Heresy or not, Thomas found himself wondering if the jailers had raped Jesus too. The Gospels had said naught of such a thing, recording only the beating and the crown of thorns. Indeed, had a rape occurred, he knew no one would have spoken of it. When one man raped another, it might be the ultimate humiliation for the victim, yet it tainted the rapist as well. Such feats were not bragged about in taverns or even confessed in secret, except on a deathbed with the red maw of Hell opening before a man's failing eyes. Nevertheless, Jesus might have been raped. After all, such an act of degradation could well have been deemed proper for a man who preached love in a time when others were fomenting rebellion and war.

Thomas shook the thought from his mind. Heresy indeed! He looked upward. No bolt of lightning had struck him for the thought, however, nor could he feel any honest guilt at his wondering. In the icy silence of that chapel, the only thing Thomas could feel was a kinship with the man on the cross. If he could not offer God a true calling to the priesthood, he could bring compassion born of torment for those who suffered. Perhaps God would be willing to tolerate that until a deeper faith took its place?

The rough stone was cutting into his knees and he shifted backward to sit on his heels. Father Anselm was so deep in prayer he did not notice. Thomas admired the man's ability to concentrate so. When Thomas had first arrived at Tyndal, he had been unable to pray at all. Even now, he could not approach God with the submissive speech of a good vassal to his liege lord. Instead, he had begun talking to God as if He had been a boon companion, a respected one, and spoke of his day, his doubts and his problems. No burst of flame had shattered the East Anglian sky to fry his body and hurl his soul into Hell. If such presumption was another instance of heresy, God was being quite tolerant of him, Thomas thought, but he did feel some envy over the pure faith of men like Anselm.

Or women like the one he now noticed in the shadows some distance from him. He rubbed his eyes and looked again. Or were there two figures in the darkness, one an indistinct double of the other? He blinked and one seemed to fade. Surely his tired eyes were playing a game with him, he decided.

The figure he could see with more clarity was slight and the length of the robe, sufficient to drape over the feet, suggested a feminine style. It must be a woman. Perhaps it was the Lady Isabelle, or more likely the Lady Juliana. The former seemed a woman more attached to the delights of the here and now, the latter more likely to long for the joys of the hereafter. Thomas shook his head. Robert's designated beloved was indeed a somber one.

He knew it could not be either Sister Anne or his prioress. The former was too tall, the latter was too short, and he was sure either or both were with Richard. The boy might be improving, but they had each told him they planned to split the watch over the lad that night when the air was more malevolent.

Ah, the lad! The thought of Richard brought some warmth back into Thomas' soul. Marriage and any legitimate issue had always been out of the question for Thomas. As a by-blow, albeit of an earl, he had had a comfortable enough home as a child but no hope of title, and, since he had not been his father's only son born on the wrong side of the blanket, he had had little chance of land. His father might have provided him with a good horse and armor if he had asked, but the life of a mercenary or landless knight, pillaging and jousting for his dinner, had never appealed. At the time he had doubted his father's wisdom, but now he knew that his best hope of a comfortable future had been that of a clerk in minor orders.

Like most of his fellow clerks, Thomas had enjoyed the favors of many women before he fell into the priesthood, but he had never desired to father a child, especially one out of wedlock. With no family to whom he could have taken such progeny for proper care, he had tried to avoid joining his seed with a woman's. Still, there had never been even a hint of any issue of his own even though he had not always been sober enough to remember to withdraw in time.

Despite all that, he had taken one look at the sick little child of his prioress' eldest brother and immediately loved him as if he had sprung from his own loins. He might not understand why, but love the boy as a son he did and he warmed with the thought of how the lad's eyes would brighten when he saw the hobbyhorse.

Tomorrow I will get the remaining leather, cloth, and rags to finish the horse's head, he thought. Richard must have his toy soon or he will be reluctant to take that bitter medicine. He quite understood. He'd hate taking the vile stuff too.

"God is gracious!"

The words startled Thomas and he shot back to his knees.

"You are smiling," the priest said with an explosion of rotting breath. "God must have given you the peace you prayed for."

"Aye, that He did, priest. Now we may return in tranquility to our beds." Thomas wasn't sure his eyes would stay closed even now, but perhaps his companion would fall into the deep sleep that avoided him and he could eventually slip away in peace from their shared room.

Anselm rose from his knees as quickly as a youth. Thomas took a little longer. His legs were numb. As he rubbed his shins and calves to bring some feeling back, he glanced in the direction of the shadowy woman he had seen before. She was no longer there. Either she had moved deeper into a more private gloom when she heard Anselm's voice or she had left the chapel entirely. He shook his head. Perhaps he had only imagined her just as he had imagined her twin. Then he nodded to the patiently waiting priest and the two men walked in silence out of the chapel.

ᏩᎥᎥᎥᎥᎩ ᏩᎥᎥᎥᎥᎩ ᏩᎥᎥᎥᎥᎩ

The air was sharp but heavy with snow. Anselm was as silent as he had been on the journey to the chapel, but Thomas was sure he saw a smile on the man's lips. He shut his eyes briefly. They burned with fatigue. By the time they got back to their shared room, it would almost be time for the Night Office, something he was sure this priest would observe. Would he never get the sleep he longed for?

They had just begun the torturous climb up the stairs to the private quarters above the great hall when they heard angry voices below them in the castle ward.

"You are a murderous, lying knave!"

"Fool! Have you buried your head so long in oxen dung that your wits have rotted?"

Thomas gestured to the priest to remain where he was and slipped quietly to a narrow window. He peered down into the darkness. Just below him he could distinguish moving shadows but could see little else, even against the lighter mounds of freezing slush. Two men must be there, or so he guessed from the noise they made, but surely no more than two.

Father Anselm was at Thomas' side in an instant, tugging fiercely at his sleeve. "We must stop them, brother," he said. "Or else they will be killing each other!"

"Hush!" Thomas ordered, but it was too late.

"'S blood, man! Someone's near," one voice called out.

"Then you'll live this hour, but more I cannot promise," the other said. In an instant both shadows had faded into the surrounding gloom.

"We must tell the lord baron about this!" Anselm continued, now clutching Thomas' arm so tightly it hurt.

"Who shall we say they were, priest? Did you know their voices?"

Anselm hesitated. "No. I could not say for cert. I fear I was lost in thought when we heard them."

"Most likely they were two drunken soldiers who will forget their mutual grievances sooner than they will their aching heads on the morrow. The baron would pay no heed to such a trivial matter."

"But a man of God must…"

"Pray, priest. We must pray for their souls that they will see their folly in the light of God's good day."

"You speak well, brother."

Thomas hoped he had, for he was quite sure he had recognized the voices of both Robert and Henry in the shadows below him.

Chapter Twelve

Thomas jolted straight up from a deep sleep. Despite the cold air, sweat broke out on his body. He would have sworn a loud noise had awakened him, but, when he looked over at the sleeping priest, Anselm was snoring gutturally, his breath filling the chamber like the stench of a dead Welsh dragon. Perhaps the sound had been from a dream.

"Will I ever leave night terrors behind me?" he mouthed silently as he rubbed his forehead with his fingers. If only he were at Tyndal, he could walk away his pounding heart and aching head in the peace of the cloisters, but Anselm would wake the minute he put foot to ground. Indeed, assuming he could escape there alone, even the chapel was no place for serene thoughts as the tortured image on the cross came to mind. Perhaps a tranquil spot could not exist anywhere in a place of war and blood. As soon as that thought took form, Thomas shook his head in amazement that he would even have such an idea. Was he turning into a bloodless priest?

A woman screamed.

Thomas was on his feet. This time he knew the sound was real, not his overheated imagination. He ignored a muffled question from the noisome priest and hurried to the door. As he rushed into the hall, others were crowding into it as well.

Baron Adam was immediately ahead of him, fully dressed, sword in hand.

Prioress Eleanor, with Sister Anne behind, emerged from Richard's chambers to join Adam.

Thomas glanced over at her door just as the Lady Juliana opened it and looked out. Her eyes were large with unspoken questions, but she stood in the partially open doorway and did not join the crowd in the passageway.

In front of him, he could see a few rumpled, sleepy-eyed servants staggering out of the stairwell.

"Please, God, no!" the prioress cried out as she came to an abrupt stop behind her father. Her voice was sharp with alarm. One hand rested on her father's back for support, the other at her mouth.

Thomas stared with equal horror at the scene over the baron's shoulder, just as unwilling to believe what he saw before them.

Standing at her chamber door was the Lady Isabelle, a fur blanket wrapped tightly around her body, her face as pale as a corpse.

On the stone floor in front of her, lying in a pool of darkened blood, was the body of Henry, heir to Lavenham. Kneeling beside that body, glistening dagger in hand, was Robert of Wynethorpe.

Chapter Thirteen

Adam and Geoffrey stood facing each other in the dining hall, just feet apart in front of the blazing fireplace. Years of friendship forged first in childhood, later in battle, and after in the companionship of shared interests and views now warred with grief and anger over the fates and actions of their respective sons. Eleanor and Sister Anne sat in chairs at the high table and watched the men's eyes shifting back and forth under hooded lids, their mouths working almost imperceptibly as they struggled to find words that each could say to the other. Eleanor longed to break the silence and comfort both her father and Sir Geoffrey, but resisted. They had been raised to scorn the comforting touch as weak and womanish, thus each alone must weigh the strength of their mutual friendship against that of grief and recriminations. Alone each must discover how the scales did balance when one man's son murdered that of the other. Indeed, she might share their agony as sister to Robert and friend to Henry, but she was a woman, allowed the luxury of public tears and the comfort of soft arms. Only before the eyes of God might a man bred to war be permitted to weep.

As if she had read Eleanor's mind and knew her struggle, Anne reached over and gently touched her hand.

Adam coughed and looked down at his feet.

Geoffrey cleared his throat and turned his head away. His voice husky with swallowed tears, he finally whispered, "I cannot believe Robert killed my son." There was not the slightest hint of accusation in his tone.

"Yet he held the dagger and Henry's blood was on his hands and cloak. How can I say he is guiltless?" As his friend opened his mouth to speak further, Adam shook his head. "Nay, Geoffrey, do not say more. You are generous to hold back your condemnation of my son, but he must and will answer for his deeds like a man. Any son of mine must take full responsibility for his actions, whether good or evil. I will send a messenger for the sheriff."

"Has Robert said anything in his defense, father?" Eleanor asked quietly.

The two men looked at her in surprise as if they had forgotten she was there.

Adam straightened his back. "He claims innocence."

"Then perhaps he is innocent." Eleanor hesitated. "I, for one, have never known him to lie. Of all of us," she said with a slight smile at her father, "he is the one who took most after you in plain speech."

Even in the flickering light of the fire, Eleanor could see her father's face turn pale with the effort to control conflicting emotions. A father's love was clearly at odds with the baron's wish to honor justice.

"He will have the opportunity to tell his tale." Her father's voice broke. He stared into the fire for a long moment, then continued. "The king's justice is equitable."

"Of that, there is no doubt," Eleanor said, then gestured at a shuttered window. "But the snow has already begun to fall thick and fast, and I fear the road may be impassable even now. No messenger can get out while this storm rages. Justice in the form of a distant sheriff will therefore be much delayed."

Adam scowled. "Then my son will have both the time and solitude to think on his sins."

"If I may be so bold, I would like to suggest that we could learn something about the one who truly committed this deed if we had a knowledgeable person look at Henry's corpse. Sister Anne has much experience…"

"A nun?" Sir Geoffrey's contempt was palpable.

"She is sub-infirmarian at Tyndal and her reputation…"

"I have heard the tales, Lady Eleanor. I have no doubt that her skills with sick children and birthing women are highly prized. My son, however, was neither."

Not exactly what you suggested yesterday at the midday meal, Eleanor thought as she felt the heat of her fury burn her face at the man's scornful dismissal of Anne. "My lord, she did learn physic from her father and she is skilled…"

Sir Geoffrey's face too had turned scarlet. "I do not care if she is a saint, my lady. She is a woman and thus, by definition, a fragile and illogical creature. As such, she has neither the ability to rationally examine in detail what she sees nor the fortitude to look on the mutilated body of…" He sobbed, turned his head and covered his face with his hand.

"Surely…"

"Enough, Eleanor!" her father barked. "Wynethorpe Castle is not Tyndal. You have no authority here. Whatever Sister Anne's skills may be, and she has indeed done great service to this house," he bowed in the direction of Sister Anne, "Sir Geoffrey does not wish her to examine his son's body. Therefore, she shall not do so."

Eleanor glanced at Sister Anne as she fought down the impotent rage twisting inside her. Although Anne's head was humbly bowed, she managed to look sideways at her prioress, then give her a quick wink. Eleanor wished she had Anne's talent for humor and tranquillity in these situations.

"Indeed, my lords," she said at last with a calm remarkable even to her own ears, "I forgot myself and do beg forgiveness." However, she decided with grim determination, if you will not have Sister Anne, then you shall surely have someone else of my own choosing.

Adam nodded abruptly.

Sir Geoffrey was wiping his eyes with the sleeve of his cloak.

After a long moment of silence, Eleanor continued. "May I ask, my lord father, where you have imprisoned my brother?"

"In the tower by the bridge over the moat. We are holding no other prisoners so the chamber is comfortable enough. I have a guard outside his door. He cannot escape."

"May I speak with him?"

Adam raised his eyebrows. "Whatever for, girl?" His tone was gentle.

"Does not a loving sister have the right to speak with her dear brother and offer comfort to him before the king's justicular judges him innocent or guilty?" she replied, her tone quite meek. Her father might be willing to put honor above family feeling and thus accept the possibility of Robert's guilt. She was not. Of course her brother might kill a man in self-defense. That she would concede. Or he could do so in the defense of an innocent victim. He would never kill out of malice, however, and, if Robert said he was innocent, he was. As far as Eleanor was concerned, it was all just that simple.

With luck, this fierce snowstorm would continue long enough to keep any messenger from being sent to the sheriff and she might yet convince her father to turn his considerable tactical skills to the defense of his son. To do so, however, she must hear the full tale from Robert as soon as possible so she might present his defense in terms her father would have to concede.

"Of course you may see him, child. I will have a soldier accompany you."

"A soldier is unnecessary, father." Eleanor glanced at Anne. "Brother Thomas will accompany me."

"Robert may be your brother, but he stands accused of murder. I cannot not take the chance that he might seize you as a hostage to gain his freedom…"

Eleanor closed her eyes to control her temper. "I assure you that Brother Thomas is sufficient protection against any such thing. He has already proven his courage and resourcefulness during the dark days just after my arrival at Tyndal."

"Robert has trained as a knight and no monk…"

"Brother Thomas is no frail ascetic," she snapped.

For the first time this day, her father's eyes briefly sparkled with laughter. "I had noticed that, Eleanor."

"I do believe he and your brother have quite taken to each other, or so Brother Thomas has said to me," Anne interjected, glancing modestly at her prioress. "There is no reason to believe the Lord Robert would hurt either one of you, and indeed he might find comfort in having a priest with him at this time." She looked over at the baron. "And should there be any problem, my lord, I do assure you that Brother Thomas is quite capable of defending your daughter. More able, perhaps, than Father Anselm, who does appear quite slight of build, if I might be so bold to say?"

Eleanor hid her smile of delight at her friend's clever speech.

Adam shrugged, then looked at Geoffrey, who nodded.

"Very well," the baron said. "Go and take your monk with you but exercise due care. I do not want to lose a daughter, or her broad-shouldered priest, in addition to Geoffrey's son."

Eleanor knew from the warmth in her face that she was blushing at his description of Thomas but drew herself up and looked back at her father with dignity. "Thank you, my lord," she said, then turning to Sir Geoffrey, she added, "and I would also like permission to bring comfort to your good wife."

"Comfort? What for? She is well enough."

Eleanor shook her head with a dismissive gesture. "It is a woman's matter. I do not doubt your wife's resilience after seeing her stepson's bloody corpse outside your chamber door this morning, but women often find a special consolation from…"

"She has Father Anselm."

"…the company of another woman." Out of the corner of her eye, she saw Anne bite her lip. Her friend had seen through her ruse. She prayed Sir Geoffrey had not. Eleanor hoped the Lady Isabelle knew something important about the relationship between Robert and Henry that would prove the innocence of her confined brother. She had to talk to her.

Geoffrey hesitated.

"Let the girls talk, Geoffrey," Adam said. "What's the harm? They have known each other since childhood, and your wife might well find more comfort from my daughter's words than from those of our priest."

Geoffrey shrugged. "Very well. I will tell her to expect you."

Eleanor modestly lowered her head in thanks to her father and his friend, then squeezed Anne's hand to acknowledge her calming influence. At least, she thought with less than humble glee, she had won more of this war of wills than either of the two men realized.

Chapter Fourteen

The prison tower guard jumped to his feet when Eleanor and Thomas appeared at the top of the stone stairs. She smiled at the soldier. He had been in her father's service since her own childhood.

He will be kind to Robert, she thought as she raised her finger to her lips in a command of silence. Soundlessly, she walked to the small barred window in the heavy wooden door of the cell, and the man offered his hand so she might stand on his stool and look in on her brother.

Robert was sitting on his bed of bare straw, head in red-stained hands, and still dressed in the bloody clothes in which he had been found. She frowned. Surely he could have been provided with a change of clothes. He had not been chained, however, and she could not smell the stench of feces. The walls might be bare of woven cloth, but her father had given him a cell comfortable enough for a Welsh prince, should the baron ever be lucky enough to catch one. She would make sure her brother had water for washing and clean, warm garments.

Eleanor nodded to the guard. As he helped her down, she looked into his eyes and saw both fear and sorrow for the duty he had been given. She smiled gently at the man and said, "I am grateful my brother has you to watch over him. My father has oft praised you for acting honorably in your dealings with all, friend or foe. Your vigilance and honesty are a comfort to our family until this matter can be resolved, and we do thank you for it." Before the soldier turned to unlock the door so she and Thomas could enter, Eleanor thought she saw a tear slip out of a corner of his eye and quickly disappear into his grizzled beard.

Robert raised his head when he saw his sister and friend enter. His eyes were raw from weeping, and his cheeks above the beard were tinted pink from the blood his tears had washed from his hands.

Eleanor knelt in the rushes by her brother's side, took his stained hands in hers and kissed them. "I believe in your innocence, Robert. Like father, you would not lie even to save your life."

As he pulled her hands toward his lips and kissed them in return, Robert gave Eleanor a tired smile. "A clever lass you've always been, sweet sister. Were I guilty of this crime, I would now be a quivering wretch, confessing all and huddled at your tiny feet after such soft words."

"No, dear brother. Had you been guilty, you would not be huddled at my feet. The weight of your anguish would have caused you to fall to your death from this very tower ere now." Eleanor looked directly into his eyes for a moment, then her eyes grew fond with the love she bore him.

"You are not only astute but have a wit so sharp no man of sense would approach you without arming himself in the finest chain mail." Robert glanced up at Thomas. "How ever do you cope with her at the priory, brother?"

"Carefully," Thomas said, then coughed, his face reddening.

Eleanor was amused at her monk's blunt response and glanced at him with a gentle look, for surely he had spoken before thinking and must fear that he had offended.

Robert's laugh was hearty. "As did Hugh and I when she was with us, even as a child. You see, Eleanor, how the men in your life respect as well as love you."

"Tell us what happened," she said, rising from her knees and seating herself next to her brother on the crisp straw. With luck he would not have noted the heat rising in her face as she wondered if Thomas bore some love for her as well. Perhaps both men would mistake her blush for womanly modesty.

Her brother's brief mirth faded and the color in his face paled, but he squeezed her hands gently as if to comfort her. "I am innocent of Henry's murder. I swear that on any hope I may have of Heaven. Aye, he and I had issue with each other. That I will freely admit, but I did not murder him. I confess that we nearly came to sword's point today. Yesterday? Which is it now?" He nodded at Thomas. "Was it not you and Father Anselm I heard earlier this morning in the stairwell to the hall when Henry and I were arguing in the castle ward?"

"Aye."

"That was not the first time we have come close to blows."

Eleanor frowned. "I remember Henry as an ill-humored boy on occasion, Robert, but he could be sufficiently pleasant too. I recall that you both got along well enough in the past, although you oft had disagreement with each other and you were closer to George. What has caused such hard strife between you now?"

Robert looked down, then released his sister's hands. He motioned to a stool. "Please sit, brother. Both you and my sister must be weary. Would you share some wine with me?" He walked over to the ewer and gestured to some cups. "I may be a prisoner here, but my father has not chosen to starve me or to withhold wine from his store."

Eleanor nodded approval for Thomas to take refreshment, then refused the same for herself. She watched her brother and waited.

"I know you await my answer, Eleanor," Robert said as he concentrated on pouring the wine for Thomas. Then he stared down at his hands and they began to shake. He quickly put the ewer down but could not manage to release the cup he held. "I bear his blood still! I fear I…"

Thomas rushed over to Robert and took the cup away from him. "I will pour for both of us, my lord, but first let me bring you a basin of water for washing."

Robert resumed his seat next to his sister and sat in silence, staring at his hands. When Thomas brought the basin and held it for him, he briefly swirled one hand in the water, his eyes unblinking as he watched the water turn pink with Henry's blood.

Eleanor rested her hand on her brother's arm. He moaned, then sagged forward, his head bowed, his back bent. For all his youth in years, he now had the look of a very frail, very old man.

"Aye, Henry was tolerable as a child," he said, at last finding his voice, "although we did quarrel even then. However, you surely knew that he has always fancied the Lady Isabelle. Being of an age, he expected they would be married." Robert's words faded into a mumble.

"As did we all," Eleanor replied, her voice soft with affection.

"When his father married her instead, Henry became quarrelsome. On the occasions when our families were together, I watched the worm of jealousy eat away at him until his humors became quite unbalanced. He grew more sullen with his father and his behavior toward his stepmother was often rude when they were alone together. Indeed, she found his manner quite distasteful."

"Did she speak of this to her husband?" Thomas asked.

"I do not know in truth, but her discomfort and Henry's behavior were surely the subject of common talk. Sir Geoffrey must have been aware, but whether he learned of it from his own observation, from his wife, or another source I do not know. Nor do I know if he and Henry had private words on the matter. The incident at the mid-day meal yesterday, however, was only one of the more extreme public scenes between father and son."

"You did know that Lady Isabelle found his attentions inappropriate. Did she speak with you about them? Was this the cause of the hostility between you and Henry?" Eleanor asked.

Robert stiffened. "She did not need to speak of her feelings. The displeasure was clear from her expression. The matter between Henry and me came to a head in another way altogether. In view of our youthful friendship and the coming union of our families, I saw no reason to avoid contact with the Lady

Isabelle. Out of respect to Sir Geoffrey, I never did so unless she was properly attended, and my manner toward her was always both courteous and most brotherly. I soon learned that Henry took offence at any speech I had with her. I decided to avoid her company for fear that my presence would add to her pain."

"But you did not continue to avoid her," Thomas said. "This morning I saw you walking with the Lady Juliana and her stepmother was walking just behind."

Robert looked sharply at Thomas. "Aye, but that was different."

"You could not have had either lady's maid with you instead?" Eleanor asked.

Her brother shook his head. "The Lady Isabelle insisted on accompanying us herself. She has joined with her husband as an ally of the marriage, and we all assumed Henry would be occupied with the family consultations over the union."

"What was Henry's opinion on this wedding?" Eleanor asked.

"He was not happy. In fairness to the man, now that he lies so foully murdered and cannot speak for himself, I will not conjecture a reason."

"I cannot understand why he would be so displeased. You would not be living with the Lavenhams, although the marriage might bring you into more frequent contact with Isabelle." Eleanor continued to study her brother's face.

Robert shrugged. "True."

"What were the circumstances of this planned union?" Thomas asked. "Perhaps a clue to his reasons can be found therein?"

"Brother Thomas' question has merit. Tell us from the beginning what the circumstances were, Robert."

"When our father asked me about the possibility of marriage with Juliana, I told him that I felt no desire for her but I did respect the lady, and such an alliance between our families would surely be a happy one. George assured me that she and I would gain contentment from such a union. Knowing us both well, he felt we would be compatible enough, indeed good companions in a life together. That was quite acceptable to me."

Eleanor smiled briefly. "Like our lord father, you are a most practical man."

Robert reached out for her hand again. "As children, Juliana and I had liked each other well enough. We probably knew each other better than most, who know nothing of the other spouse until their first intimacy in the marriage bed."

"Well said, Robert," Thomas replied.

"Surely Henry did not object to the lack of passion between you," Eleanor said.

"Nay, George told me that Henry would object to any marriage for Juliana. He wanted her to take the veil."

"Why?" Eleanor asked. "He would have saved little by that. A nun must bring land or coin to the convent as surely as a wife does to an earthly husband."

Robert shook his head. "I should not suggest reasons that Henry can neither refute nor defend."

"The sheriff will not have such scruples, sweet brother. I would rather hear what your thoughts are than a stranger's."

"Perhaps he was afraid that any marriage would take more from his inheritance than he cared to give, that he would surrender less to a convent than to a husband. Perhaps he thought it would bring any man into closer contact with Lady Isabelle and his jealousy could not bear the thought. I have suspected both at one time or another but cannot say which is the more accurate. If either."

Perhaps such would be questions to pursue with Sir Geoffrey's wife, Eleanor thought. "In truth, Isabelle's behavior was not always an example of modesty and propriety from what I saw. She did tend to fuel the fires of jealousy. At dinner, I saw her hand on your thigh, Robert, something a wife does not do to a man who is not her husband, unless..." She hesitated. "Was such behavior common between you?"

Her brother flushed. "Nay, sister! It is true that she does love to put flame near wood. Nevertheless, her pleasure is only in watching the fire char the branch. Indeed, what she did last night was more accidental than deliberate. She had had too much wine at dinner."

How speedily he has come to her defense, Eleanor noted with concern. She glanced at Brother Thomas and saw his frown. Perhaps he, too, questioned her brother's all too quick response. She took a deep breath and continued. "Perhaps she had, but now I must ask how it happened that you should be found with Henry's body, a dagger in your hand, outside the Lady Isabelle's room while she cowered close by with no sign that her husband was near."

"I had had a confrontation with Henry before the midday meal which our father broke up."

Thomas nodded.

"That you were a witness to as well." Robert's look darkened, although the monk could not tell if the cause was anger or fear.

"By accident, my lord. I swear it," Thomas answered quickly. "I was not spying on you," he added, his tone gentle.

"Indeed, I am grateful you were there. Such witnessing may lend verity to the rest of my tale. At that time, as you saw, Henry continued his crude jesting with his stepmother. Later, he and I had, but for the presence of you, brother, been ready to draw arms against each other again. Why he was in the ward at such a late hour, I cannot say. I had been making plans to feed our livestock with this heavy snow upon us and was just returning to the barracks. Perhaps he and I had been too much in each other's company the last few days, but it seemed we could not bear the sight of one another yesterday without fire sparking tinder. After I left him the second time, my spirit was sufficiently disturbed that I could not sleep."

"A reasonable thing, my lady," Thomas blurted out.

Remembering Thomas' own history of nocturnal wanderings at inopportune times, she nodded. "Indeed, I doubt it not. Go on."

"I decided to visit our father and seek his advice. He is often up before cock's crow, and I thought we might talk about the marriage and Henry's difficulties over it, as well as how I should handle the discord with my future brother-in-law. As I climbed the stairs to the quarters, I heard low voices. I stopped, not wanting to invade the privacy of, well, perhaps some lovers who did not want their tryst known. Then the voices stopped and, after waiting a bit, I continued up the stairs to the hall. I reached the top but saw no one. Suddenly, I tripped in the shadows and fell. My hands landed in something wet and sticky. After I picked myself up, I could see they were stained dark. When I smelled the metallic odor, I knew they were bathed in blood."

"Are you saying there was no light but moonlight? When Father Anselm and I passed through, the rushes were dim but lit," Thomas noted.

"They must have gone out before I arrived. It was quite dark with the snow falling and all windows barred shut. I did not know I had tripped on Henry's body so I felt for what had caused me to fall. At first I thought it might be a large animal, a dog perhaps, but quickly realized the shape was that of a man. The body was warm still, but I could not tell who it was. I thought two drunken soldiers might have strayed into the family quarters, an easy enough thing to do, then gotten into a fight where one had fled after wounding his fellow."

"How did you light the rushes?" Eleanor asked.

Robert hesitated. "When I stood up, Isabelle was standing in the door. She had a candle in her hand and reached out to give it to me. I lit the rushes with that, then knelt to see who was lying on the floor. I saw to my horror that it was Henry and the dagger lay beside him. I picked it up. Why I did that, I cannot say. Everything seemed so like a dream. I could not believe what was before me. As I took the knife into my hand, the lady screamed. I froze in horror as I looked down at the blood, which had also soaked into my clothes from my fall on the body. He must have been bleeding freely still. Then the next thing I heard was your voice, Eleanor. The servants grabbed me. You know the rest."

"You saw no one else, heard nothing, not even the echo of footsteps running away? No glimpse of a garment?" Eleanor asked.

Robert shook his head wearily.

They were all silent for a while, then Eleanor looked over at Thomas. "You are lost in thought, brother."

"Aye, my lady." He turned to Robert. "You say you saw no one yet you had heard voices, perhaps lovers you thought. You must have had reason to conclude that the voices were those of a man and a woman."

"I did not recognize them and cannot be certain one of the voices was that of a woman. The pitch of one voice may have been somewhat higher. That is all. Now that you ask me, I cannot say for sure that it was not two men."

As he watched Robert lower his head and look down at his feet, Thomas was sure he was lying. The man was not practiced enough at deceit to look another directly in the eye while he twisted the truth.

Once again, Robert's shoulders slumped with fatigue and hopelessness.

Eleanor reached over and hugged her brother. "You must rest. Perhaps more details will come to mind later. In the meantime, I will send for clean clothes and enough warm water to bathe away the blood you are not guilty of shedding." As she stood, she nodded at Thomas. "Please stay a while and bring my brother some comfort for his soul. Then we must all pray that we find the truth before this storm ceases and we must send for the sheriff to take my brother away to crueler lodgings."

Chapter Fifteen

Thomas watched his prioress' brother lean back on his heels and cross himself. Robert had just finished his confession but had said nothing that would guarantee him a greater place in Hell than any other mortal man.

He had denied the murder. He had denied even wishing Henry dead, although he grieved over his desire to do him at least some bodily harm for insults he had made against the Lady Juliana and for the death of Hywel, an accident Sir Geoffrey had explained was the result of Henry's thoughtlessness. The nature of the insults against his betrothed he had refused to specify lest they befoul the reputation of the lady. Even with the shadow of a hangman's rope swinging above his head, Robert of Wynethorpe was a most chivalrous man.

"You will feel better after you have gotten a tub for bathing and clean clothes, my lord," Thomas said at last.

Robert's lips twisted into a bitter smile. "You are kind, my friend, kinder than my condition warrants."

"One may be kind to a guilty man for the judgment of God is nigh. An innocent man deserves courteous treatment."

"Do you not believe that I am innocent of Henry's murder, Thomas? Your tone is harsh."

"Then you misread the meaning. I cannot believe that a man would lie in confession, knowing he could never deceive God and must soon face Him. That aside, I do believe you are innocent, yet my opinion means little while the truly guilty remains hidden. The harshness you hear in my tone is from worry. I pray the murderer may be discovered ere long."

Robert turned away. "Perhaps the killer has already made confession to his priest." He hesitated. "Has no one ever lied to you in confession?"

"If anyone ever has, I would not be the one to suffer. Whether or not a man chooses to hide his sins from me is irrelevant. God's justice will always prevail."

"Of that I have no doubt, but, since I am still of this world, I find comfort that you have faith in my innocence."

Thomas smiled. "Aye, Robert, that I do. I do not think you killed him."

"I did not murder him," Robert said quickly, then fell silent. "Had I done so, I would have confessed that."

Thomas blinked. Was there some significance in his friend's choice of words? "Can you tell me nothing more about what you saw and heard?"

Robert stared into space, his brows furrowed with thought. "Nay."

"Think on it carefully. Might you not have seen someone when you entered the hall outside the chambers Sir Geoffrey shared with his wife? Something you saw that seemed but a shadow at the time? Your life is in the balance, Robert. Give me even the thinnest thread to follow!"

Robert stood and walked over to the basin of water that Thomas had put on a small table. For a long moment, he dabbled his fingers in it, staring as the water circled around them. "Nothing," he said, his whispered voice hoarse.

"When you heard the voices, however..."

"In truth, now that I think more on it, I must confess that I spoke too quickly when my sister was here. I heard nothing, unless it was voices in the dining hall. Aye, it must have been that and thus my confusion. It would have been the servants. Nay, I misspoke, Thomas. I heard no speech between two people."

Thomas frowned at this sudden and doubtful retraction. "Such a quick abandonment of your previous statements,

Robert? But surely with the body so warm there must have been someone nigh, someone that could have escaped down the passageway to other stairways. You must have seen or heard…"

Robert swirled around, his eyes angry but focused on the wall behind Thomas. "I saw no man. I heard no one, and I did not murder Henry. That may not be enough, Thomas, but that is all I can say."

"Hywel's wife? Might she have come to confront Henry…?"

"His wife was given a draught by the woman who took her away from his corpse this morning. After I left the dinner, I paid a visit to offer what comfort I could, and the old woman assured me that the drink she had concocted would put the wife into such a deep sleep for so many hours that she would awaken with a lesser grief. She has, after all, young children she must comfort and cannot afford to suffer such deep sorrow herself."

There was clearly no purpose in pursuing anything further with Robert. The man's eyes had glazed over and his color was now a gray pallor. If need be, the story of Hywel's wife could be easily confirmed.

Thomas rose. "Will you promise to send word if anything else comes to mind, my friend?"

"Aye," Robert replied. His words were barely audible, his head bowed, and his expression was hidden.

As Thomas left the prison cell and the guard closed the door behind him, he asked himself how carefully Robert might have chosen his words. Indeed, the man did seem to make a distinction between *kill* and *murder*, but with greater interest Thomas noted that Robert had said he had told him all he could *say*, not all that he *knew*.

Chapter Sixteen

Later, as daylight finished wrestling the last of the lingering shadows into the crevices of the rough corridor wall, Brother Thomas stood outside Isabelle's room, stared down at the dark stains of blood on the stone floor, and shivered.

I might have a man's body but a child's heart still beats in my chest, he thought ruefully.

In his youth, he had often awakened in the deep night to the sounds of scuffling and moans outside his room, and he had cowered in terror, waiting for the sun to chase away those demons he knew must be waiting for him just outside his door. In the morning he would rise, open the door and, with bravery bought with sunlight's coin, look out to see just such stains on the stone floor. He imagined the marks must from the blood of giant gray werewolves struggling with great black demons, until an older man took some pity on him and said that the blood was from mortal men fighting over petty things, and nothing to fear at all. He had been relieved that the creatures were not supernatural, but some fear had remained with him although he was no longer a little boy alone in the dark.

"I am a man, not a lad anymore," he reminded himself with some success, then bent to look more closely around the area where Henry had been murdered. After a few minutes he shook his head. There was nothing here to suggest anything had happened than the most obvious. An examination of Henry's body would reveal more details, of course, but he feared there was naught here to help Robert's cause.

He hunched his shoulders as they began to ache in the cold and considered the possible ways of escape from this place. Henry had been killed right in front of the guestrooms assigned to Sir Geoffrey and his wife. Their chambers were at the opening to the staircase that wound down to the dining hall and then out to the castle ward. That was one exit. The rooms also faced the point where that inner passage turned and led toward one of the defensive towers at the corner of the wall surrounding the inner ward. That would be the only other way a murderer could have escaped because, in the other direction, the corridor ran straight down to the room Thomas shared with Father Anselm and abruptly ended there as if the workmen had never finished it.

"When Robert first claimed he had heard voices as he climbed the stairs but saw no one," Thomas said aloud, "the speakers might have been anywhere. In the stairwell, in the dining hall, near the guestrooms or further into that tower passageway."

Since the stairs were deliberately designed to be steep and sharply curved so any attacker would have difficulty swinging his sword against defenders above him, it was not surprising that Robert could not see anyone just ahead of him. Had Robert been near the dining hall when he heard the voices or had he been beyond that and closer to the living quarters above the hall? He could not remember if the man had said. Now, of course, Robert was denying that he had heard two voices at all so it would be useless to ask him, and, needless to say, Thomas did not believe his abrupt retraction.

"If the voices had come from the dining hall," Thomas continued, "the speakers might have remained there until Robert passed that entrance, then retreated down the stairs he had just climbed. If, however, they had come from this higher level, the murderer, or murderers, might have heard him coming and escaped down the passageway to the tower before Robert emerged from the stairwell. Those are the only ways to escape."

What if the speakers were further down the corridor where there was no exit? They might not have heard him climbing the stairs and that meant they might not have been able to escape before Robert emerged and would have been trapped. Thomas closed his eyes and tried to picture exactly what he had seen last night.

He and Anselm were in the very last room in that corridor. When the Lady Isabelle screamed, Anselm had been asleep. Thomas could confirm that he was there and no one else was in the room. Nor had the priest ever emerged. He had been sitting at the edge of his bed, pale and quaking, when Thomas returned with the grim news.

Next to them were the baron's chambers, and as Thomas was leaving his room, the baron was rushing from his own door. He had been fully dressed and had his sword in hand. No one was in the corridor between those two rooms. That Thomas could confirm as well.

Thomas hesitated and opened his eyes. "Was it odd that the baron was fully dressed at such an early hour?" Perhaps not, he decided, for Robert had said that his father was often up before cock's crow. Still, the hour had been very early. Any cock would still be enjoying the lush charms of his hen of choice and not yet sated enough to bring forth his morning boast. Perchance the Baron Adam had also just returned from the warmth of another's bed. Or, like Thomas, suffered sleepless nights alone. He would think more on that.

The baron was, in fact, now residing in Robert's usual quarters. When his grandson fell ill, he had given up his rooms with their luxuries of a curtained bed and hearth for warmth. The room next to the baron was now where Richard lay. The prioress shared it with Sister Anne as well while they cared for him. Of course, he had seen his prioress leave the room just behind her father. Sister Anne had returned to be with Richard as soon as Henry's body was discovered, so Thomas had looked behind him as she left. Again, no stranger was in the corridor.

Next to the boy's sickroom was the chamber assigned to the Lady Juliana. Had he seen her? He closed his eyes. The image of Juliana's face peering around the door of her room came to mind. He could recollect nothing but her head.

Her head? It was covered, covered with a hood as if she had just returned from a walk and still had on her cloak. Indeed, she was dressed in a cloak, now that he thought more on it. Odd, that. With whom might she be walking at such a black hour? Not Robert, surely. Not alone? Or was it? Perhaps they had been together and Robert had wanted to protect... Nay, there was no need to protect his lady's virtue. Few would begrudge a betrothed couple the right to sample a bit of marital pleasure before the final vows were spoken. After all, a betrothal was binding in the eyes of God...but there was no betrothal yet. Might that be Robert's reason for wanting to protect the lady?

"If the two had spent some hours in bed together, they would have done so in Juliana's room surely, since Robert had moved to the barracks to provide room for the guests when the Lavenhams arrived. Thus she would not have needed her cloak." Thomas rubbed his eyes where a dull ache had taken up residence.

Unless it had indeed been she who was in the chapel when he had gone with Anselm to pray. He had thought she had left before they did, had he not? Nay, now he remembered that he had thought the woman might have moved further into the shadows. If she had left before he and the priest had returned to their room, she would have had time to undress for bed. If she had left so much later that she was still in her cloak when Robert was discovered with Henry's corpse, however, she must have seen something. Surely...

"Yet she has said nothing. Could Robert have just left her bed and, to cover her nakedness, she threw on the cloak? But why do that when a blanket would serve as well?" Again, he could not imagine that she would not have confessed their tryst with her soon-to-be-betrothed when his life was at stake. "There is something amiss here, yet I cannot grasp what it is."

Had Wynethorpe been like many other castles, Thomas thought, there would have been a private entrance to the chapel from the lord's solar or indeed from any of the other chambers, especially that of the resident priest. Whatever the reason for the omission of such a comfort, Thomas had heard from Father Anselm that it was the source of one of his most joyful trials. No matter how foul the weather he had to wend his way down those perilous stairs past the dining hall, into the inner ward, and around the quarters to that small entrance in the inner ward wall. Thomas had caught himself thinking at the time that the trip to the chapel in a heavy rain might be the only time Father Anselm ever got a bath. He smiled at the thought of the priest sprinting through the open ward to avoid even God's attempt to bathe him.

"Nonetheless," he muttered, "the lack of such a private entrance does eliminate any other possible escape routes."

At least the Lady Isabelle seemed to have been in bed, as they all should have been, and asleep when the murder occurred. When he saw her, she was standing in the corridor with her fur blanket thrown around her body for warmth and to hide her own nakedness. It was her scream that had roused them all. Still, it was curious that she had been calm enough to hand Robert a candle to light the rushes yet had screamed when he picked up the dagger. Had Robert been correct about the timing of those events? What had awakened her? Had she seen or heard anything outside her room…

Suddenly Thomas remembered how the lady had played with Robert under the tablecloth at dinner. "Could Robert have been in bed with the Lady Isabelle last night?" he exclaimed in shock at the realization. "Could it be her honor he is protecting?"

Thomas rubbed his eyes again. The ache did not diminish. Indeed, this new question added even more complications to an already murky situation. He understood from Robert that Sir Geoffrey, being a husband who found a woman's monthly courses distasteful, had chosen to spend his last nights in the barracks rather than with his wife. A woman who did not expect a husband in her bed usually had her maid for warmth or company, yet Thomas had seen no maid with the Lady Isabelle. Perhaps the maid had not come to the door. Perhaps her mistress had kept the maid back so she would not see the horror of the corpse? Or had the maid been sent away so Robert could come to Isabelle that night? The baron's manservant had appeared, for it was he that arranged to take the corpse away. Perhaps Thomas had just failed to see the lady's attendant in the confusion of the moment.

At least he had been able to confirm that Hywel's wife had slept from early evening through late morning with the old woman in attendance. That was the only question that had been resolved, however, and too many others gnawed at him, not the least of which involved his fondness for the man accused of Henry's murder. Could this man, to whom he had taken such a liking, be a killer? Or was he an honorable man who would die before he would betray someone he believed should be protected? His instincts told him Robert was innocent of murder, although he was surely guilty of something. If nothing else, he was lying, even if the cause was a matter of honor.

An examination of the corpse would either raise more questions or settle some. Baron Adam had ordered the body removed to the chapel and had locked away the dagger found in Robert's hand as evidence for the sheriff to collect when he could be summoned. Thomas thought it interesting that Sir Geoffrey had trusted Robert's father to keep the dagger, considering it was his own son who was accused of killing Sir Geoffrey's.

"On second thought, maybe it is not so odd," Thomas muttered. "When the servants brought Sir Geoffrey from the barracks, he seemed as distraught over the idea that Robert had killed Henry as he was over the death of his own son."

Perhaps the years of friendship between the two men allowed each to feel the grief of the other as much as they felt their own loss. It touched Thomas that such might be so.

Suddenly he heard a soft rustle behind him and he spun around. The tiny outline of his prioress was barely visible in the gray shadows at the top of the stairs. He wondered how long she had been watching him and what she had heard him mutter to himself.

"My lady?" He bowed.

"I was on my way to visit with the Lady Isabelle, Brother Thomas, but I am glad to have first found you alone. I must briefly speak with you in confidence, and I beg that you will answer me with forthrightness when I ask you two important questions."

He hesitated, suspecting what she wanted to ask. He struggled with his reply to one of her questions, then quickly made his decision less on logic than on what his heart told him. "On my hope of Heaven, I will keep your words in confidence and will answer you with honesty, my lady."

"In addition, I must also ask of you a favor."

"To do you any favor would bring me both pleasure and honor."

"For all of this, you have my deepest gratitude." She stepped into the pale light and looked up at him. "As you may know, I love my brother as much as any sister could and believe I know him well, what he could and could not do. I am, however, still a sister, a weak mortal, and my judgment may be clouded." She gestured at the stains on the floor. "There is nothing here that acquits Robert. I'm sure you have found the same. I fear that a court will look at the evidence we now have and hang him."

Thomas nodded sadly. "Aye, my lady." Eleanor's eyes were the color of storm clouds, rimmed in red from tears he was sure she was too proud to let anyone see her shed.

"Then my first question to you is this: Do you think my brother has told us the whole truth?"

This was the question he dreaded most and, when he replied, he lowered his head for he could not look her in the eyes. "No, my lady," he said, his voice barely audible. "I do not."

"My second question is: Do you believe he is innocent?"

"Without question, I do," he said, the answer undoubted in his heart as he raised his eyes to meet hers, "and we must discover who did this terrible act. Quickly."

"Then you will carry out the next task I request?"

Thomas nodded.

"You must examine Henry's corpse with due care and bring me your observations as well as conclusions."

"My lady, I will do so as I promised, but my skills are poor and I could miss a crucial lead. Surely Sister Anne is a far better…"

"Sister Anne has been forbidden to do so. Your name, however, was not raised, and, since no one has said yea or nay to your examination, I see nothing to stop you from performing the task. To ease your mind about this, Sister Anne will be with me when you report what you have seen."

Thomas looked down into the gray eyes of his prioress and wondered whether those who thought they had thwarted her knew just how thoroughly they had been bested. Not for the first time, he found himself most grateful that he would never have to face this woman as an opponent in battle. "I will do as you ask, my lady."

As Prioress Eleanor of Tyndal reached out and squeezed his hand, gently and in silence, Thomas might have thought that her eyes shone with love had he not known better.

Chapter Seventeen

Eleanor rapped once on the door. No servant came to open it. She hesitated, sure she had heard muffled words. She knocked twice.

"If you be not Satan's imp, enter and cease the din!"

Eleanor opened the door.

The bereaved stepmother sat lolling on a stool, legs spread, her robe pulled up around her knees and her back braced against the bed. Her sole companions in the room were a large pitcher and a mazer cup perched on the wooden chest next to her. Indeed, the wife of Sir Geoffrey was quite drunk.

"I came to offer comfort," Eleanor said. "I could return later."

Trying to rise in greeting, Isabelle grabbed at the chest. Her hand slipped and knocked the empty wooden cup onto the floor. It bounced and rolled under her stool.

"It's you," the woman announced with conviction. She swung down to swipe up the errant cup, missed, then snagged it on the second try. "Wine?" she asked hospitably.

Eleanor shook her head.

"Another vow, I suppose."

Eleanor shrugged noncommittally. "The air is bitter cold. Wine warms both body and spirit on such a day." As well as loosening your tongue, she thought. You will more likely tell me things after another cup or two than you would say with a more sober mind.

"Vows make no sense."

"Have you never taken a vow, Isabelle?" the prioress asked as she studied the woman in front of her. Her playfellow of more innocent times might now have difficulty focusing her eyes, but Eleanor could see the sober glitter of hostility behind the unclear gaze. Could this be the same person she once knew or was the person sitting in front of her a demon in the likeness of Isabelle? The change was that dramatic.

The woman leaned back, waving Eleanor to another stool. "*Have you never taken a vow, Isabelle?*" Sir Geoffrey's wife twittered in malicious imitation. "Oh, aren't we ever so arrogant with that proud tone of voice. Have I never taken a vow, you ask? Doesn't marriage count?" Isabelle wobbled her head back and forth, pursing her lips as she did. "Perhaps not to you. Marriage reeks of lust, does it not, and you have surely taken a vow against that. How you have changed since we all made merry together that last summer before you returned to Amesbury, Eleanor."

"We have all changed since then." Eleanor kept her voice even. She could almost smell the bitter enmity well mixed with the woman's wine-infused sweat.

"Some more. Some less." Isabelle waggled her finger at the prioress. "Now you are given in marriage to God's Son, but did your bridegroom know before your vows that you were less than chaste when you came to him?"

Eleanor knew that silence was the wisest response.

"I know your secret!" Isabelle said in a loud whisper. "Did I not see how you and George played with each other the summer before you took your vows? Do you think I have forgotten?" Her expression darkened as she leaned forward. "Did you not give him your paps to suck by midsummer's eve as if he were a hungry babe, and did he not wiggle his fingers like eager min- nows in your private places?"

Eleanor paled with anger. "Did George tell you such tales?"

"Nay, he is too much the courteous knight to brag of your secret times together in the forest glade, but I know the ways of men and women. He may not have broken you and taken you for a proper ride, but most surely you did buck under his hand 'til calmed." She poured wine from the pitcher and gulped the cup dry. "Are you certain you won't take a cup of wine to ease the day's chill?"

Eleanor sat back and closed her eyes for a moment to regain her calm. Showing anger would mean taking the path Isabelle wanted her to follow and away from the real reason the woman had gone on this attack.

"Games played in the heat of youth are only games," Eleanor said at last. "You attracted enough bees to your honey as I recall, but no ill came of that. Where then was the sin in what we all did that summer?"

A drifting fog born of wine fumes veiled Isabelle's eyes as she tried to pour unwatered wine into her cup and missed by half. A rivulet of red meandered across the wooden chest and dripped down to the rushes beneath. "In the fall that came after, perhaps, but what would you know of that, my lady? You went off to Amesbury and sent not a word to any of us."

Not quite true, the prioress thought as she struggled to find a clue to Isabelle's bitter confrontation. Surely it could not be concern over George's broken heart after all these years. Isabelle's account of what had passed between George and Eleanor was more colorful than the reality of it, but George had loved her. If Eleanor had written him, he would have harbored hope when there was no possibility of any consummation. She had therefore chosen the lesser cruelty of silence. Nonetheless, she had written to Juliana on occasion and had certainly included Isabelle as well, but the correspondence had become sporadic as often happens between friends whose lives take different routes. The last letter she had written was on the death of Juliana's mother. The reply had been proper but no more. Isabelle had never sent her any message at all.

No, Eleanor was sure that Isabelle was not harboring such hot anger on behalf of George's thwarted dreams. Had she resented the greater friendship Eleanor had had with Juliana? Nay, she doubted that. The woman in front of her, drinking yet another mazer of wine, had never sought such closeness with Eleanor. Whatever was troubling her so?

"Perhaps some important message was not delivered to me, Isabelle, or a letter I sent you all was lost? I did write on the death of the Lady…"

"We received it."

"I did not hear the news of your marriage to Sir Geoffrey…"

Isabelle snorted. "Marriage?"

Eleanor heart skipped a beat. Had she hit on it?

Isabelle put her head back and roared with laughter. "You call what I have a marriage? Aye, maybe a nun in holy wedlock would call it such. Yet when I took my vows, I swore to honor the marriage bed, not undertake chastity. What strange things vows are. In truth, I am as much a nun as you, Eleanor."

"I do not quite understand…"

Isabelle splashed more wine into her cup. "Don't play the innocent with me. Or are you really that dull of wit?"

Now was the time for a display of temper, Eleanor decided. "Indeed, I may have taken other vows, but I did not take one of stupidity. If you have something to say, out with it, but I have no desire to pry into things you might not wish to tell me."

Isabelle slapped her belly. "What is there to hide? Have I quickened with child since I became a wife?" She bent forward, her reddened eyes trying to focus. Her breath smelled like soured milk. "I am a young woman and was with child on my marriage day, but I have not quickened since. What does that tell you? The world would say that Sir Geoffrey may warm the bed with his body but his lust cannot warm his wife's seed. Many would advise him to set me aside for a woman who could conceive."

"If he got you with child before…"

"Got me with child, you say?" Isabelle's laugh stung the prioress' ears. "In truth, his member has withered with one of those vows you hold so precious, Eleanor. He promised God he would remain chaste if He saved the dying mother of his children. Although God did not hold to His part of the bargain, my husband apparently decided to keep to his, despite a new wife, until the Judgment Day."

"Then how...?"

Isabelle reached out, lifted the pitcher of wine over her head, and shattered it at her feet. Bits of pottery flew, one large piece rocking to rest at Eleanor's foot. Red wine splattered their robes, then slowly began to seep into the rushes between them.

The two women stared at each other. Isabelle's face changed from red to white and back again. Eleanor remained silent in the face of so much anger, so much grief, and too much drink.

"One night, Sir Geoffrey came to my chambers," Isabelle began, her voice low but each word spoken with an abrasive clarity. "I poured him much rich wine and soon he was quite drunk. As we lay dressed upon my bed, I let him kiss and play with me. Then, when he had passed out, I stripped him of his braes. Poor man! Despite all our merry games, his member was still as tiny as a babe's! On the morrow, he awoke with me naked beside him. I pointed to the blood on the sheet and wept, saying he had taken my maidenhead. A little chicken blood, the oldest trick in the world, but he believed it. Of course he did not remember the act, but such proof that he was no longer impotent gave him so much joy." She put her head in her hands and swayed with mirthless laughter.

"If not he, then who did get you with...?"

"In truth?" Isabelle sneered, bending so close to Eleanor that she could feel the heat of her breath. "It was Henry. He was the father of that child. He had raped me...."

Chapter Eighteen

After Eleanor had entered the Lady Isabelle's chambers, Thomas went back to his own. He wished he had not given his word about examining Henry's body. With great cheer he would pass the duty on to almost anyone else, but give his word he had and there was naught he could do to take it back. Nonetheless he would delay the task for an hour. The corpse might wait just a bit longer. After all, the living should take some precedence over the dead. Children most of all.

Walking through the door to his chambers, he smiled, then picked an object up from the corner where he had propped it. He tucked it under his arm and gave a boyish skip of joy before walking back down the hall with a gait more seemly in a man.

ᕼᕼᕼᕼᕼᕼ

"You are recovered," Thomas exclaimed as he walked into Richard's sick room and found him standing beside the bed.

Sister Anne was carefully tucking the hood of the boy's cloak around his neck for warmth. "If not fully so, well enough that I would have to tie him to the bed to keep him in it."

"I am fine, Uncle!" Richard hopped like a rabbit toward the monk, then stood grinning up at him. Had all men ever looked so innocent as lads, Thomas wondered as he smiled down at the boy. Then he shook his head. If the boy had not burrowed into his heart before like a puppy seeking warmth, he would surely have done so now.

"Sister Anne, would you say our young knight was well enough for a short ride on his brave new steed?"

"The hobbyhorse?" Richard's eyes grew large. "Oh, yes! Please, Aunt Anne, please say I may?"

Thomas grinned at Anne and silently mouthed, "Say yes, *Aunt!*"

Anne struggled to keep her expression stern. She had, however, utterly failed to banish the twinkle from her eye. "Very well," she said, "but only a short ride around the room. Then you must get rest and take your medicine."

Thomas whisked the hobbyhorse from behind his back where he had been hiding it. "One short ride then," he said, kneeling to the child's level to give him the toy.

The boy squealed with joy, hugged the horse to him, then held it out at arm's length and studied it with a gravity that had the stamp of his grandfather's face. "I name you Gringolet," he said at last, "and we shall have many adventures together."

"Aye, lad. There are dragons to slay and damsels to save," said Thomas.

Richard wrinkled his nose. "More dragons to slay, Uncle, and fewer damsels to save, methinks."

"What do you say to your uncle for bringing you such a fine horse, Richard?"

Without letting go of the toy, Richard threw his arms around Thomas and hugged him. "Thank you, Uncle! I love him, I do. Gringolet is the finest horse in my grandfather's castle!"

As Thomas hugged the boy back, he hoped Sister Anne did not see the tears of happiness in his own eyes. "Well," he said as he cleared his throat and stood up, "I had better show you how to hold those reins. Gringolet is a very spirited horse."

Soon the boy was trotting around the chambers on his fine wooden steed and Anne bent to Thomas' ear. "I have yet to meet a man who is not still a boy," she whispered.

As Thomas turned to smile at her, he felt the heat of a blush spread across his face.

Chapter Nineteen

"Henry raped you?" Eleanor stared at the woman in front of her. A torrent of feelings, horror and sorrow mixed, flooded her heart.

Isabelle nodded her head once. The fire of her anger banked, she sat hunched and wizened on her stool.

With gentleness, the prioress reached over and took her companion's hand. "Was there no one you could have told?"

Isabelle shook her head.

"Would you care to tell me more of the story?"

Isabelle said nothing.

"You may find some peace in the telling."

Sir Geoffrey's wife shook off the prioress' hand, then began to draw lines with one finger across the puddle of wine on the chest. "I had long known of Henry's wish to marry me," she began in a hushed tone. "The family hoped to retain the income from my lands, of course, but he lusted after me as well." She hesitated. "Many told me how fortunate I was that he longed for the woman as well as what wealth the woman would bring to him, and I would nod in agreement. Indeed, he is handsome enough to the eyes of other women. Or so some have said. Nonetheless, I dreaded the very thought of his touch, and I sickened at what I must endure on the wedding night."

"He knew this?"

"How could I tell him? And what difference would it have made? I knew that I had little choice in this marriage so prayed that I would come to feel...*nothing* instead of loathing when his fat fingers groped me." Isabelle grabbed Eleanor's arm with a ferocious strength. "Can you understand this at all. At *all*, Prioress? Bedding with Henry was like bedding with my natural brother! It was as unnatural and sinful to me as incest."

That Eleanor could indeed understand, yet she knew there was more to come. She nodded in silence. She did not want to stop the flow of the story.

"At first, his attentions were almost charming, childlike and innocent, but, as time went on, he began to plague me with incessant demands. I allowed the occasional kiss, but I could not bear his hand on my breast. My flesh froze at his touch, and I began to push him away when he fumbled with my clothes. I hoped he would take my hesitancy for maidenly modesty, but he became angry at my refusals. One day, he found me alone in the garden and would not stop with a kiss. He covered my mouth so I could not cry for help. Swearing I would now spread my legs for him whether I wished to or not, he pulled me to the ground and raped me."

"You could have told your priest."

"What an innocent you are, Prioress," Isabelle sneered. "Are you so removed from the world that you are ignorant of the assumption that any woman who quickens with child from sexual contact must have found pleasure in the act and thus may not cry rape? If you are, let me assure you that many of your cherished monastics accept that theory even more than those who remain in the world. Now tell me how could I claim rape when my courses ceased and I began to vomit every morning?"

"Indeed, Isabelle, not all believe that pregnancy equates to pleasure in the act. My Aunt Beatrice thought such a conclusion odd for she knew women who begat many yet remembered feeling no pleasure in the begetting, while others who had felt great joy in the act never had children."

"Your aunt was not in residence at Sir Geoffrey's estate."

"I might then understand why you hesitated to say anything after your courses had ceased, but surely you could have spoken before…"

"It is well that you did escape the world, Eleanor. You are too innocent to have long survived outside your convent walls."

"Not all in the world are without compassion, Isabelle."

Isabelle ignored her, then looked around, her mouth twisting with anger. "How can you breathe in here, Prioress? The air cuts like ice crystals." She looked over at Eleanor. "But then Wynethorpe Castle has always been a bitter place, especially when the winds howl and bring snow to this horrible land." Great beads of sweat began to break out on Isabelle's forehead and her face turned a pallid green. "Have you never had a dream that haunted you?" she abruptly asked, her voice dropping to a whisper as if she feared someone might overhear her words. "I have."

Eleanor blinked at the suddenness of the question, then quickly said, "Tell me about it."

"It came to me after the rape." Her eyes glazed over as the memory of the dream took hold of her. "I was in a meadow, naked, and the sun's gentle warmth flowed over me. A breeze, soft as baby's breath, caressed my body. As I glanced down, I saw that the silkiness under my feet was a tapestry of wildflowers: flecks of white, dots of lavender, bits of yellow hiding under green leaves as if shy of any notice. With a sigh, I bent my knees, extended my arms, and slid into the petals as if I were slipping ever so slowly into a tranquil pond. The flowers were as soft as angel feathers against my breasts."

Eleanor watched with fascination as Isabelle became bound with the spell of her dream.

"As I breathed in the comforting fragrance from the undergrowth, I remember thinking how foolish I had been to suffer so when the solution to all my problems was right before me. Indeed, I realized, the problem was no problem at all. Then a feeling of great peace coarsed through me. I closed my eyes and just lay there, listening to the sweet twittering of the birds in counterpoint to the delicate hum of insects.

"Then a gentle voice began to sing. The song was ancient, the voice long unheard but so dear I ached to hear it. Nay, I remember thinking, there was no need to feel the old pain. The singer's arms were open at last, and I could seek the refuge I had longed to find these many, many years. With a cry of welcoming joy, I turned on my back, stretched out my arms, and…" Isabelle closed her eyes. Her face glistened with sweat.

"The body that fell upon me was hard as castle stone. The man's jagged nails scratched my breasts like dull knives." She curled one hand between her legs as if protecting herself. "His rough hand bruised me here when he forced my legs apart." She opened her eyes wide, her gaze shimmering with horror.

"All I could see was black hair, hair heavy with encrusted knots that stung my face like nettles. The man cursed, then grunted as he rammed his sex into me and began to rasp away as if he would cut my body in half."

Eleanor reached out a hand to comfort her.

Isabelle swatted it away. "I tried to scream but no voice came forth, only a hot liquid flowed from my mouth, metallic and bitter on my tongue. It was blood, blood coming from my mouth. Once again I tried to scream for help. Once again there was only the mockery of silence." Her voice began to rise in pitch like a woman screaming in her sleep.

"Isabelle…"

"The man jerked, then collapsed on me and was still. I lay without moving. He did not move. I pushed at his body, then tentatively pushed again. He was motionless, his weight heavy as lead and his flesh cold as river ice." She took a deep breath. "Finally I was able to push him away, and I turned to see his face." The sweat was now dripping like water onto her robe. "The blood in my mouth was not mine."

Eleanor turned cold, suspecting what would come next.

"The man's skull was crushed, you see. The hair I had thought was black was dyed dark with his blood. It was his blood that had flowed from that grisly wound, over my face, and into my mouth."

Eleanor felt bile rise in her throat. She swallowed hard.

Isabelle closed her eyes again, then bit her lips. "I knew I was cursed. I knew that everyone would blame me for what had happened. And I knew they would hang me for it. Hang me until my tongue turned black as that man's blood. Hang me until my neck cracked, ever so slowly, in two."

"But..."

"No!" Isabelle shrieked. "Please, my lords, I did not do this!"

"It was but a dream!" Eleanor shouted, reaching out to grasp the woman's arm.

At the prioress' touch, Isabelle blinked as if suddenly awakened. "Don't you see? I knew then that no one would ever understand. There would be no help, not for me." Then she laughed with a sound so sharp it cut through the air like a sword. "I lay abed for days after that dream. All I could think about was the pain of my ruptured maidenhead and shattered honor. Soon I had a fever no one could diagnose. It was a taste of hellfire for my carnal sins, I suppose, yet I wanted to die, eternal damnation or not. When the fever left me and I finally did rise from my bed, the pain was supplanted by shame. I lost my will to speak. If this was the pleasure I was supposed to feel from the union of Henry's seed with mine, then I could understand why many women like you chose the convent."

Eleanor was still reeling from the shock of what she had just seen and heard. "Henry would have married you," she said without thinking. "Had you been willing, a lawful union would have banished shame." Instantly she regretted her words. She should have remained silent.

"And he would have, but do think on this, my lady prioress. Would you have married such a man?" She wiped the salty sweat from her eyes. "I think not. Even you could not spend enough time on your knees in prayer to avoid having to lie on your back when he commanded it."

Eleanor struggled to regain her calm. "So you would not marry the man who had violated you, a man you had once found too much the brother to be a bed partner and now regarded with repugnance for what he had done to you. That, I can well understand."

Isabelle shrugged. "How kind of you," she said, but there was little sting in her retort.

"What I do not understand is why you decided to trick Sir Geoffrey into thinking the child was his. If you would not marry Henry because you thought of him as a brother, how could you bed a man who had reared you like a father?"

"In truth, Eleanor, I meant him no ill. You must believe me. Sir Geoffrey is a good man. He took me into his family as an orphan, and his first wife became the mother I had lost to that horrible fever. Indeed, I love this family, and the lands I brought with me could stay with the Lavenhams for all my caring." Isabelle's words were slow, hesitant. "Nor did I expect much bedding. I had overheard tales aplenty about his impotence and much jesting about his feeble rubbings against servant women after his lady wife had died. Whether grief or age withered his manhood, I do not know, but I hoped he would think the child his own and marry me out of gratitude for one night of renewed virility. After a few failures in bed thereafter, I did not think he would demand a husband's marital rights, but I did hope the child would give him some happiness. Thus I could stay with the family I had grown up with but not have to endure Henry's coarse assaults…"

"Yet you lost the babe…"

"…to the grief of both my lord and me. It may have been Henry's child, but it was the only gift I had to give my husband in exchange for my protection. Odd as it sounds, even to my own ears, I loved the babe that grew inside me. Indeed, I had come to think it *my* child, not Henry's."

"You have gotten the chaste marriage you hoped for, however."

"Indeed, Sir Geoffrey's nights of tilling fields are quite finished." Her eyes gazed without focus into the distance, then, turning to the prioress, she hit herself sharply in the breast with her fist. "The plowman's plow has broken and this field of his must remain forever fallow, it seems."

As true as that might be, she was a field that cried out for seeding and desperately at that. How tortured a mortal's life could be with so many contradictory desires, Eleanor thought. She considered Isabelle's lewd playing with her brother the day before compared to her expressed desire to marry an impotent man. She surely hated the rape, but she did not hate the child and resented her current barrenness. She had lied her way into a safe but loveless marriage yet wanted to give Sir Geoffrey some joy for marrying her. Eleanor shook her head. The world was not as black and white as we are taught it should be, nor are decisions so easy to make.

Suddenly one more twist to this already tangled tale came to mind. "Did you not realize that any such marriage with the father would be found void if it became known that you had had sexual relations with the son?" She waited for a reaction.

It came sooner than she expected. Isabelle rushed to the chamber pot and, with hacking gasps, vomited sour wine.

With a touch gentler than some of her words had been, Eleanor wiped the pale face of Sir Geoffrey's wife with a dampened cloth that lay next to the bedside basin of water. Although she had asked nothing about the murder, she knew that Isabelle was no longer in any state to talk. Indeed, she had gotten all she probably could from the drunken woman for now, but she did wonder if Isabelle knew she had just made herself a suspect in Henry's death. Had Isabelle's nightmare come true?

Chapter Twenty

The body of the murdered man lay covered on a trestle bench in the sanctuary of the castle chapel. Thomas looked around on the vague hope that someone would appear to order him off or perhaps bring him the comfort of companionship. He was, however, quite alone.

He stood quietly beside the corpse for a moment, then pulled back the cover to reveal the butchered body of a man who was once a son, a brother, and perchance even some woman's lover.

Although the chapel was bitterly cold, the smell of decay was unmistakable. The sickening sweet odor of overripe flesh from the corpse's pale skin drifted into his nostrils. Thomas coughed. He wanted to vomit but would not allow himself such a weakness.

"Courage, man!" he muttered to himself. "You may have taken monastic vows, but you are no less a man than you were before them." He shrugged. "And the man you were probably wouldn't like this any more than the man you are." Thomas smiled at his weak attempt to draw bravery into his heart.

The corpse lay on its back. Thomas held his breath and bent to examine the body. There were marks on the face. Scratches perhaps. Thomas could count three, perhaps four, jagged lines along the left cheek. There was also a deeper cut on the left side of the face. That wound had bled freely but would not have been fatal unless it had festered. It looked cleanly done. A sharp knife perhaps?

Gingerly, he turned the body over on one side. "Here the killer plunged the knife into Henry's left side just under his arm," he noted aloud, the sound of his own voice echoing back at him from the crudely rounded roof over the sanctuary. "A short slice on the face from ear to jaw. Then a blow to the left side? Might there have been two men who attacked him? One behind him who held a knife under his chin, thus cutting him in the struggle, and one who delivered the blow from the front and under his arm?"

Thomas frowned in thought. If Henry had been surprised by the attack from behind, the assailant could have slit his throat easily. There would have been no need for the second wound. Had Henry become aware of the threat in time to struggle free after a slight wound to his face, he would have called out. From the rooms along that corridor, the baron, the priest and Thomas could have rushed to his aid and frightened the assailants off before a fatal wound was struck against a man who was fighting back. Neither sequence of events matched the wounds. Why?

The wound in the side was a strange one as well. If he had been facing his murderer, surely he would have been stabbed in the heart. Had he twisted somehow? Thomas turned this way, then that. No motion quite fit the blow.

Finally, there were the scratches on his face. What were they from?

Thomas flipped the body all the way over. In the back of the corpse was yet another very deep wound. "If he had been killed with the blow under the arm, why stab him again in the back?" he wondered aloud. He bent down and looked more closely at the wound. He made a fist as if holding a dagger and pretended to strike at the corpse. This wound seemed to have been made by a blow from above; the cut was higher on the right and slanted down to the left. Why would someone have faced Henry only to reach around him and stab him in the back?

He looked again at the side wound and compared the size of that entry wound under the arm with the one in the back. The one in the back was large enough to suggest that a blade had been plunged all the way into the body. The smaller wound in the side indicated one of two things: a very small blade had been used or only part of the knife had entered Henry's side. More likely the latter, Thomas thought. "The knife may have entered Henry's lung at the side wound, but it would not be deep enough to reach his heart. It surely would have been fatal eventually," he whispered, "but the one in the back would have killed him at once."

Thomas spent another few minutes looking over the body but saw nothing else of interest. Then he stood back to get a cleaner breath of air before he turned the corpse over on its back, an act he did with as much gentleness as if Henry had still been alive. He carefully pulled the cover up to hide the man's body from curious eyes and fell into silent thought.

As with any man, Henry would have had his faults and perhaps even deserved punishment for them. But this? Thomas looked at the outline of the corpse under the sheet. No man or men had the right to murder him. Indeed, what right had any imperfect mortal to steal another's life?

His own time in prison might have made him more hesitant than others to conclude that any man had the right to decree how another should die. That Thomas freely admitted. If he were yet more honest with himself, he would acknowledge that he secretly thought that only God, not men, should decide fit punishment for crimes that now required the burning, hanging or quartering of a fellow man. Since one mortal's idea of fair punishment was another's definition of excess, or laxity, could either be right?

Last summer, he had seen human judgments rendered. One he had even abetted. Now, looking at Henry's mutilated body, he wondered if he had been right to do so. Might not severe penance have been the better choice until a natural death took the person to face God's justice? He hesitated. And should the sinner himself have a choice?

"If the sinner understood the depth of his sin, might he not have the right to seek God's eternal judgment quickly?" Thomas immediately dismissed the idea in fear. "May God forgive me for such a thought! That path suggests that self-murder would not be sin if it would allow a man to face God sooner, a most heretical idea indeed!"

He turned away from the body. He should not be thinking on any of this. Such questions were better left to philosophers and saints. In too short a time, he had been faced with much violent death, and he had been graced with neither the calm faith of a monk called to the vocation nor the temperament of a soldier hardened to such things.

Thomas walked away from the body on the trestle, then stopped. Surely, he had seen something move. Just in front of him toward the door.

There it was again. He was sure of it. Something had moved in the shadows. Then he heard a light scuffling sound.

Taking care not to let whoever was watching him know that he was privy to their presence, he crossed himself as if he had been in prayer, then bowed his head and walked on, slowly, meditatively, toward the chapel door.

As he reached the place where he had noted the movement, he bent down to examine his shoe, meanwhile shifting his eyes to peer carefully into the darkness. A darker shadow moved once again. Thomas stood up and turned toward the shifting gloom.

"What are you doing here, Richard?" he asked.

Chapter Twenty-One

"My grandson was doing *what*?" Adam's mouth twitched with irrepressible glee. Although he ran his hand down his mustache and over his mouth, hoping to hold the laughter back, mirth bested his efforts with ease. "And in the chapel?"

"Indeed, my lord. Hunting dragons in the chapel was what he told me," Thomas replied.

"Did he find any?" Eleanor asked.

"Only me," Thomas said with a grin. "I told him it is not in the nature of dragons to be about chapels in winter so he does understand now how profitless such hunts would be."

"Just how did he escape his room?" The baron's smile faded.

"It seems he crept out with his hobbyhorse…" Sister Anne began.

"…down the stairs and into the snow and freezing wind." A flush of anger spread over Adam's face. "Nay, sister, do not say it was your fault. I said myself that his nurse was responsible and you could leave him in her care. I curse my judgment and place the blame on her. Where was she, I'd ask? Curled up asleep, snug and comfortable most likely, while the boy risked death making his way from the warmth of the hearth to the cold chapel."

Anne shook her head. "Indeed, my lord, I swear the boy is made of iron. One day he is at death's door and the next he is racing through the castle corridors like a wild man."

Eleanor nodded. "Just like his father."

"Be that as it may, she was too lax and shall be punished for such carelessness in her duties." Adam raised his hand to beckon a page.

Eleanor reached over and caught his arm. "Be kind, father, and forgive. She has been most diligent and loves the boy beyond reason. He has so progressed in health that we all thought him past danger. Her short nap was no abandonment of duty. She had the right to it for Richard himself was sleeping when Sister Anne gave him up to the good woman's care."

"Or pretending to do so," Anne said in a low voice to Thomas.

Having overheard them, Adam glanced at the two and smiled with concurrence.

"Any of us might have made the same mistake," Eleanor continued.

"That I doubt, my child, but I will be merciful for your sake. Indeed, he came to no harm."

"At least he did not see the corpse," Thomas whispered with more care into Sister Anne's ear. "My first fear was that, but he told me he had just come to the chapel as I was leaving."

Eleanor nodded in the direction of the monk. "Brother Thomas has, I believe, frightened him off from further adventures in the chapel, or anywhere else unattended."

"I did my best, my lord. I told him that he had endangered Gringolet's safety by taking such a young horse into unknown territory without proper training. I allowed him to ride forth only with proper attendance and within the living quarters until his steed has gained some experience in the skills of hunting dragons in dark places."

"When will Gringolet have gained such prowess?" The baron's smile had regained a hint of amusement.

"Your grandson asked the same question, and I told him he could ride unattended when I have done the proper training and confirmed that the horse was skilled enough in such pursuits."

Adam nodded. "That may work. My grandson has heard tales of the warrior monks and thus has no difficulty accepting a cowled man with knowledge of horses and battle strategies.

Were I Richard's age, I would find the argument sufficient, albeit hard to accept." Then his face lost all joy. "Setting that aside, you had something to tell me, daughter, something about this foul murder?"

"I do, father." Eleanor proceeded to tell them what she had learned from Isabelle, omitting only the woman's cruder insinuations and softening the more tactless remarks. The dream she mentioned not at all.

"If I may say so," Thomas said at the conclusion of her story, "that would give Sir Geoffrey's wife good reason to kill Lord Henry."

Adam shook his head. "I have never approved of my friend's choice for a second wife, if the whore may still be called that considering Henry's prior knowledge of her. Now rage at what she has done to a decent man blinds my judgment even more."

Eleanor bit her tongue. Her father's easy equation of the violence of rape with the bland "prior knowledge" might strike her woman's heart sharply, but now was not the time to argue the point. That he listen with a clear mind to what Thomas had found after examining Henry's corpse was of greater importance. After all, he would not be pleased that she had maneuvered around his prohibition against Sister Anne doing the same, and she feared his displeasure over Thomas' examination might take precedence over the importance of his findings. She forced her anger into firm retreat.

"How I handle this ugly truth of her deception," the baron continued, "and what I say to Sir Geoffrey are issues I must decide after a cooler reason returns. Nonetheless, even now, when I would love to concur with the possibility of her guilt in this murder, I confess I hesitate to conclude that a woman could have done this deed." Adam looked over at Thomas. "She might have wounded him, if she surprised him, but not with a deep or fatal blow. I cannot see her successfully stabbing him to death except by stealth. The body would tell some of the tale, of course."

"Brother Thomas did examine Henry's corpse, my lord," Eleanor said. She could not tell if her father's surprised look held anger or not, but she knew better than to think she had won any easy victory over the man.

"Indeed," he said at last in a dangerously composed voice, "and what expertise does a contemplative man bring to the study of wounds gained from violence?"

"If I may speak on the good brother's behalf, my lord?" Sister Anne said quickly.

The baron's smile was grim. "Why not?"

"Brother Thomas regularly assists me at Tyndal's hospital. We often have cause to treat knife wounds when men from the village drink too deeply or find they share the favors of the same woman."

Adam leaned back in his chair, his expression unreadable as he looked back and forth between the nun and his daughter. "Sister Anne, I respect both your skill and your plain speech," Adam said at last. "When I denied my daughter's demand to allow your examination of the corpse, I did so to honor the request of my grieving friend, not to insult you."

"I took no offense at your words, my lord."

"And respected them more than did my own child," he said with a side-glance at the prioress. "Yet your strategy worked well, Eleanor. I give you due credit for that and for coming to a solution which may be the most useful and equitable. Despite having far greater knowledge in such matters from my days on the battlefield than either Sister Anne or Brother Thomas could possibly have, I cannot look on Henry's corpse with any impartiality. It was, after all, my son who held the bloody dagger. Neither Sir Geoffrey nor any of his men has the requisite detachment either, for it was his son who was killed. He and I may not put the burden of impartiality on anyone under our respective commands since it is a man's nature to look first to his master before he looks to the facts."

Eleanor resumed breathing.

The baron turned to Thomas. "We must therefore trust you, as a man whose only true master is God, to give an objective and informed opinion while the body is still uncorrupted and until this snow storm ceases and the sheriff comes."

"May God be merciful and this storm continue," Eleanor said under her breath.

"So, brother, what did you discover?" The baron sipped at his wine and nervously rapped his knuckles against the underside of the table.

"Henry suffered several cuts and abrasions on his face and under his arm, although the deepest wound was in his back." Thomas continued to describe the wounds in detail.

Adam shook his head in thought. "Not a clean killing then. Perhaps Henry was grabbed from behind but struggled free before his assassin had time to cut his throat? I also find the wound under his arm troubling. It would appear that one man attacked in front and one from behind Henry? Could there be two men? Robbery perhaps. Nor can I understand the scratches on his face. What is your conclusion, brother?"

Eleanor began to allow herself hope that her father shared her confidence in Robert's innocence. Although she instinctively believed he must share her conviction, she did not know that as a fact. The circumstances were so very damning, but for the first time his words suggested that he might entertain the idea that another had done the deed. If convinced, he would work hard in his son's defense.

"Sir Geoffrey would know best if anything had been stolen," Thomas was saying, "yet I saw a gold brooch on Henry's cloak while his body lay in the corridor. I could not check for his purse at the time, of course, but surely a thief would have taken the brooch. It would have been so easily removed even if the thief had been frightened away before he finished plundering the corpse."

"You must be with me when I ask Sir Geoffrey what might have been taken from his son," Adam said, his fingers now tapping impatiently on the top of the wooden table. "His wounds. What is your interpretation of them?"

"Some would certainly suggest a woman's hand, my lord: the scratches on his face, perhaps even the wound in his side." Or so Sister Anne had thought when he related his findings to her. However, he did know better than to reveal his consultation with Tyndal's sub-infirmarian. "The latter was a small and a shallow one, I believe, although the knife may have punctured a lung. More I cannot say. A strong and angry woman could definitely stab a man deeply in the back. I saw such done once, but she was successful only because she surprised him. He had not seen her knife when he so unwisely turned his back on her." Thomas glanced quickly at Sister Anne, who concurred with an almost imperceptible nod. "No man would turn his back on a woman with a knife in her hand," he continued. "He would disarm her. I thought there might be two assailants as well, but the sum of the wounds does not point to a clear answer."

"If I may say something, father? The Lady Isabelle may have had enough anger and cause to kill her stepson, but she would not have had success unless Henry had turned his back to her. Henry might have been a small man but he was quick with his sword, according to Robert, and fast on his feet. Nor, may I add, did she mention he had visited her."

"Now if she had been the one to kill him, she would not have done so, would she, daughter?" Adam rose, wincing as he flexed his bad leg.

"Two questions, if I may, my lord?" Thomas asked.

Adam nodded.

"There was only one knife found at the site?"

"Yes. I have it locked away. There were no identifying marks, if that is your second question."

"What was the size of the knife?"

Adam frowned in thought. "Now that you mention it, the knife was a small one. The size one might take to table, not to war."

"Then it could have been a woman's dagger as well as a man's." Eleanor frowned.

"Again you point to Sir Geoffrey's wife. However agreeable the thought and as much as I may hate her, I would still conclude that two men attacked Henry," he said. "We will handle this matter with the utmost fairness, no matter what the consequences. I have, of course, arranged for the questioning of the soldiers, servants and tradesmen who were here between the closing of the castle gates for the night and the opening for the morning trade. Perhaps the murderer hides in those ranks and we shall quickly find the truth of what happened there."

Thomas coughed and glanced nervously at his prioress.

She nodded permission for him to speak his mind.

"My lord, might this murder have any connection with the death of your retainer?"

"I have thought of that. Henry was a thoughtless whelp, and, although I do believe that Hywel's death was an accident, it would not have occurred if Henry had been taking due care with his own horse. Perhaps there are some here who would wish to take revenge, although I pray that such is not the case. I have worked hard to gain the trust of those in my service. Nonetheless, the possibility will be investigated and should be resolved when everyone in the castle has been questioned."

Thomas opened his mouth to continue, but the baron raised his hand to signify he would hear no more. It was clear to all that they had been dismissed.

"In the meantime," Anne said in a low voice to Eleanor and Thomas, as they left the hall, "we must pray for the snow to fall unabated, thus keeping the sheriff with his chains from Wynethorpe Castle until we can present him with those who did this to Lord Henry."

"Indeed," Eleanor whispered back.

Chapter Twenty-Two

Sunlight had never quite won the battle over the stubborn murkiness of the day. The gray light, increasingly obscured by tumbling snowflakes, was now retreating into a twilight sometimes called the blue hour before black night once again took precedence over the land.

Thomas leaned against the hard cold stone near the window in the stairway between dining hall and living quarters and, lost in thought as vague as the dying light, looked down on the castle ward from his vantage point. The Baron Adam had been as good as his word and with impressive efficiency had gathered together those tradesmen and servants who had been in Wynethorpe Castle overnight. A few dark shapes were still leaving the hall, some singly and a few in pairs.

The townspeople had been brought to the dining hall where the crackling hearth had provided warmth for those waiting to be questioned. In addition, the baron had shown no meanness in providing all with warm, spiced ale, sufficient to increase comfort, foster good will and encourage a greater willingness to talk, yet not enough to promote an unprofitable jollity or querulousness. Perhaps the tradesmen saw this as more their due, being largely an English group of some affluence, but the mostly local Welsh servants sipped their unexpected bounty with silent appreciation of the equitable consideration this Norman lord had shown to his underlings.

Adam had asked Sir Geoffrey and Thomas to assist him in developing what would be asked and in what order so there would be consistency and equity in the investigation. As the baron said, each of them brought his own objectivity as well as self-interest to the asking that neither of the others did. Thomas had realized he had been chosen for balance between the two other men and, as a stranger to the castle, he took his choosing as a compliment. With some amusement, he noted how alike father and daughter were in the ways they used the abilities of those under their command. He wondered if they saw the similarity as well.

One English sergeant had been assigned to the questioning of the English tradesmen. Respect was shown for the needs of their businesses, a tactic that warmed a few hearts along with the ale. For those who did not know the King's tongue, a Welshman, loyal to the family and one who served as the house steward, had been assigned the inquiry of local townspeople. Soldiers were held in the barracks and interrogated by the other trusted sergeant. The process had taken all day but was finally coming to an end.

A rank draft wafted under Thomas' nose. He did not need to turn around to know who had just joined him in the stairwell.

"You missed a fine supper, monk," Anselm observed with great cheer. "Baron Adam was most generous to those of us who remained for questioning." He looked carefully at Thomas' face. "Perhaps you have been fasting?"

"Thinking rather. I forgot the time, and, with this icy storm, night and day seem to have blended more than usual." Indeed, Thomas had been mulling over the events of the previous evening, trying to find something odd, something out of place, but nothing had come to him. Now that Anselm had mentioned the meal, however, his stomach began to growl.

"This world is an evil place, brother. There is much to think on."

"At times evil stalks the earth with more vengeance than at others. Last night was such an occasion. Murder is an especial evil, I think."

"So you say, but I do believe that evil is always with us, waiting to catch us unawares. Being frail mortals, we are often blind to its presence until it wears a brighter cloak to catch our eye, as it did when the Lord Henry's blood was so sinfully shed."

"Perhaps."

"For a tonsured man, you express many doubts."

Thomas smiled. "As my name would suggest."

Anselm blinked and then grinned, showing several gaps in his brownish teeth. "Ah, of course, Doubting Thomas who asked for proof that it was our resurrected Lord who stood before him! You were being witty, brother, and I fear I am not accustomed to such a thing."

"Does no one in Wynethorpe Castle jest?"

"All have become rather more somber in recent times. With Lord Hugh off on crusade with our King's son, the summer raids of the Welsh and the de Montfort rebellion, there are many scars which are still tender and have left us with unabated worry."

"The residents of Wynethorpe have you to give them spiritual comfort, however, and that must fill their hearts with much peace in these troubled times. You have served the family and soldiers for many years, I believe?"

"I have."

Thomas noted with gentle amusement that Anselm had replied with a straightened back that suggested just a modicum of earthly pride. "You know the Lavenham family as well?"

"From better days than these."

"Perhaps happier times as well?"

Anselm shrugged. "There was more merriment when Sir Geoffrey's first wife was alive and in good health. More frivolity and a joy in earthly things. I must say that I thought the change to a more restrained manner after her death was a good one at first for it surely pleases God when men jest less and pray more." He looked at Thomas and frowned. "Do not misunderstand me, brother. There is no sin in happiness. Our Lord was known to smile himself and we have the marriage feast at Cana as evidence for that."

"Of course, brother. Men must be joyful in the Lord for therein they find their heart's peace." For a moment, Thomas wondered where he might have previously heard such thoughts. They surely were not of his own making.

"Well said, brother! So you see, I soon realized that the new solemnity came, not from a turn to a greater pleasure in godly things, but from lack of all joy. Peace deserted the family after the marriage of Sir Geoffrey with the Lady Isabelle."

"The marriage was a matter of discord in the family?" Thomas leaned back against the edge of the window.

"I could not say." Anselm sniffed a little sanctimoniously, then fell silent.

"Do not think I was asking for secrets from the confessional," Thomas quickly added, then waited until the priest recovered from his fit of self-righteousness. "Rather I do not know the families involved so did wonder what had been the origin of such discord between Robert and Henry that murder could be the result."

Anselm shook his head. "I was quite surprised myself that such did happen. Lord Henry had always been a willful boy, thoughtless and selfish often, but not cruel as I recall. Lord Robert has never been close to him, but I thought that was due most to the difference in their ages. Henry was the elder and looked with contempt, as children often do, on the antics of younger siblings. He treated Robert and his own brother and sister with an equal disdain."

Thomas smiled. "I hear the voice of experience in your words. You must come from a large family yourself?"

Anselm blushed and lowered his head. "You have read my words well. My elder brother and two sisters were much older than I, my parents having lost several children to a kinder world between our births, but my father and mother had further offspring after me. I fear I followed my elder brother in his sinful pride with regard to those younger brothers."

"Yet you were wise and learned it was a practice well put behind you along with other games of childhood."

Anselm actually beamed. "Nonetheless, my younger brothers never fail to remind me of my past sins against them, albeit in good grace, when they visit here. Their words prompt me to strive for greater humility."

"Henry did not learn as you did?"

"Perhaps it is sinful for me to judge so, but Henry did not gain in restraint as he grew older. He wanted his way and he tried everything he could to get it."

"What could Henry have possibly done to so provoke Robert that he would kill him, a man he'd grown up with and a man who would soon be his brother-in-law?"

"This I find as strange as you, my friend. The two may not have been close in youth, but they were not enemies. They maintained a correct, however stiff courtesy when together. It was not until recently that I saw anger between them."

"What changed?"

"I do not know. I first saw the change when the two families came together to discuss the marital union."

"Do you think Henry resented the loss of lands?" Thomas then shook his head in disagreement with his own notion. "Nay, I do indeed think that too petty, for he would have known that any man who married his sister would receive something as her marriage portion. At least the lands would not go to a stranger if Robert were her husband."

"I cannot say, brother, for I have heard nothing about the cause for conflict. I would agree that such a reaction would be excessive even for Henry. Despite his selfish and fleshly nature, he would more likely prefer the lands go to the amenable Robert. I do believe he knew this brother-in-law would be more generous than most in providing additional funds should the Lord Henry find himself in difficulties from worldly excesses."

Thomas was quite surprised at the priest's observations. For all his austerity, Anselm was no innocent.

"Henry was in debt?" Here was a new idea. Perhaps the murderer was a man to whom he owed money.

"I fear he had not yet learned that price of sin, although he was well on the way. He refused to burn long with any worldly desire even to save his own soul from a hotter, eternal fire. I have seen him rampant as Pan with a milkmaid against the cowshed wall, and the soldiers of Wynethorpe Castle greeted his arrival with joy because he fattened their purses when he joined them in games of chance. His own priest has told me that the man had long ceased to listen to his admonitions. I, too, was mocked for my efforts."

"Now with the fires of Hell lapping at his feet, he must rue his failure to listen to wiser counsel." Thomas moved away from the icy stone, put his hands into his sleeves to warm them, and winced at his own hypocrisy. Had he, after all, ever listened any more in his days before imprisonment than Henry had? Would he care what anyone advised if Giles appeared before him now, arms open and eyes shining with love?

"I include him in my prayers."

Thomas was touched by the sincerity he heard in Anselm's voice. The priest would no doubt do the same for him, he thought, no matter how foul he believed his sins to be. He smiled at him with more fondness than he had ever shown before. "You say Henry broke many a maidenhead against the wall and in the straw. Were you not surprised when, at dinner and in public, his father mocked his son's manhood?"

"Nay. I did not think Sir Geoffrey meant to mock his son's virility, monk. Rather, I believe his father meant only to shame him back into a more Christian manhood, one in which the young man would marry and, with due and devoted solemnity, produce proper heirs."

Thomas would not have equated Sir Geoffrey's gesture of tossing the boar's testicles into his son's lap with a Christian hope that Henry might stop swyving milkmaids.

"Enough of idle gossip," Anselm said with a tug at Thomas' sleeve. "I thought to look in on the boy, Richard. I have heard he loves good stories and have quite a modest store of instructional parables to share. Then I was going to the chapel to pray. Will you join me, brother?"

Thomas was moved by the priest's wish to do something for the lad. Unless dragons played a strong role, however, he rather doubted Richard would care much for tales of saints. "Nay, I fear my fast has gone on too long, priest, and I am feeling weaker than even God would deem prudent. I will join you soon, but first I must seek a bit of bread from the kitchen."

Anselm scowled. "I know that look, brother. You seek meat. Avoid temptation! Fall on your knees with me and beg God to give you the strength your frail body lacks!"

Thomas managed not to laugh. "It is not meat I seek, priest. It is a kitchen wench who is lusty with desire…"

Anselm's face paled in horror.

"…to warm my stomach with a bit of ale so I may better kneel in prayer. Or a cook willing to feed my body with a bit of cheese so I may raise my voice with more vigor to heaven. Go. I am sure you will still be in the chapel when I join you."

As the men parted, Thomas turned and looked back at Anselm as the man began the slow climb toward the living quarters. For all his teasing of the priest and for all his disdain of the man's less than pleasant traits, he realized that Anselm had a generous heart. Thomas was surprised to realize that he was growing rather fond of him.

Chapter Twenty-Three

"Don't play the innocent, daughter!" Adam slammed his hand against the tapestry on his chamber wall. "He was standing over the body with the bloody dagger in his hand. What more would any judge need to know to hang my son?"

Eleanor could feel the skin on her face grow taut with a rising temper. "What more to know, you ask? Only that Robert would never kill a man in anger."

"What man would not?"

"My brother. Your son."

"You know little of men then."

"An easy assumption, my lord, but an inaccurate one. In case you were not aware of my duties at Tyndal, allow me to remind you that I must direct men as well as women in their daily lives. I must also assume you had not heard of the violent events which occurred at the time of my arrival last year, since my priory is so far from the king's court." She, too, was shouting back.

"Your tone is insolent, child."

"Nor am I a child, father. I have long since arrived at a woman's estate." With great effort, Eleanor lowered her voice to a quieter tone.

As red-faced as his daughter, Adam opened his mouth to reply but instead sank down with a tired sigh into his chair. "I have no wish to argue with you, Eleanor. Yes, of course, as a bride of Christ, you are fully grown, but please understand that a father finds it difficult to accept such a thing when it only reminds him that he is not the virile youth he wishes he still were."

"You are more vigorous than most of those callow youths you claim to envy, father. Indeed, it is they who will look to you as an example of manhood in its prime." Eleanor relaxed somewhat with his conciliatory tone, then smiled. "Arguing will do neither of us any good. Nor Robert for that matter."

"Agreed. To further the peace between us, I will also tell you that I have indeed heard of your time at Tyndal. In full detail. Your priory is not so remote that those at court do not speak highly of your competence." His expression grew strangely sad. "I have heard much to make me proud that I am your father, Eleanor."

"You are over kind, my lord, but if you feel pride in your daughter's acts, remember that it was you who sired her." Then she bowed her head to hide the sparkle of joy and pride she knew he'd see in her eyes.

"It is said by those who claim to know, that strength of character in any child comes from the vitality of a father's seed. Perhaps I should not argue with those who are more knowledgeable about such things than I, yet I must confess that I see much of your mother in you."

Adam turned his head away, but not before Eleanor saw tears starting down his cheeks from a grief that had not lessened in the fifteen years since her mother had died. She reached over and took his hand to comfort but chose her words to save his pride. "And Robert? Which parent does he most resemble?"

"Ah, but you have my stubbornness, I see." Adam squeezed her hand and, quickly wiping away his tears, laughed. "Robert, you ask? I will concede you a point there. Unlike your mother, who would have gone off on crusade and conquered the Holy Land all by herself had the Pope given permission for women to so do, Robert is mild-mannered. Indeed he is much like his sire in that." His eyes twinkled with a teasing humor.

"My very point, father. Robert would only fight if provoked. He also shares another quality with you, if I may be so bold..."

Adam raised one heavy eyebrow in question.

"You are a man of unquestionable courage who has learned that mediation is most often preferable to war, a cast of mind much like that of our king, I believe. Still, you have never hesitated to tell the truth as you see it, no matter how honeyed the words, if such would be the more effective road. Only when all that utterly fails will you turn to the sword. If I correctly remember the tales I've heard told, you warned King Henry many years before the rebellion about the dangers in Simon de Montfort's actions..."

"De Montfort was not that different from his father and his father before that. He was as clever and devious as Odysseus but ambitious beyond his station. Nonetheless..."

"An observation which the king ignored to his detriment."

"What has this to do with Robert?"

"You did your best to resolve a dangerous situation with words but then did not hesitate to draw your sword and fight in defense of your king when de Montfort attacked him. In like manner, my brother would rather reconcile than draw blood, but draw it he would if all else failed and he was attacked."

"Are you suggesting that Henry attacked him first in the corridor that night?"

"He has said he did not murder him and, although I believe in Robert's innocence, the manner of his telling makes me wonder if my brother is withholding something for a reason deemed sufficient to himself. When Brother Thomas spoke with him, he carefully used the word *murder*, for instance, rather than *kill*."

"Surely he would have admitted to a killing in self-defense. Such is no violation of the law, God's or man's."

"Perhaps I have found too much subtlety in the use of that one word, but I noted that he did take some time in the telling of the events when I first visited him. I wondered if he did so in order to decide what to tell and what to omit. I wish I could honor his decision to keep to this silence, but, if the sheriff will not believe my brother's story as he chooses to tell it, we have only his character to fall back on." A thought occurred to her suddenly. "His character is something to which even Sir Geoffrey might bear witness."

"He might indeed. Sir Geoffrey seems as grieved with the suspicion hanging over my son's head as I do, despite the agony he must feel with his own son's death." Adam scowled. "His generosity to my son is testament to our friendship and his chivalry. To ask him to testify to Robert's likely innocence, however, is something I would find hard to do under the circumstances."

"Then we must find who did the deed, or, if Robert did kill him in self-defense, we must find out why my brother refuses to say just that." Eleanor sat quietly for a moment. "Although Brother Thomas' suggestion that revenge for Hywel's death might be involved has merit, I know your reputation for fairness amongst your Welsh retainers. Surely someone would have approached you for justice first in this matter before taking Henry's life."

"Indeed, I would hope the same. Nonetheless, I have told those doing the interrogations to be alert for any hint of desire for such retribution."

"Have you heard nothing to help our cause from the interviewing of those within the castle walls last night?"

"Not yet. I told those in charge of the questioning to report to Sir Geoffrey, your monk, and me when all was done. We are conducting the final interrogations of the soldiers from the last watch in the barracks as you and I speak. I expect to hear nothing until morning. Of course you are right that we must find the truth before this storm ceases and a messenger can get through to bring the sheriff. To deflect justice by simply pointing hither and thither is…"

"False and dishonorable. You speak as your son has done himself. Just before I came here, I took him some clean garments and presented just such an argument to him then. He told me in some anger that he would refuse to be released on such ignoble terms. He wants the real murderer found first."

"That is the son I know."

"Of course, Robert would like to assist in the hunt, however guarded he might be…"

Adam smiled grimly. "He will stay in his cell, Eleanor. Do not insult me by assaying such feeble tactics. That one was quite unworthy of your skills."

She bowed her head to hide her frown. Of course she knew such a weak line of reasoning would not fool her father, but she had promised Robert she would try the plea on his behalf. "Indeed, my lord, you are right and I beg pardon." She hoped her tone was sufficiently deferential to temper her father's irritation.

"There is nothing for which to beg pardon. Your devotion to Robert reflects what is in my own heart." He looked at her in silence for a long moment. "Do not interpret my lack of tears for lack of caring. Ever."

Eleanor nodded and neither spoke for a while. Then she continued. "I cannot persuade my brother to tell the whole truth of this to me. Could you get Robert to break his silence?"

"I should not be the one, Eleanor. He is the accused and he is my son. Any confession to me would be suspect in the eyes of the law."

"Nevertheless, might he tell you the truth of it? It could give us the means to present the real murderer…"

"Robert must believe that some honor demands his silence or he would have spoken before. I cannot force him to betray that, and no son of mine would chose life over honor."

Were the circumstances less dire, Eleanor thought, she might find a wry amusement in how obstinate with pride the Wynethorpe men could be, father and son. The circumstances, however, were dire. "Since he will not speak to me of it," she said aloud, "perhaps Brother Thomas could…"

"The value of your monk's testimony is also questionable. Brother Thomas could be accused of breaking the sanctity of the confessional if Robert did tell him the truth. No, this would not help my son's cause."

"You do believe that your son is as innocent of murder as you or I, don't you, father?"

"Aye, lass, in my heart I do, but God must help us prove the right of that."

Eleanor gathered her cloak closely about her as she knelt in a corner of the chapel. Even here the cold was bitter and her lungs hurt just to breathe in the sharp air. Her father had invited her to break bread with him and share a simple dinner, but she refused and had left him at the entrance to the dining hall while she went on to pray. The day had been long and her head ached with tension. As much as she loved her father and even though they had made something of a peace between them, she yearned for the familiar.

Castle Wynethorpe had not been home to her for most of her life. If she could not be in Amesbury with her aunt or at Tyndal in her own quarters, she preferred to retreat to a quiet supper with Sister Anne, a woman in whose company and friendship she found a deep comfort. First, however, she needed solitude and prayer to help soothe her weary spirit.

Eleanor heard steps and opened her eyes. In the shadowy gloom barely penetrated by a smoky candlelight, she saw a figure enter the chapel and kneel in front of the altar. With her somber dress and short stature, he must not have seen her kneeling further back in the darkness.

A loud moan came from the kneeling man. It was Sir Geoffrey. As he raised his eyes to heaven, she heard more groans, then harsh sobs, and knew that he was weeping uncontrollably. She grieved to see this man in such agony over the loss of his son, and her heart longed to offer him solace. Her comfort, however, would not be welcome. A man might shed tears without shame before God, but he would never show such weakness in front of the woman whose brother lay accused of killing the son he mourned.

Briefly she wondered how deeply he must now regret the scene at dinner where he had so humiliated Henry. Indeed, considering what she knew about the circumstances of his remarriage and the strained relationships with his adult offspring, he might well have much more to regret and other sins buried in his soul for which now to beg forgiveness.

As she listened to the man's sobs and mumbled prayers, Eleanor looked for a way to leave without disclosing her presence and thus embarrassing the knight. There was only one entrance to the chapel, but the chill draft she felt on her back meant he had probably left the door ajar. She decided that his groans of anguish were loud enough that she could try slipping behind him and out the door without his hearing her light footsteps. Later she might return to the chapel, perhaps with Sister Anne and Brother Thomas, to honor the next Office of prayer. For now she would leave this man alone with his God and his pain.

She was fortunate. She slid soundlessly through the small opening of the chapel door, and Sir Geoffrey would never know she had been witness to his tears. For once, she was glad she was so tiny and light of foot.

As soon as she entered the dark courtyard, the raw wind struck her with a knife's sharpness, slashing at her face with frozen pellets. During the day, the temperature had warmed just enough to melt some of the snow, but now the temperature had dropped once more to freeze the slush into sheets of treacherous ice. Although the cold bit deep into her bones, she was grateful for it. No one could travel to summon the sheriff. The prolonged storm gave them more time to prove her brother's innocence. She bent her head to the wind, but it continued to lash at her cheeks.

Just as she approached the entrance to the stairs leading to the chambers above the dining hall, she looked up. No more servants or tradesmen were leaving from the hall. Apparently, all questioning was finally done. Would anything of use be discovered? Might someone, out of fear or shame, have confessed to the deed?

Distracted, Eleanor stumbled. She reached out to catch herself as she fell, and her hands landed on something soft and warm.

It was a man's body, just dusted with snow.

"Someone bring a light," she shouted into the wind.

A young soldier with a burning torch in hand emerged through the curtain of thickly falling snow. "Are you hurt, my lady?" he cried out.

When the torchlight illuminated the ground where she had fallen, Eleanor gasped. The body was that of her family priest, Anselm. In the weak and flickering light, she could see his dark blood turning to ice under him. As she looked closer, she saw that some did still flow sluggishly from a wound in his head.

"Get Sister Anne and some men to carry him inside. Quickly!" Eleanor ordered.

As the soldier disappeared into the white night, Eleanor brushed the snow off the body, then bent and listened carefully. The priest was still breathing, albeit very, very shallowly.

"Surely God will understand this," she said to the darkness, then she hunched over and gently put her arms around the priest, hugging him close so the warmth from her own body would keep him from freezing.

Chapter Twenty-Four

Richard lay huddled under the covers, his pale face turned to the wall.

Thomas sat on the edge of the bed and put his hand gently on the thin little shoulder. "Lad, what's wrong?"

The boy's body quivered as if with a fever, but the monk could feel no unusual heat. The boy said nothing.

Thomas looked over at Sister Anne and asked his question silently with a slight movement of his head toward the mute child.

She stood up and pointed toward the door. Thomas gave Richard's shoulder a gentle squeeze, then followed after the nun.

As soon as they were in the privacy of the corridor, she shook her head. "He has no fever but refuses to speak, brother. I had hoped he would say something to you but even that has failed."

"What happened? Has he fallen ill again?"

"I am at a loss to know what has happened. After his encounter with you in the chapel, he was in fine spirits. He broke his fast with good appetite and even took my advice about a nap, especially after I told him that Gringolet must rest as well. While he was sleeping, his nurse came and begged to sit with him. She was quite grieved about the incident when he escaped her care and wanted to make amends, but I left him in good health. The baron had told me of a Welsh herbal some of the villagers used and said I might find it of interest. I left Richard and fear I lost track of time studying it where it is kept near the barracks."

"So he sickened while you were gone?"

"As his nurse told the tale, Father Anselm came to visit the boy and assured her that he would stay and tell him tales while she fetched some supper from the dining hall. Richard was quite lively when she left, but, when she returned, Father Anselm was gone and Richard was back in bed. She thought he was asleep, but then he began to cry."

"Cry?"

"She ran to his bed, but he screamed when she touched him. His face was red and she thought he was delirious from a returned fever."

"She sent for you?"

"No. Richard calmed, and, when she felt his brow, it was cool to the touch. She concluded he had awakened from bad dreams and sang him soothing songs. By the time she began to wonder why he had neither moved nor spoken, I had been fetched to see how Father Anselm fared. When she heard my voice in the corridor, she begged me to examine Richard as well."

"Are you saying that a plague of some sort has invaded Wynethorpe Castle? Is Anselm ill too? We had met in the stairwell just before he came to see Richard. He told me that he was going to the chapel afterward." Thomas chuckled nervously. "Tell me instead that he did catch a mild chill from too much kneeling on the chapel floor."

"Laugh not, brother. Father Anselm is unconscious and I fear for his life. There is no strange sickness here, unless Death may be called such. As our prioress was returning from the chapel, she found him lying in the snow near the entrance to the stairwell leading to this corridor. Perhaps he slipped on the narrow stairs and fell, but, whatever the cause, he has suffered a grievous head wound. Had it not been for our prioress, he would surely have frozen to death. He may yet die of the wound."

"May God forgive me! The man may be an odorous pest, but he is a good man at heart and I wish no evil on him." Thomas fell silent for a moment. "You say he was found outside the stairwell. In the ward?"

Anne nodded.

"There were no witnesses?"

"None that we know about."

"After I left him, I went to the dining hall for some supper. Not long after I got there, the baron arrived. We spoke of plans for the morrow to go over the statements made. Now that I think on it, I did see the nurse. She came into the hall and skulked along the wall so Baron Adam would not see her. His back was to her and I said nothing about her appearance. Our prioress must have been in the chapel." Thomas was counting people off on his fingers. "That would leave Anselm and Richard in the living quarters. Do we know where Sir Geoffrey and his wife were?"

"Our lady did mention seeing Sir Geoffrey in the chapel. His wife may have been in her chambers, although I fear she might not have heard much. It seems she has been spending much time with a pitcher of good wine for company."

"A strange way to grieve over a man who had raped her."

"Unless it is no grief at all but the violent act of murder which has so unsettled her humors."

"We'd be wise to leave the questioning of that lady to our prioress for she knows her better than we." Thomas frowned. "I do find the accident strange, however. The stairwell is a narrow one." He looked up at Anne. "Has anyone found the reason for his fall? Was there something on the stairs to cause him to slip or trip?"

"No one has said so, nor, do I believe, has anyone yet looked. What are you thinking, brother?"

"If he slipped, he might well have hit his head, but he would not have fallen far. The stairwell is too narrow and the twists too sharp. If the accident happened just at the first curve, he might have fallen to the stairwell entrance but not into the open ward. If he fell further up toward the living quarters, he would have been found still in the stairwell or quite dead from the fall to the stones below. Either way, it would have been impossible for him to have fallen into the ward."

"Nor could he have crawled with the wound I saw."

"Has he been conscious? Did he speak at all of this accident?"

"Despite my best efforts, he has been unconscious from the moment of his discovery. As to details, there are few. Considering the amount and freshness of the blood flowing from his head, I would say that our prioress must have stumbled upon him not long after he fell. Those are the details."

"You say you fear for his life? What is the nature of his head wound?"

"I fear that his skull has been fractured. We have treated the external injuries as best we can, but a binding of yarrow with a wine cleansing has its limitations. I am not skilled at surgery, brother, but I know how difficult it is to determine the extent of such a wound. I looked for fragments of broken skull but found none. At least the cold did help keep the swelling down, but I cannot judge whether there is pressure on his brain from the injury. I fear this could be fatal, but we must leave it to God's mercy. Father Anselm requires our prayers."

Thomas nodded and turned his head away from Sister Anne. As close as he had become to the sub-infirmarian of Tyndal, there were some things he could not speak to her about. One of those things was his inability to pray. "Was the head wound in front or in back?" he finally asked.

"In front. As if he had fallen forward."

"Surely, he would have put out his hands to break his fall even before he hit his head on the stairs. Has anyone found where he injured his head? There must be blood."

"It was dark when he was found and carried back up the stairs. As I said, I doubt anyone has looked."

"Then perhaps we should, sister," Thomas said as he grabbed a torch from the wall and hurried to the flight of stairs.

The stairwell was too narrow for more than one person to walk through at a time with any ease. Thomas handed Anne the torch, and she followed the monk as he slowly descended, studying the stones of the stairs and wall as he went. It did not take them long.

"Here it was. See?" Thomas had just reached the fullness of the first curve below the living quarters and pointed to the wall.

Anne turned and looked behind her. "He must have slipped at the top then, but I noted no impediment, nothing that should have caused him to fall."

"A mouse running across his path? A rat might have startled him." Thomas knelt, looked at the bloodstain on the wall, then studied the stairs just above and below it. "You say he lost much blood?"

"Indeed he had," she said, kneeling to look as he moved down a step to give her room. "I believe I see where your thoughts are leading. With such a blood loss, there should be more blood here, or perhaps stains all the way down the stairs if he slipped further on after the injury."

Thomas stood and gestured for Anne to bring the torch closer. "Look here. What do you think this is on the stones of the window?"

"Blood."

The monk leaned over the stones and looked down into the open ward. "God must surely love this priest. Had the winds not driven the snow into a good drift against this tower, Father Anselm would have suffered more than a cracked skull."

"You think…"

"I suspect he was pushed out of this window, sister. After he was shoved down the stairs."

Chapter Twenty-Five

The baron closed his eyes.

Eleanor watched him and frowned with concern. "Richard is getting the best care possible, father," she said.

He looked at her in silence, eyes dark with fatigue and anxiety. The lines in his face had deepened.

"Sister Anne tells me that he has no fever and that he did take some watered wine this morning."

"Lass, I question neither your judgment nor Sister Anne's ability as a healer, but tell me, if you can, why God has chosen to curse me so? I have failed to protect my family, my retainers, and my guests. This castle has become not a fortress against unnatural death but rather a place to embrace it. The first was Hywel, a man I shall sorely miss, killed by misadventure. Then Henry is foully murdered under my very roof and my son stands accused of the deed. Father Anselm meets with calamity, and now my dear grandson lies in a sick bed once again. What horrendous sin have I committed? As a woman closer to God than this old warrior could ever be, can you answer that?"

"Job committed no sin."

"Job was a saint. I am not." Adam rubbed his hands across his eyes. There were circles the color of bruises under them.

"I have faith that Richard will recover and my brother found innocent. Hywel's death was accidental. That could have happened to anyone and at any time. No one could predict that Henry would be stabbed to death, especially you, and we do not know exactly what happened to Father Anselm. It may have been an accident as well." The latter she did not believe at all.

Adam slammed his fist on the table. "You may have your faith, Prioress Eleanor, but my charge remains a more earthly one: to protect all within the walls of Wynethorpe. In that, I have failed. As to the nature of my priest's *accident*, do not insult me so. I have spoken to Brother Thomas, who seemed quite sure that the poor man's head was pushed with force into a wall and his body tossed from a window to finish the deed." He smiled grimly. "Surely, you do not now doubt the judgment of a man whose praises you sang to me so recently?"

Eleanor said nothing until the fires of her father's exhausted anger had sputtered and dimmed. Silence was a woman's wisest response until a man's choler cooled and reason regained a seat in his soul, her aunt once said. It was man's nature to swing at flies with an ax at such times, however much he might later rue the consequences. "Nay, I trust him implicitly," she said at last, her tone gentle.

Adam snorted. "Good! While Sister Anne has been tending to Richard and Brother Thomas has been piecing together evidence with perceptive logic, I assume you have contributed to the search for justice by offering sufficient prayers so the murderer will be found before my son is taken away to be hanged?"

"Dare you suggest that prayer is not effective, my lord? Such would be heresy," Eleanor snapped, but her pride was wounded. "Perhaps you might tell me what you have discovered from your questioning of those within the castle?"

For just an instant, she saw the fury she felt reflected back at her from her father's eyes, then the fires were banked and he replied in a calm voice. "Every man in this fortress has been questioned about where he was the night of the murder by one of three under my command I trust the most. So far, all have either been where they should have been, passed out with drink, or with some woman, wife or no. Nor was there any indication that anyone did more than wish Henry's soul a hotter fire in Hell for the accident he caused."

As Eleanor began a question, he raised one hand and continued. "At your suggestion, I did approach Sir Geoffrey about his thoughts on the murder when he came to the dining hall this morning to break his fast. As I suspected, he is a most generous friend. He said he could not believe that my son could have done the deed and thinks someone else must have killed Henry. Robert simply came upon the body at the wrong time, he said. He would be most willing to present other possibilities at any trial. As the most likely event, he suggested that Henry ran into a drunken soldier in the halls of Wynethorpe and was murdered for no better reason than the discordance caused by too much wine or a gaming debt. Henry was known to play at dice and rarely won the rolling of them."

A noble gesture but an indefensible supposition, she thought, considering the results of the questioning. "You told me none of this until I asked. May I know why?"

"Because I am lord of Wynethorpe!" he thundered. "The accused murderer is my son and the murder occurred in my castle. I have been far too tolerant of your involvement. None of this is woman's business."

"First you accuse me of doing little to help Robert and then you dismiss me as a weak woman who could do little if I tried. You may not have it both ways, my lord. As to what is woman's business and what is not, may I remind you that I have full responsibility at Tyndal and there is no question there about what is and is not my authority. In addition, need I remind you that Robert is also my brother, whom I love as well as any sister can, and that Isabelle, Juliana, Henry and George are almost kin to me in my heart. Although you are, without question, lord of this place, I am your daughter. As such, I have the right to be involved and know what is happening by the love I bear for all concerned."

The baron turned pale, then sat down on the bench with a heavy thud. After a moment, he continued, his voice hoarse but calmer. "Let us make peace, daughter. I do not wish to argue with you."

From the pinched look around his eyes, Eleanor realized that her father was in as much physical pain from his old wound as he was emotional pain from the accusations against his son. She took a deep breath and let it out slowly. "Nor do I wish to argue with you, father. Please tell me all that Sir Geoffrey had to say."

Adam stretched out his leg and began to massage it. "Little of help. He said he had never seen Robert strike in anger and he has known him from a time he was younger than my grandson. Of course, my son and his have never been close, but they were of different ages and temperaments. On the other hand, he said he had never known Henry to raise a sword or fist to anyone either, although he had seen a change in the lad recently."

"His father mocked him cruelly in front of all at dinner the other night. Did he taunt Henry for his lack of manhood often?"

Adam snorted. "Geoffrey was sick of the boy's whining. Henry had taken it into his head that he would wed the Lady Isabelle. When Geoffrey announced he would have her instead, the boy acted like a baby whose wet nurse had taken away the tit."

"Surely Henry had reason to believe Isabelle would be his wife after all these years. Perhaps he had even grown to love her."

"I would have agreed with you once, but, if I may be so blunt, a man does not rape the woman he loves. And he did rape Lady Isabelle, did he not, if we are to believe her and I understand that you do?"

It was Eleanor's turn to be surprised at her father's words. "Indeed, my lord, I do believe her tale if for no other reason than she did herself no favor in the telling."

"Well reasoned. I would agree."

"I must wonder, however, why Henry never told his father about his bedding of Isabelle. He might not have confessed to a rape as such, but the act would have prevented his father's marriage with the lady and guaranteed the success of his own wishes."

"According to Sir Geoffrey, Henry did swear that he had bedded the woman."

"Yet…"

"There was blood on the sheets when Geoffrey awoke next to her. In her grief at losing her virginity, she pointed that out to him and he believed her."

"Smearing a little chicken blood on the sheets to prove virginity when the gate had already been breached is an old trick. I wonder that a man of Sir Geoffrey's experience could be duped with such ease."

"By God's right hand, whatever are they teaching girls in convents these days?" Adam laughed. "That you should know such a thing is…but never mind. If you have enlightened me about how much nuns know about worldly tricks, let me perhaps enlighten you about the nature of good men."

"Do," Eleanor said. The earlier tension between them had dissipated and she began to relax.

"My dear friend is a true innocent with women. Although he may have dallied as boys do before marriage, I know that he was never once unfaithful to his first wife after they took their vows at the church door, even when her pregnancies would have given him cause to seek relief elsewhere for his own health."

"Yet surely he knew that women do such things…"

"He chose to believe Isabelle's story and disbelieve that of his son. As I have said before, he is besotted with his ward or, since we are speaking unadorned truth here, besotted with the idea that he had regained his virility and that it was he who had gotten her with child."

"Thus he also chose to believe that his son had lied. Men cannot be such fools, surely."

"My child, we are all mortal, men and women alike. Fools we have always been and fools will we always be, especially when our greatest frailties breach the walls of our better sense."

"I have learned from you, my lord. But please continue. I did not wish to interrupt."

Adam smiled with gentleness at his daughter and continued. "Indeed, once Geoffrey married his whore, she was no longer available to Henry whether he loved or lusted for her. As my old friend said, a man, after being unhorsed, picks himself up and finds another horse to ride, but Henry whined and whined like a whipped pup. His father tried to make him see what a fool he was becoming and he mocked to press the point on him. That is all, but Henry continued to force his attentions on the lady and that angered his father even more. It is unnatural for a son to pursue his father's wife like a lovesick pigeon."

Eleanor shook her head. "If I may be so candid, father, Sir Geoffrey's public ridicule of Henry was as excessive as beating an unweaned pup. Would you have so mocked either of your sons?"

"My sons have always known their duty. As a consequence, I have never been driven to treat either as Geoffrey did Henry. Still, I think I may say with some reason that both Hugh and Robert have gained respect amongst their peers. Henry had few friends and even fewer admirers. Have you forgotten that Henry so angered someone that he was killed? Someone, perhaps, who was less tolerant of his peevish manner than Geoffrey? He would have done well to take his father's advice and behave in all ways as a man should. No matter how blind Geoffrey was about the woman he took to wife, he takes responsibility for his actions, something his son had yet to learn."

Eleanor held her breath for a moment before saying what was on her mind. However angry it might make her father, she had to speak the thought. "You do not think that Sir Geoffrey might have done the deed himself?" she said at last, not daring to look her father in the eye. "You do not think that he might have been so outraged at his son's rape, real or purported, that he killed his own son in revenge or even to silence him from forcing an annulment of the marriage by claiming prior sexual knowledge of his father's wife?"

Adam snorted. "Nay, I do not, daughter. For all his blindness about his wife, he is a man of mature years who has suffered and overcome trials severe enough to test the limits of any mortal man. Henry, on the other hand, had no iron in his backbone. It is more likely, therefore, that Henry would have killed his father for taking away the sugar teat."

"Then I must ask this, father: Although both you and I believe in Robert's innocence, do you think he might have been bedding the Lady Isabelle? Could Henry have come upon them that night and attacked my brother out of a jealous rage…"

The baron smiled. "Ah, Eleanor, do you remember how shocked we were when Hugh brought that babe to us and confessed it was his?"

The prioress nodded.

"Know then that Robert confessed to me, as I proposed the marriage with Juliana to him, that he has had no knowledge of women except in his dreams when Satan sends his whores to tempt us all. Although he would swear otherwise, I think he would have found a monkish vocation quite suitable if you had not already taken vows." He stopped and studied his daughter's face for a long moment before continuing, "Now, however, although he might have made a fine abbot, he will be, as he always has been, a loyal son and will do as I ask, even to marriage."

"You are truly blessed in your sons, my lord, if not in your daughter."

"One of my children had to take after me," replied the baron as he rose, leaving Eleanor to wonder which he meant.

Chapter Twenty-Six

The woman had been standing immobile near the stones of the parapet for so long that miniature drifts had formed against her feet. Oblivious to the chill, the Lady Juliana continued to stare into the gray void filled with swirling flecks of snow.

Thomas shook with the cold. Even the thick cloak and decent leather boots, loaned to him by his prioress from clothes left behind by Lord Hugh, were barely sufficient to keep the wind's ice from his bones. How the woman in front of him could endure the bitter cold in lighter attire was beyond his imagination. Was she in a trance, he wondered, possessed perhaps, or simply mad?

"My lady," he shouted into the wind. "Should you not seek shelter?"

When she finally turned to him, her face was without expression and her eyes blank of recognition.

"Fear not! I am Brother Thomas of Tyndal. I came with Prioress Eleanor and Sister Anne. Will you come inside for some spiced wine to chase away this cruel chill?"

She continued to look at him in silence. Although the falling snow obscured her features, her eyes glowed black amidst the pale flakes and Thomas felt uneasy under their unbroken gaze. Shifting his weight to keep his feet from growing numb, he found himself thinking that the woman could not be possessed, for surely Satan preferred fire to this ice when he tortured souls.

"Wine?" she asked at last in a tone that suggested his offer was some fantastic thing.

The snow continued to whirl in the wind. Thomas watched one snowflake, delicate as lace, land on his sleeve and slowly blend with its fellows. Beauty can be so fragile, yet so deadly, he thought, remembering how the snow had nearly frozen Anselm to death last night.

"If you will come inside," he said, stepping forward with hand outstretched to pull her from the castle wall if need be, "we have much to discuss."

"You wish to question me on my desire to enter Tyndal as an anchoress," Juliana said as she started to walk slowly toward him.

"Aye," he replied, "and perhaps more."

"If you wish to speak of death, we should remain here, brother, where we are closer to it." She stopped and gestured toward the parapet.

She was quite mad. Thomas was now sure of it.

Then she smiled with such warmth that even her grim words were melted into a jest. "I will come with you, brother," she said as she pulled her cloak more closely around her and hurried to his side. "You have no need to stand in the cold waiting for this foolish woman to come out of it. I did not mean to make you suffer for your courtesy."

꩜ ꩜ ꩜

Despite the warmth of the hearth and the heaviness of his borrowed garments, Thomas could feel his hands and feet just now begin to sting with returning feeling. The woman who sat on the other side of the table with a cup of spiced wine looked untouched by her time in the freezing storm.

"You say you wish to enter Tyndal as an anchoress, my lady," Thomas began, his teeth still chattering. "There is no enclosed cell for you next to the church. Would you not come to us as a nun instead?"

"I do not require a hermitage enclosed with stone, brother. I know of no rule, beyond current custom, that requires someone of my stern calling to anchor in a space surrounded by stone and mortar. A cave or hut in the forest would suit me as well as it did men and women in times past. Amongst God's verdant gifts, He has given us many quiet places where we may find the solitude to contemplate and hear His voice with greater clarity. It has never mattered whether those who seek Him retreat into the burning wilderness of the desert fathers or England's dark woods."

"My lady, please understand that it is not I who will decide whether or not to approve your plea or the details thereof. The bishop and our prioress will do that." Thomas poured more hot, spiced wine into her cup as well as his own. Perhaps women did dwell in forest huts long ago, he thought, but such a request by members of the weaker sex was quite unusual now. Still, she was right about one thing. Removal from the joys of London to the more austere East Anglian coast had given him more time for contemplation, as had the new joys of his work in a hospital and listening to the novice choir's simple lyricism whenever he wished. His new sea-scented residence might not be as dour as a desert, the wind-pruned forest near Tyndal might not match the grim darkness of others less buffeted, but surely the reek of fish and rotting seaweed held some position of merit in God's eyes.

Thomas glanced up and caught Juliana smiling at him. The look was not mocking, but it unsettled him. "Since I am the confessor to the nuns of Tyndal," he quickly explained, "your welfare would be my responsibility; therefore, Prioress Eleanor thought it wise that I question you on the basis for your decision to become an anchoress."

"Ask what you will, brother." Juliana crossed her hands and leaned back in her chair.

Indeed, Thomas had little to ask, but when his prioress requested that he question Juliana on her vocation, he had had no good reason to refuse. Surely he was the least qualified to judge if someone were suited to any form of monastic life since he had not chosen such himself with whole-hearted willingness. On the other hand, some might say that the choice of life over being burned at the stake by an admirer of that *exquisite punishment*, a concept regaining strong popular support amongst clerics, might be deemed whole-hearted enough. Perhaps he should be flexible about her reasons for finding her vocation as well.

Thomas cleared his throat and asked the obvious first question: "Why do you want to enter a monastic life?"

"You ask me an easy question first." Juliana smiled. "The simplest answer is that I feel called to it."

The change in Juliana from the person he had coaxed from the castle parapet was dramatic. Unlike that deathly pale creature with eyes like burning coal, this woman positively glowed with a most womanly warmth. Had he been wrong to think her mad? Might she not be that rare creature who was filled with grace, perhaps even gifted with visions? "Why?" Thomas asked. Indeed, he truly wanted to know.

Juliana leaned forward. This time her steady gaze comforted rather than unsettled him. "I think we might understand each other in this, brother. I feel called to it because worldly things no longer give me joy. In my case, I have enjoyed the love of good parents. My brothers were a happy trial when I was growing up." She laughed and Thomas watched a memory dart across her eyes. "In addition, I have felt the pain of lust, and, if I may repeat a secret I told in confession, I have experienced the joy of it as well." Her brown eyes twinkled with a comfortable sensuality.

Thomas realized his bones no longer ached with cold. "Our Lord…"

"…does not require virgins as brides. As I recall, he not only saved the life of Mary Magdalene but also honored her. It was to her, after all, that Jesus announced his resurrection at the tomb, not to Peter or John."

"I was about to say much as you did."

"Then you are wiser than many priests." Juliana fell silent for a moment, her eyes unashamedly examining the auburn-haired monk. "Not to say I questioned the choice of Tyndal for my hermitage, but knowing that you are there is further sign of its merit."

Thomas felt his face flush.

"Be at peace, brother. I have no more designs on your very fine body than I believe you have on mine." She shook her head. "Do not protest, for you did think that was my meaning. But do answer this for me: am I right that you did not come to the monastic life as a child?"

Thomas nodded, deciding it was best to see where her questions led before saying anything further.

For a moment Juliana said nothing, then closed her eyes as if profoundly weary. "I find comfort in the knowledge that I shall confess to a priest who had a full taste of the world but was wise enough to reject its corruption for a peace that only God can bring."

He waited.

"Forgive me, Brother Thomas. Please continue to ask me your questions, and I shall reply, as is meet, with more modesty. Playing the hare to your hound is contemptible in a woman who longs to become an anchoress." Juliana's face paled as her smile disappeared. "Although that day of peace seems as far away as the softness of spring is from this bleak winter."

As he watched the light fade from her eyes, Thomas felt the unease returning that he had experienced with her on the walls. "You have wearied of this world then?" he asked with a gentle tone.

"Wearied? Perhaps. Once I reveled like a child in earthly pleasures. Now they stink in my nostrils like night soil in the summer sun. Once I believed that anyone with a good and faithful heart could remain pure. Now I know that all mortals are tainted with violence and evil. Should I stay in this world, I fear I would try, time and time again, to reclaim the lost Eden, something no mortal will do. Thus my desire to leave a world that rots under my hand may be as much due to fear of my own sinful nature as it is to weariness. I long to seek God's wisdom and all-forgiving love, something I can only find in the solitary life."

"A solitary life is possible in a monastic setting. You would be shut away enough from the rest of the world. Why ask for the more severe life of an anchoress, closeted in a isolated cell and separated even from the comfort of other nuns?"

"Because the company of women would be a burden to me. I seek a place where I will hear only the sound of God's voice singing in my ears. I cannot bear the voices of the children of Adam and Eve."

"People may come to beg wisdom from you. Many anchorites and anchoresses are judged to be closer to God than most religious."

Juliana's eyes sparkled in brief amusement. "Fear of the strange woman in the glade will frighten most away, I trust, and Tyndal will protect me should that not be sufficient. In the meantime, I promise that your visits to shrive me will be welcomed, and Eleanor's voice will never intrude on my contemplations. Your voices I shall bear."

"What caused you to so turn against the world?"

"God."

Thomas sat back and stared at her. "God does not hate His creation."

"God has willed this."

"His voice? A vision?"

"If you will."

"Could it not be Satan who spoke to you, not God?"

"Satan loves his comforts, brother. He would be happier with me if I followed the lusts of my body rather than the harsher ones of my soul."

"You have been candid with me, my lady, but now I must be blunt with you in return."

"You may be as forthright with me as need be. It will make your task and mine easier."

In spite of himself, Thomas smiled. "Might not your weariness with the world be grounded more in disappointment than in a true belief that mortal joys are shallow ones?"

"That was not plain enough speech! If you mean to ask whether I am jealous because my dearest friend married before

I did, then the answer is *no*. I must differ with my father on this."

"Nonetheless, you and the Lady Isabelle have quarreled much since she married with your father."

"We have fought less than my father has suggested. She and I are not suited to the roles of stepmother and stepdaughter. That is true, but the memory of our youth together remains strong in our hearts."

"Yet I have seen your sorrow and silence in her presence. You did quarrel. Why?"

She sat back in her chair and sighed. "Do you not remember when the innocence of childhood fled? Each of us is doomed to repeat that bite of apple given by the serpent in Eden, I think. One day we laugh together in play; the next we look at each other and raise our hands to strike those very loved ones. Is there a reason or is it the nature of our mortal sin?"

"I am a simple man, my lady, and have no easy answer to that…"

"You are neither simple nor prone to facile answers, brother. One day, perhaps in the peace of my forest chapel, we will speak further on that subject, and you will share your own experiences with me." She shook her head as Thomas was about to respond. "Forgive me. We were talking of my calling, not yours. Yours was a direct question that should be answered in an honest fashion. No, I am not running away because my dearest friend married before me. I do not, as has been suggested, fear marriage and its pains, although I confess I feel unsuited to that state. Yes, I wish to escape the world, but my reason is a longing to fold myself completely into God's love and forgiveness much as a child does into her mother's arms. Compared to that, all worldly joys are flawed and feeble things to me. Does that satisfy you, brother?"

Thomas looked at the woman sitting peacefully across from him and felt the sharp stab of regret. If only he had her clear-eyed vocation, perhaps he would rest with contentment. "You speak convincingly, my lady."

Juliana reached out her hand. "Then let us try to become friends, for I do believe we share a special kinship found only amongst those who reject earthly things."

Although he did not understand why, Thomas felt peace at her touch. It was not until after she left the dining hall, however, that he realized she had never answered his question about the specific reason for the quarrel with the Lady Isabelle.

Chapter Twenty-Seven

Dinner that night was a sour affair, both in taste and in mood. The storm had prevented anyone from bringing fresh meat from the hunt; thus the stew was cooked with salted-down venison and tasted too strongly of the garlic used to mask the flavor of meat past its prime. Although the cheese was a good one and the bread fresh enough, neither could make up for the ice-cold stew, congealed after a trip from kitchen hut to dining hall through the snowy mist of evening.

Adam took a deep swallow of the wine and winced. It was his second best and had already turned sour. He scowled, then looked up and his expression grew even grimmer. The Lady Isabelle approached and slipped into her chair, all too near his. She was quite late to table.

"My apologies for my tardiness, my lord. I was waiting on my husband."

"Did your husband give you no reason for missing this fine meal, my lady?"

Her hands traced vague circles in the air. "I have not spoken to him since midday. He said nothing to me at the time about any plans to cause such delay, which is why I waited for him to bring me in to table."

"I wonder how he can speak to you at all," Adam muttered, not softly enough to avoid being overheard.

The lady reached for her wine, and a servant promptly filled her goblet. Either this wine had come from a different barrel or

Isabelle was less fussy than the baron about taste. She downed her cup in one and held it out for more.

Other than the sound of scuffling feet, as servants brought or retrieved platters and replenished wine, and the weak attempts of a less than talented musician at the further end of the hall, silence reigned amongst the rather cheerless diners.

Surely the poetic abilities of the Welsh have been vastly over-rated, Thomas thought, as he listened with pain to the off-tune ballad now being sung. He tried to make a bread ball from the thick, grainy slice on his trencher, but it would not hold and he tossed it down next to the half-eaten cheese. He, too, was infected with a dismal mood.

How could any of them not be? Two men lay dead by mis-adventure. Richard had taken ill once again. Robert, accused of murder, was locked away in a bleak room until the sheriff could take him away for hanging, and Anselm was still unconscious and in mortal danger of dying. His new nephew and compan-ions from an earlier meal had not fared well, Thomas thought, and he had accomplished nothing in finding either cause or the guilty ones.

He glanced around at those currently picking at their food. The prioress was staring into the distance, a small piece of cheese raised halfway to her mouth, then forgotten as her thoughts took precedence over eating. Sister Anne was sitting with her hands resting on either side of her trencher, her eyes lowered as if in prayer. The faces of both women showed the weariness of caring for a silent boy and an even more silent Anselm. The baron was audibly grinding his teeth on the tough stew meat. The Lady Isabelle had refused all solid food and was now into her third cup of wine. Juliana had touched nothing.

To make matters worse, Thomas had noted a change that evening as he walked from chapel to dining hall. Softness had crept into the air that boded well for warmer bones but ill for a man accused of murder. The storm was showing signs of abat-ing, the snow would melt, and that meant a messenger could be sent for the sheriff all too soon.

He broke off a slice of the cheese on his trencher and swallowed it, this time letting the rich flavor fill his mouth with some pleasure as he watched Isabelle and Juliana look over at each other, briefly and at the same time. Neither smiled. Isabelle turned away and gulped more of her wine. Juliana lowered her head and closed her eyes.

If anyone were lost in prayer, Thomas decided, it would be this woman. Sister Anne, however devout she might be, had learned to nap while seeming to be awake after all her years caring for the sick. She could be doing so now for all he knew, but not the Lady Juliana. He sighed. Tyndal might benefit more from her being there than she would from residing at the priory.

She could truly be a saint. Priories often prospered with such in residence, whether in the shape of a living being or in the bonier form of a relic. The long line of eager penitents begging for her touch or wise words would shatter her solitude. And if she were mad rather than a saint? Well then, she might not find the peace she sought at Tyndal, but she would find kindness. Sister Anne and Prioress Eleanor would make sure of that.

A bang shattered Thomas' musings. The door to the dining hall crashed against the wall as a soldier rushed through it to the high table.

Adam jumped out of his chair. "Satan's balls! Have the Welsh set siege to the castle?"

The soldier knelt. Thomas could see him sweating despite the cold. "Forgive the rude entry, my lord. Although the Welsh have not broken truce, the wicked murderer has attacked. Another man has fallen victim to him."

Adam paled. "Who?"

"Sir Geoffrey, my lord. We found him behind the stables. He was stabbed and left to die."

ᏬᎾᏟᎦ ᏬᎾᏟᎦ ᏬᎾᏟᎦ

Anne shook her head as she watched the men carry Sir Geoffrey away with great gentleness on a litter.

"Will he live?" Adam asked, his voice catching.

"He has lost much blood, my lord, and is still unconscious. The wound itself may heal well enough if it does not fester, but he was bleeding for some time. God was merciful, however, for the cold may have slowed the blood loss enough." She looked around. "It was fortunate he was found in time at all. On such a cold night, no one else would have come here."

"We must be grateful for a stable boy's loose bowels, it seems," Adam said, his tone flat.

"When did you say you had last seen your husband?" Eleanor turned to the Lady Isabelle. The woman's gaze was as fixed as if she were seeing a vision in the dark stain of her husband's blood in the snow. "My lady?" she asked again.

Isabelle looked up. "Forgive me, but I did not hear what you said."

"At dinner you said Sir Geoffrey had not come to escort you to table, that you had not seen him since midday. Do you remember if he said anything to you at all about his plans for the day? Perhaps he mentioned something last night or this morning which would cast light on what has happened?"

A light flush spread over Isabelle's face. "My lord husband does not share my bed while I have my courses. We were not together last night, nor in the morning."

Eleanor looked at her father with a question in her eyes.

Adam shrugged.

"Perhaps you know where he slept last night? If you would rather tell me in private…" Eleanor gestured toward their lodgings above the hall.

Isabelle shook her head. "I do not know. He never speaks to me of women he might lie with for his health."

God will surely forgive such public deceit to protect the private humiliation, Eleanor thought, then asked: "You saw him at midday, did you not?"

"Briefly. I was resting and suddenly he came into my chambers without knocking, looked around as if searching for something, and left."

"He said nothing to you?" Or was he just checking to see how drunk you were this day, Eleanor thought.

"He smiled at me as if pleased but said nothing."

"Has his behavior been unusual in any way?" Eleanor pursued.

"He has been much distracted since we came to discuss the marriage of Jul—my stepdaughter, that is, to your brother."

Adam frowned. "Our negotiations over rights were not so dour as to cause him grief. Your husband and I have long been friends and the marriage was to have been of mutual benefit. He had nothing to fear from me and he knew that. It was Henry who seemed most upset by the talks. Perhaps something else had distressed your lord husband?"

"If so, I knew nothing of it. He did not discuss his concerns with me."

"Nor would I," Adam muttered, turning his head at a sound of footsteps coming through the stable.

As Brother Thomas approached the solemn group, the joy on his face was obvious. "Your men have guarded Robert well, my lord. Despite their fondness for him, they have chained him in his room at night and never left him alone, nor has he attempted bribes or asked for a lax watch. He could not have done this deed."

"Then he is innocent of Henry's murder as well, father," Eleanor said in a low voice. "Surely this is the act of the same man. The air at Wynethorpe has never fostered such a pestilence of unlawful death."

Adam turned to his daughter and for the first time since her childhood she saw tears flowing down his cheeks in public. "He is surely free of blame for this act and may be of Henry's murder as well, but I cannot free him until we find those guilty of one or both acts. My son was found with the dagger and Henry's blood on his hands. I cannot free him until his innocence is without question."

"Then, my lord, the answer is quite simple," Eleanor said, straightening her back and looking around at the assembly. "We will find the person who did it. And soon."

Chapter Twenty-Eight

"Simple? Simple!" Thomas threw out his hands in disbelief as he and Sister Anne strode down the corridor. "If I did not know our prioress better, I would swear on God's very breath that she has lost her wits. It is no simple task to find who killed Henry, perhaps pushed our priest down the stairs and has now stabbed Sir Geoffrey. And to do it all, I might add, before the sheriff gets here and takes Robert off to some dungeon until he can be tried and hanged." He took a deep breath. "Perhaps the most mercy we can hope for is that they'll let us pull his legs to break his neck and put a speedier end to his misery."

"Do you have a brother?"

Thomas skidded to a stop from the shock of the unexpected question. "Why ever do you ask?"

Anne's smile was a gentle one. "Not to pry. I meant only to ask if you have never loved someone so much that you would move heaven and earth to save that one person's life?"

Thomas paled as the image came to mind of one he had loved that deeply, but he said nothing. Not even the kind Sister Anne would understand his love for Giles.

"I see the answer on your face, Thomas," Anne said, putting her hand on his arm. "Then perhaps you will understand how our prioress feels about her Robert. She has told me of their closeness. In the years after she was taken to Amesbury, it was Robert who wrote her missives full of love as well as family news.

It was he who remembered special occasions and sent her special gifts. A frog for her birthday once, I've been told."

"A frog?"

She formed a rather large circle with her hands. "A big one. He was quite proud of catching it, our prioress said, and her aunt let her keep it in the garden pond. I'm told it became a veritable Methuselah of frogs and serenaded the nuns at Amesbury for longer than any thought possible."

Thomas laughed. "For the gift of a raucous frog she would save his life? Most sisters might feel differently."

"Our prioress is not like most women."

"Aye," he sighed, "there is truth to that."

"Meanwhile," Anne said, "we have our small hospital here to attend. Let us see how our patients are doing."

Thomas followed as she pushed her way through the wooden door.

⚭ ⚭ ⚭

"Am I in Heaven?" Anselm's eyes opened wide as he gazed up at Sister Anne's smile. "Are you our Holy Mother?"

"Far from either, priest," Thomas said with a grin as he looked over Anne's shoulder at the awakened man.

Anselm winced. "I know that you are no angel, and my head would not hurt so if this were Heaven."

"Nor would you have the breath of an eater of animal carcasses in your nostrils."

"Be gentle," Anne scolded back at Thomas. "Our brother is still a very sick man." She put the back of her hand on the older man's cheek.

Anselm cringed. "Touch me not, woman! I have taken vows…"

"As have I, brother, and I assure you that I am no more tempted to sin with you than you are to sin with me. I am Sister Anne, sub-infirmarian at Tyndal Priory, and…"

"A man! A man should tend me!"

"Relax, priest," Thomas said. "This nun has saved your life, and the only man in the castle who might tend you works best with horses and mules. Although you may resemble the latter at this very moment, I doubt you'd prefer his manner of physic."

Anselm sputtered and his look was still wild, but he let Anne examine his head wound.

She lifted her opened hands when she was done as if to show she had stolen nothing of value from him. "Did that hurt?"

"What have you done to me, daughter of Eve?" the priest growled.

"Tested you for fever. You have none. Checked your bandages and found no foul discharge. Changed your dressings to make sure the strength of the herbs remains potent."

Thomas sniffed the air. "And someone has bathed you for your scent is now quite sweet."

Anselm opened his mouth wide at the horror of what Thomas had just said. "I will die of your care, woman! It is ungodly to bathe."

"Our good brother is jesting with you," Anne replied as she scowled at Thomas. "We would never do anything ungodly to you. We are as dedicated to holy service as are you."

Thomas nodded solemnly. He knew full well that Anne believed in the effectiveness of frequent washing and had most likely ordered the reeking priest sponged off before he was placed on this mattress, freshly stuffed with lavender, tansy and sweet woodruff. Nonetheless, he had no desire to upset Anselm. The man needed his strength to heal, not joust verbally with Thomas. "I do jest indeed, priest. Forgive me."

The priest looked at him balefully. "Do you swear on your hope of Heaven that nothing untoward has been done to me as I lay in the charge of this woman's unclean hands?"

"I swear it on my hope of Heaven." At least he could be honest enough about that, Thomas thought with a smile. "You have been attended with all due propriety and have not sinned, however unwittingly, while you lay unconscious."

"Indeed, Brother Thomas speaks truly for he assists me in my work at Tyndal."

"A monk who *assists* a woman?" Anselm tried to frown disapproval but his head hurt too much.

"We are of the Order of Fontevraud," Thomas replied.

Anselm nodded, then winced. "A strange sect, that," he mumbled, but overall he seemed more at peace.

"Perhaps rest would be wise," Anne said. "While you sleep, Brother Thomas will sit with you. After you awaken, some vegetable broth might suit, after which we would like to hear what you remember of your fall."

Before Anne had even finished her sentence, the priest was snoring with a smile on his face.

⌘ ⌘ ⌘

"Alas, my lady, I remember nothing," Anselm said. His eyes brightened with the offer of more broth from the manservant.

Eleanor sat with back straight and hands primly folded in her lap, a position she felt gave her the dignity her youth could not. "Perhaps in the telling of what you do remember, there will be something to help. Are you strong enough to tell us that?"

The priest sucked at the broth with noisy appreciation, then took a breath and continued. "I remember having a discussion with Brother Thomas. About the dangers of eating meat, I think. He is quite a bright and promising young priest but suffers the follies and passions of youth. Although his blood still has that youthful heat, I do believe he will be a good religious one day if he would only avoid…"

"Yes, we think he will," Eleanor said with slow patience.

"Oh. He is one of yours, is he not?"

"I am sure you have advised him well as you have us all at Wynethorpe, Father Anselm." She hesitated to avoid any appearance of impatience. "After you left him," she continued, "what do you remember?"

Anselm frowned in concentration. "I left him in the stairwell, I believe. We had agreed to meet in the chapel later for prayers. First, however, I wanted to visit the young Richard. I had heard he loved stories and I had some edifying ones I thought he might enjoy. Saint George and the dragon for one."

Eleanor coughed and raised one hand so she could hide her smile. The priest was not as insensitive to the interests of little boys as she would have once thought. "Aye, a good tale, that."

"After a few such sagas, he grew restless and took up the hobbyhorse. Like a flash of lightning he was out the door, and, when I stepped into the passageway, he was riding his hobbyhorse down the corridor at a fierce pace. He had a stick for a lance and was charging at some imaginary target with all the ardor of a true knight. A miracle, it was, his recovery, and I stood watching him in wonder at God's grace."

Eleanor blinked as a thought began to take form in her mind. "Indeed, his recovery was a blessing from God, but what happened next?"

Anselm blushed. "I am ashamed to say I became like a boy myself with joy at God's kindness."

Eleanor smiled. "We all become innocents at such times, good priest. It is nothing to feel shame over."

"I confess I lifted my robes and raced after him, joining in his innocent pleasures. I became his dragon and we chased each other up and down the corridor outside the chambers. I wouldn't let him go down the passage to the tower but, on one turn, he did ride toward the stairwell to the dining hall and disappeared. I feared he might tumble if I cried out for him to stop so I continued in the game and shouted out to him, as I stopped at the entrance to the stairwell: 'Hi ho, knight, I have seen your deeds but would hear more of them from you! Come here to me!'"

"Richard would have been delighted to entertain you with his exploits against the dragons of the castle," Eleanor said. "Did he not return to do so?"

"I don't know, my lady. That is the last thing I remember until I awoke, my head on fire, with your sub-infirmarian and Brother Thomas bending over me as I lay here."

Eleanor frowned in thought.

"I fear I have not told you anything of merit." Anselm winced with a sharp pain.

"On the contrary, Father, you may have given me the balm to heal my nephew."

Chapter Twenty-Nine

Sister Anne was spooning a very similar vegetable broth into Richard's mouth. The boy was sitting upright and had been cooperative with his feeding until this moment. His face, however, was without expression.

"Another sip for you," she coaxed, putting the spoon up against his now firmly closed lips.

Richard turned his head away, shook it with minimal motion, then slipped back down into the bed and burrowed his head against that of his hobbyhorse. The head of the toy shared his pillow.

"Do you think Gringolet would like some of the broth?" Thomas asked from the doorway.

Richard wrapped his arms around his horse, turned his face to the opposite wall, and pulled the covers up over his ears.

"I cannot believe what has happened to our brave knight," Thomas said, walking up to the bedside. He took the bowl of broth from Sister Anne and nodded toward the door where Eleanor stood waiting. Anne rose and walked out of the room with the prioress as Thomas sat on the bed.

Richard remained silent.

"I do not doubt his courage. He has faced and slain too many dragons." Thomas reached over and stroked the horse's head. "Perhaps it is his noble steed. Could Gringolet be sick? Has he thrown a shoe? Is he lame?"

Richard clutched the hobbyhorse closer to him. A tear escaped from one eye, flowed over the bridge of his nose and disappeared from view. "Not sick," he whispered.

Thomas tried not to smile. Those two words were the first the boy had spoken since taking to his bed. "Fear not, lad. I will not let anyone take him from you, nor did I think this fine horse was mortally ill. Nonetheless, you must tell me what is wrong so we two can physic him back to health, for you cannot stop riding the halls of Wynethorpe for long. The dragons have heard it is safe to roam again and we need you to protect us."

A twitch of a smile came to the boy's lips.

"Hmm. Now let me see," Thomas continued in the best Welsh country accent he could manage considering his short time here. "His eyes are bright. His mane is, well, it could stand some combing. Maybe his master hasn't groomed him yet?"

The boy put his hand over his eyes and wiped the remaining tears away, but this time he was smiling. He shook his head.

"Well, he will soon. We know him to be a good man with a horse. He'd never let his steed go without care, would he now?"

"No," Richard mumbled into his arm.

"I think this horse is fine. There is nothing to worry about, but I'd also say he needs a good rubdown, some fresh hay and a good rest. Perhaps he has returned from an arduous journey and is weary. Methinks his master is too." Thomas put his hand gently on the boy's shoulder.

Richard turned pale.

"Let me tell you a story, lad," Thomas continued, dropping the accent. "Would you like that?"

Richard nodded.

"Once upon a time, there was a brave knight who had a noble steed. Together they roamed the countryside, slaying many dragons, saving maidens (a few) in distress, and taming nameless other monsters (many more of those) that threatened the king's peace. Their exploits were legendary throughout many lands, and no enemy dared attack such a well-protected realm while the knight and his horse stood guard over it. Then one day, a villainous creature in the service of an evil king, who hated the noble king of this happy land, slipped across the river and into the good king's very castle." Thomas hesitated for a moment, looking down at the boy. Richard was watching him, eyes wide and unblinking with concentration.

The monk continued: "This villainous creature could blend into the color of night and hid in the castle corridors, causing great fear during the midnight hours amongst those who lived there. Even the king himself did not know what to do. So he called the brave knight and his noble steed to court and begged them to save the castle. The knight swore he would, but he had never faced such a creature before and knew that courage alone would not be enough. So he took his confessor with him for extra protection from evil. Each night he rode the corridors on his horse with his priest in attendance, hoping to force an honorable confrontation, but the creature evaded him. Then, one night, the creature slipped up behind the knight…"

Richard cried out. "He did!"

"Aye, lad, he did, didn't he? But the man the creature attacked was not the knight. He was the good confessor, was he not?"

Richard nodded vigorously.

"And the creature lifted up the priest to throw him down from the top of steep stairs…"

"Yes."

"Although the brave knight wanted to save his confessor, he found he could not, for he was suddenly frozen in place. The creature, it seemed, had put him under a spell. He had rendered the knight speechless and without the ability to move. The knight was powerless to save his confessor from the creature's attack…"

"Yes!"

"As we all know, good always overcomes evil, and the knight's courage and true heart were stronger than the evil of the creature. So do you know how the knight overcame the creature and saved his confessor?"

Still clutching his hobbyhorse, Richard wiggled back to a sitting position. "Tell me how he did, Uncle."

"The brave knight lay where he had been put under a spell until a wandering priest came upon him. The priest looked down at him and saw that the knight was under an evil spell but knew that the knight's heart was pure because he was the knight's uncle. So the priest said to him: 'Knight, your heart is pure. Rise and speak to me of what you saw and your courage and goodness will conquer the evil creature.'"

"That was all he had to do?" Richard asked in a whisper.

"Aye, lad. All he had to do was tell his uncle, the priest, what he saw and his courage in so doing would slay the villainous creature and save the confessor." Thomas reached out his arms and said in a gentle voice, "So tell me, lad, who pushed Father Anselm down the stairs?"

Richard threw himself into Thomas arms and began to sob. The monk hugged the quivering boy, tucking his small head under his chin, and rocked him gently until the tears began to slow. As they sat together in silence, Thomas closed his own eyes tight, willing the boy to speak.

Finally, in a barely audible voice muffled by the monk's woolen robe, Thomas heard Richard say: "It was Sir Geoffrey, Uncle. It was Sir Geoffrey."

Chapter Thirty

"Who will believe a child?" Adam was pacing. Thomas, Sister Anne and Eleanor sat watching.

"Do you, my lord father?"

"Do I believe that a man at whose side I fought from Poitou to Evesham, a man who covered himself in honor at tournament after tournament, a man who was the exemplar of knightly virtues to those he faced in battle, that such as he would try to kill a priest? For what reason? Tell me that! Whatever for?"

"The last thing Brother Anselm remembers saying might suggest to a hidden listener that he had seen Henry's murder," Eleanor said.

"Forgive me, my lady prioress, but no one could possibly conclude that a priest chasing after a child on a hobbyhorse and shouting about knightly deeds was referring to a murder." Adam glared at his daughter.

"Unless Sir Geoffrey, or whoever else it might have been, heard Father Anselm saying that he 'had seen your deeds and would hear more of them'? Perhaps he thought the priest had seen him and was coming to confront him?"

"A conclusion that stretches the bounds of credulity, my child."

Eleanor had hidden her hands in her sleeves and was gripping her arms until they hurt to keep her calm with her father. "Not if Sir Geoffrey was coming down the passage from the tower and only heard Anselm's words. If he did not see Richard and saw only Anselm standing outside the chambers he shared with his wife, he might have concluded that our priest had come to confront him about the murder of his own son."

"Still a far-fetched conclusion when weighed against what I know of Sir Geoffrey's character."

"I ask again, father. Do you believe Richard?"

Adam slid into his chair with a wince. He said nothing, only reaching out a hand to touch the design on his mazer of wine.

Eleanor waited with great patience and in silence.

"He is a good lad," Adam at last said in a low voice.

Eleanor nodded.

"An honest one as well."

She nodded again, gripping her arms more tightly.

"Not given to telling wild tales as if they were true." Adam hesitated, then turned the mazer cup in a half circle. "When asked, he says he only fights play dragons." He turned the cup the rest of the way around. "He told me that one day he might find real ones to fight but the dragons here were just for practice, like the stuffed figures dressed in chain mail at practice tilts." Adam smiled in spite of himself.

Eleanor relaxed her hands. Her nails no longer cut into her arms. She still said nothing, waiting for her father to say what she hoped he would.

"Oh, very well, lass! Yes, I believe the boy thinks he saw Sir Geoffrey. Maybe it was someone who looked enough like him to confuse the lad. I just cannot believe the man would have tried to kill Father Anselm! And it was Geoffrey who was most adamant about Robert's innocence. Why would he want my son freed if he were the murderer? Does not a guilty man seek to cast his culpability onto another? How could he kill his own son, his heir and his own blood? Are these not enough contradictions to raise reasonable doubt that he is the murderer?"

Eleanor bowed her head. "Surely you know better than I that mortals are full of contradictions, father, but let us then say that he did not kill Henry but knows who did. Perhaps he wants to save Robert, because he is the honorable man you know him to be, and does not wish your son, an innocent man, to take the blame when he knows who did the deed. Perchance the person who did kill Henry is someone whom he also loves? Thus he may be the one who tried to kill Father Anselm but may not be the one who killed his son."

Adam frowned. "Killing a priest is not the same as killing another man. Yet," he hesitated, "I might believe that love or loyalty could drive him to it. Whom do you think he might be protecting?"

"Who is closest to him? George is not here. Henry could not have stabbed himself in the back and thus committed the sin of self-murder. That leaves his wife and his daughter." Eleanor hesitated. "Unless you know of someone else in his company…"

"Nay, lass, you've named them all." Adam took a sip of the previously untouched wine. "You have not yet explained his own wound. Could it be that Robert killed Henry and someone else attacked Sir Geoffrey?" He held up his hand to silence the expected protest. "Do not misunderstand me. I believe Robert is completely innocent and this latest attack makes such a conclusion credible, but we must consider all possibilities if we are to prove my son's innocence. He was, after all, still found with dagger in hand, blood staining his hands while he bent over Henry's corpse."

Eleanor looked over at Thomas and Anne. Their wine was untouched, and they were watching her with quiet concentration. "I find the conclusion that there are two murderers loose in the small confines of Wynethorpe Castle as illogical as the idea that Robert is the head of a band of masterless men with some purpose in killing off the Lavenham family, one after the other. If the same person did not attack both father and son, then the motive for attacking Sir Geoffrey separately remains unknown and the likelihood of two separate attacks for two separate reasons is doubtful. We may live in troubled times, father, but Wynethorpe Castle is well disciplined and, as I have already said, not a breeding place of lawlessness."

"Well argued, Prioress of Tyndal," Adam replied with a smile that bespoke some pride in his child.

"Thus," Eleanor continued, "we have three prime suspects in Henry's murder: Sir Geoffrey, his wife and his daughter."

"And in the attack on Sir Geoffrey?"

"The same three."

Adam slammed his hand down. The cup bounced and wine splashed on the table. "I find it impossible to believe that a woman could kill two adult men, including one who was well-versed in fighting. I find it equally impossible to believe that my friend could have so grievously wounded himself."

"Why not his wife and daughter, my lord? Certainly Juliana and Henry were of much the same build. Henry was more muscular, for cert, but he was small compared to most men and not inclined to sport, which suggests he had less strength than many, despite his quickness. Might not both Isabelle and Juliana have been the guilty ones?"

Adam shook his head. "Nay, women are weak creatures, my child." He raised his hand as Eleanor began to speak. "Let me finish. Although you may argue that two women might have overpowered Henry, Sir Geoffrey is a trained warrior." Suddenly, Adam looked down and frowned. "Still, you may have a point. Few men were equal to Geoffrey in a fair fight, yet no man can be prepared when someone he trusts and loves attacks him. Either his wife or daughter might have done this. They are both dear to him and could have gotten close enough to stab him before he knew what was happening."

"You have discounted revenge for the death of the Welshman then?" Thomas asked with some hesitancy.

"I have, brother." Adam sipped at his wine. "Although someone might have killed Henry for that, none would have had reason to attack Geoffrey. Indeed it was he that gave the widow a fat purse filled with coin for the orphaned babes. It was accepted as a fair blood price so I do not believe anyone killed Henry for revenge either."

"Blood price?" Thomas asked.

"A Welsh custom. Perhaps I should say 'law', although we do not accept such and find the practice barbaric. The Welsh take money in payment for the death of a loved one."

Thomas shook his head in amazement.

"That aside, we did question the Welsh just as we did the English and all were elsewhere, with witnesses enough to prove it, at the time of Henry's death. Nay, I have no reason to think it was a killing for revenge. We may find the customs of the Welsh strange, brother, but they follow them as honorably as do other men. Once the blood price was accepted, the widow and orphans most certainly continue to grieve, but they would demand nothing further."

"Then we are back to considering why wife or daughter might have killed Henry and if Sir Geoffrey would be willing to kill a man of God to protect either or both. The murder of a priest is not the act of a man who would later turn against either woman, telling what he knew to the king's justicular. Thus I ask why these women would kill a man who was protecting them, a man who is husband to one and father to the other. In this you are more knowledgeable than I, Father, for I am long away from the days when Isabelle, Juliana, and I frolicked amongst the summer flowers."

"Not so far, Eleanor. To begin, you know the reason why his daughter might as well as I. She wishes to enter a convent and her father wants her to marry."

"A woman who is called to become a nun usually does not commit violence to obtain her way."

"Then I ask this: what would you have done if I had not granted your request to leave the world and, instead, ordered you to marry George?"

Eleanor bent across the table and touched the back of her father's hand. "Your wisdom, my lord, is known by all in this land, and you are wise as well in your kindness. For this I have always loved and honored you. Had you rejected my plea to become a nun, I would have grieved, but I would have respected your choice. I might have thrown a wine cup against the wall in anger, but I would not have tried to kill you."

Adam turned his head away, but not before Eleanor saw the flush of pleasure on his cheeks at her words. "I am most pleased to hear that."

"What say you about his wife then?" Eleanor continued, her hand still resting on her father's.

"As I promised you, I will be blunt. Sir Geoffrey has had problems with potency in this marriage. I had heard rumors that his wife has been less than understanding. Her youth may be blamed, perhaps, but there is tension between them."

"Has he told you as much?"

This time, Adam did not bother to hide the flush of embarrassment. "He did confirm those rumors. In his cups one night at court, he told me that he has been unable to sustain his manhood with her. She has continued to share his bed but does nothing to help him as some wives…"

"I understand, father, but has she mocked him?"

"That she does not. As he has told me, she waits until it is clear he is impotent, then turns away from him and falls quickly to sleep, leaving him to suffer his humiliation alone."

"Has she taken other men to her bed?"

"Sir Geoffrey feared such. He saw her tantalize other men in front of him as if he were not her husband. He confronted her. She claimed she meant nothing by it but youthful good spirits and gaiety, but he remained troubled. When he first arrived here for the marriage negotiations between our children, he suggested to me that he feared she had finally taken a lover, but he would not name him even when I pressed him to do so in confidence."

Eleanor thought back to her own discussion with Isabelle. "Might he have thought Henry was the one? They were of an age and once believed they would marry."

"That I doubt," Adam replied instantly. "Even before you told me of the rape, it was obvious to all that she wished to avoid Henry. It was Henry who was pushing his attentions on her. I saw it, as did Robert. She had taken a dislike to her old playmate after her marriage."

Eleanor said nothing but wondered once more if the rape might be good reason for Isabelle to have killed Henry. Had he tried to force her again? Might he have told her of some plan he had to void her marriage to his father? Had Sir Geoffrey found out and tried to protect her, overprotection perhaps for a woman he could not pleasure but whom he did seem to love for his own reasons. After all, he did believe that he had been potent with her once.

"We seem to be wandering in circles, child. You have presented good reasons for reducing the number of suspects to three. Now I wonder where you would have us go from here?" Adam asked, looking over at his daughter.

Eleanor sat back, then turned to Sister Anne. "Before I answer, I must first ask: how does my lord of Lavenham?"

"Weak but gaining strength, my lady. He is a strong man and I rather think he will recover from his wound unless gangrene appears."

"In that case," Eleanor said, turning to her father, "hear my plan."

Chapter Thirty-One

Bright dots of red splotched Sir Geoffrey's cheeks, a macabre contrast to the almost luminous pallor of the rest of his face. Sitting next to his bed on a stool was Isabelle. Juliana stood just behind her stepmother, one hand resting lightly on her shoulder. Behind the baron was Anne. Eleanor stood to one side of her father. They all faced the knight.

"I know how you love your grandson, Adam, but the boy lies." Geoffrey's eyes narrowed in anger as he looked at his old friend.

Adam now flushed an angry color. "After all these years, you must surely know that indulgence in blind emotion has never been one of my flaws. Nor have I become such an old fool that I cannot see the flaws in those I love. It was I who assumed Robert's guilt in your attack."

"It was I who said he could not have done it. I have always believed in your son's innocence, but your grandson is a child with a child's imagination. Perhaps he did not mean to lie. Perhaps he believes he saw something he only made up. Or perhaps he saw someone he did not know and thought he had seen me."

"I will not argue with you, my friend. Let us go on to what is most important here. Who did this deed to you?"

"I do not know."

"You were stabbed in the chest, not from behind. You must have seen who did it."

"It happened so quickly, Adam! I was walking behind the stables where I could find some solitude, deep in thought about the plight of your good son, when I heard a sound. I looked up. I saw something move toward me from the shadows. There was little light, as surely you noted yourself. Before I could react, I felt the pain and remember nothing more. If my son had enemies, they were not mine. Why should I fear an attack on me at Wynethorpe Castle? I was surprised, ambushed as we would have said in the old days when we were comrades-in-arms." Sir Geoffrey smiled weakly but with fondness at Adam. "I never saw the face or even the figure of the man who did it."

There was a knock at the wooden door. Sister Anne went to open it and Thomas entered the room. He whispered something in her ear and she beckoned to Eleanor.

Adam turned and looked angrily at the three. "What is it? I will have no whispering here!"

Eleanor's hand fluttered to her heart. "My lord, perhaps we have good reason..." Her voice was as tremulous as her gesture.

"Silence, child! This is my domain, and, as I breathe, I am the lord and master here. What means this mumbling?"

Eleanor bowed her head in meek obedience. "My lord, Father Anselm has just awakened. It seems he has recovered wits, speech, and his memory."

"That is good news!" Adam said, looking down at Geoffrey. "Perhaps he can give us a clue to the monster who is attacking good people at Wynethorpe."

Eleanor nodded to Thomas, who stepped forward. "That he can, my lord," he said.

Geoffrey looked quickly at his wife, his dark eyes widening.

"He saw who pushed him?" Adam asked.

"More than that." Thomas shifted nervously and looked down at his feet.

"Out with it, man! This is no time for monkish meekness. Who?" Adam shouted.

Thomas coughed and looked sheepishly at Eleanor.

"Speak, brother. You have my permission," she replied, her lips set in a grim line.

"He did not see who pushed him, but he did see who murdered Henry."

Adam strode over to Thomas, put his hands on the monk's shoulders and shook him. "Who, monk? Who killed Henry?"

"My lord, I hesitate to say."

"Must I lock you up? Perhaps a few days in the dark of the keep will speed your decision to speak…"

"Father!"

Thomas paled. "There is no need, my lord. Father Anselm was at the chamber door of the murderer when he was attacked. The person who killed Henry was the Lady Isabelle."

⁂ ⁂ ⁂

Isabelle's scream rent the air.

Sir Geoffrey, his mouth open in silent horror, reached out to grasp his wife's hand, then fell back, groaning in agony from his wound.

The Lady Isabelle stood, one hand shaking as she extended it in supplication. With the other, she clutched the fabric of her dress over her heart. "My lords…" she began in a whisper, looking in terror first at her husband, then at Adam, and then at Eleanor.

Juliana stepped forward. As she did so, she turned and caressed her stepmother's face, tucking a loose strand of fair hair back under her wimple. "Hush, my lady," she said in a soft voice. "You have nothing to fear." She looked around at the staring eyes of the assembled group. "Innocent people must no longer suffer from the terrors of this mystery. I had hoped Robert would be found innocent of Henry's murder. After the attack on Father Anselm, I thought he would be released for he could not have done such a thing from his prison cell. Then I hoped the attack on my father would gain the good man's freedom at last. Indeed, Robert should not have suffered but for the accident of finding my brother's corpse, and I never would have allowed him to die for something he did not do."

Sir Geoffrey, coughing in pain, turned to stare at his daughter. "You could not know who did these deeds, my daughter. Be careful whom you accuse in your ignorance." His voice was weak, his words hesitant.

"I speak from knowledge, my lord," she replied. There was a calm confidence in her voice and countenance.

Time seemed to slow as Eleanor found herself thinking that the woman she was watching had the serenity of a saint and could not be the mortal Juliana she had known years ago. "Who did it?" she asked at last, her own voice rough with tension.

"It was I."

Chapter Thirty-Two

"No!" Geoffrey shouted. "You lie, daughter. You did not kill anyone. You did not stab me. You did not push the priest. You are innocent!"

Juliana smiled with serenity at her father. "Surely you know that it was not your wife who attacked you."

Geoffrey struggled to sit up in his bed. "Nor did you!"

"How can you be so sure? You claim you did not see who did the deed." Juliana sat carefully on her father's bed and took his hand. "You know the Lady Isabelle is a weak woman, but you know me better, father."

Geoffrey turned his head. "You did not do any of this."

"I was the one who ascended trees to the very top as a child. Isabelle stood on the ground and cheered my efforts, but she could never make it to the first branch. She has always been far more womanly than I."

"Don't do this, child," Geoffrey whispered, squeezing her hand.

"In our youth, when Henry turned rude, it was I who leapt upon him and wrestled him to the ground, pulling hair from his head and clouting his ears. Did he not come to you and complain of me?" Juliana laughed softly. "Do you not remember how often you had to separate my brother and me when we quarreled?"

"They were squabbles. Things that children do. They were not serious. Do not try to make them so, Juliana."

"Henry never forgave me for shaming him."

"You did not humiliate him in front of other boys."

"It was all in front of Isabelle, father. He never forgot that and took revenge. As he grew into manhood and began to lose his fear of my hard blows, he told vile stories about me to all that would listen. It is hard for any woman to defend her honor when her own brother stains it. Did you not see what was happening between us?"

Tears were beginning to flow down Sir Geoffrey's cheeks. "You had always been quicker of wit than he. I assumed you would always best him. Indeed, he had complained to me…"

"But he had stopped, had he not?"

"He and I were estranged. You knew that well, but you are exaggerating the seriousness of your quarrels."

"Am I? The rumors Henry spread would have made any man hesitate before taking me to wife. Any convent would have been reluctant to welcome me amongst a company of nuns no matter how rich the dower. For the sake of my honor, I had reason to kill Henry. And you have just said how quick of wit I am. Then surely I would have known when you were most vulnerable to attack." She took a deep breath. "Isabelle is innocent, is she not?"

Sir Geoffrey muttered something unintelligible.

"Speak up, Geoffrey," Adam said. He stepped up to his friend's side. "Was it your wife who did this to you?"

"No. Juliana is right. She did not. Even had she reason, she would not have had the strength." He looked at his wife with great sadness.

Adam looked over at Juliana. "Then what say you to your daughter's confession, Geoffrey. She is the only one left with motive to kill Henry and the cleverness to…"

Geoffrey swung his handless arm at his old friend. "I will not lose yet another child to this accursed trouble."

"If it was not your wife, and we have found no other person who could have done the deeds, then your daughter's confession must be accepted." Adam turned to Thomas. "Call two of my guards, brother. We will escort the Lady Juliana…"

"Nay! It was not she. It was not my wife and it was not Robert!" Geoffrey shouted.

"Then who was it, my good friend?" Adam asked sadly.

The wail from the old warrior cut like a scythe across their hearts. "May God have mercy on my black soul, Adam! I murdered my first born. I tried to kill your priest, and I attempted to send my soul to Hell for both deeds by trying to take my own life."

⊙⊙⊙ ⊙⊙⊙ ⊙⊙⊙

The two men looked at each other for a long time. Tears hovered at the rims of their eyes, then each blinked them back. Geoffrey turned his head away first.

"I would never have let Robert die for what I did, Adam. You must believe me. When I found he had stumbled on Henry's body and you had imprisoned him as the accused, I did everything I could to prove he did not do the deed. I tried to find a way to show his innocence."

Adam nodded. "Why did you do it, Geoffrey? Why kill your own son?"

"I was convinced that my son and my wife were making a cuckold of me." Geoffrey stopped and looked at his wife's tear-lined face. "Your complaints about his attentions were too quick, my love, too contrived after all the years you had known each other. I thought you were trying to deflect my suspicions away from the one man you were bedding, out of the many with whom you flirted openly."

"Yet they were not putting the cuckold's horns on your head." Adam's voice was gentle.

"Indeed I know that now, yet my reason had fled for some time, along with my manhood. When you claimed your courses had come, wife, I wondered whether they might have come earlier than usual…"

"In that you were right, my lord," Isabelle replied, her voice barely audible.

Her husband smiled weakly. "I assumed you wanted me out of our bed so you could invite my son into it. I waited outside your room, in the shadows just down the corridor that leads to the tower, where I could hear but not be seen. Finally, I did see a man come to your, our, chambers and knock. You opened the door and I rushed forward to find you in Henry's arms, his back to me..." Geoffrey hesitated as he looked at his wife and back at Adam. "...and I was blinded with rage at the thought he had come to share her bed. I stabbed him."

Isabelle looked at them all, then put her face into her hands. "Please hear me on this, good people. Henry did not come at my invitation. I swear it!" She raised her face, tears streaming down her cheeks as she turned to her husband. "I only opened my door because he claimed, in a voice much like yours, that he was you. You must believe me!"

"Silence, woman. This is my tale to tell." Geoffrey looked up at Adam. "My wife tells the truth. We have talked, she and I, since that horrible night. She has explained that my son was besotted with her and did much threaten her when he knew I was not there to protect her. She did not tell me the full tale of his actions out of love for him as my son. Aye, the demons of jealousy have ceased to possess my heart and soul, but too late."

"And Father Anselm?" Eleanor asked after a long silence.

"I pushed him. I did not see Richard but did hear the priest cry out at my chamber door that he had seen my deeds and wanted to hear more of them. I assumed that he had seen me kill my son. I waited until he had turned away from me, then I came from behind, grabbed his habit and tossed him against the stone wall of the stairs, head first." He looked down at his scared stump and shook his head. "My strength is not what it was when I had the use of both hands so I saw I had not killed him. When I bent over him, he was motionless but I could hear him breathing, so I tossed him from the window. If not the fall, I knew that surely the cold would do the final deed."

"The priest claims he saw your wife kill your son."

"A dream. A fantasy." He looked sternly at Isabelle. She neither moved nor spoke. "Monks are often like women. They imagine things that never happened."

"Nor is it uncommon to have such strange thoughts with such a severe head wound," Anne added.

"Your grandson did not lie, Adam. He must have seen me although I did not see him."

Once again the two men stared at each other in silence.

"Adam, I would not have harmed a hair on Richard's head even if I thought he had seen me killing Henry or the priest."

"Why should I believe you?" Adam said, his voice unnaturally low.

"Because I fell on my own dagger to force suspicion away from your son. No one attacked me. I found a place apart from the rest of the castle and stabbed myself, hoping to die and, in so doing, provide proof that Robert was innocent. He could not do both deeds and I thought no one else could ever be accused. Henry's death and mine would remain unsolved crimes."

"It is a sin to take your own life," Adam said.

"I had already murdered my own son and tried to kill a priest. Would the taking of my own life have made my soul's fate any worse? It had already won quite enough land in Hell."

"I must tell the sheriff of your confession," Adam said.

"You needn't put too many guards at my door, Adam, for I am too weak to run," Geoffrey replied, gesturing at his chest.

"Why not just confess? Why try to kill yourself instead?" the baron asked, taking his friend's whole hand in his.

"I am bred for battle, Adam, not the rope. Surely you understand this. Had you and I been in the Holy Land and surrounded by the enemy with no chance for escape, I would have killed you first so you would not have had to suffer whatever humiliations the enemy would delight in inflicting. Then I would have fallen on my own sword. Do you doubt that either of us would have flinched from such acts? Such are honorable deaths for a soldier. Thus I did indeed want to die before the hangman took me. I had sinned so much that one more rotting spot in my soul would mean nothing."

"Facing a hangman for the crime of killing your son is not the same as dying in war."

"I did not want to face the humiliation of the rope, Adam. I have seen men hanged. They kick their feet, their bowels loosen, and their pricks rise while those who witness the event jest at their shame and disgrace. It is no death for a knight who has, until now, tried to lead his life with honor."

Adam nodded. "You have the right in that."

The corners of the knight's mouth quivered.

In silence and in sorrow, Adam and Geoffrey looked at each other for a very long time. The baron stood, wincing with the pain of his old wound. "You are weary. Perhaps it would be best if we all departed and Brother Thomas sat with you. You might find some peace in giving him your confession and seeking the solace a man of God can bring you, Geoffrey. Will you give permission, my lady?" He glanced at Eleanor and she nodded. "While he hears your confession and gives you counsel, I will release my son, bring guards for your room, and send for the sheriff."

Geoffrey nodded. "As is only right, my friend."

Adam turned to Thomas. "When you are done with your priestly duties and he has rested, come for me. I must explain further to Sir Geoffrey what he can and cannot expect from his imprisonment here." The baron closed his eyes. Whether from fatigue or grief no one could tell. "You are my dearest and oldest comrade, Geoffrey. I owe you no less courtesy than I owed my son."

"As you will it, my lord," Thomas replied.

Chapter Thirty-Three

The light of the following morning brought no joy. Thomas' face was drained of color. He was the most reluctant of messengers.

"Be assured, my lady, that Sir Geoffrey died peacefully," the monk said, quickly tucking his hands out of sight as if they were stained with blood he wished to hide from the widow's sight.

Isabelle's wail would have sent tears down the cheeks of the most hardened of men.

Juliana drew her friend into her arms with the tenderness of a mother, resting her cheek on the top of Isabelle's head. "Then he was not in pain last night when he died, brother?" she asked, her eyes as dark and inscrutable as they had been when she and Thomas stood together on that snow-swept parapet.

"Bleeding to death is a gentle passing. Moreover, your father's soul was at peace. As Baron Adam asked, I remained with your father for his confession, after which he said I could leave for I had given him all the consolation he needed. In that you may find comfort."

"Was my lord father able to see him after the confession as he wished or was Sir Geoffrey too weak?" Eleanor's look was sympathetic. She poured a mazer cup of wine and handed it to Thomas. "Drink, brother. You need this."

Thomas gratefully took the offered wine and swallowed with more enthusiasm than thirst. "He was weary but begged to see your father. I waited outside the door in case either of them needed me. When the baron left Sir Geoffrey, he said the knight had fallen into a calm sleep and that no one, not even Sister Anne, should disturb his friend's rest. Indeed, he said, Sir Geoffrey would have little enough peace in the days to come. At least your father was able to see him before he died." He took another long draught of the wine. "I cannot help wondering if there was something I could have..."

"Nay, brother, wonder not," Eleanor said. "You could have done nothing to prevent his death. Of that I can assure you. Sister Anne has said that Sir Geoffrey was so agitated when he confessed his guilt that his wound might have reopened, but the bleeding would have been slow. None of us could have noticed it until it was too late and, when my father thought Sir Geoffrey was falling asleep, he may have been slipping into God's hands."

Eleanor turned to the two grieving women. "God's many mercies are often mysterious. We all heard Sir Geoffrey say he wanted no part of the hangman. Perhaps God answered his prayer. His soul would have been at peace with God so soon after confession, and God must have been at peace with Sir Geoffrey to have granted him such a kind death."

Thomas drained his cup. The prioress poured him another.

"Be at peace too, brother," Eleanor said. "Thanks to you, Sir Geoffrey died with a cleansed soul and will be buried in consecrated ground, which would not have been possible had he died at his own hand." Then she reached over and lightly touched his arm. "Sister Anne might need your help with Father Anselm. And with our mutual nephew. You may go to them now, if you would."

Thomas continued to stare into his empty cup, then started as her words registered. He looked up at Eleanor. He could feel a modest heat flood across his face. With some surprise, he noted that his prioress' face was also flushed.

"Yes, brother, I did hear that I have gained one more brother and one more sister than were kin to me before this winter. Sister

Anne has told me that Richard calls you *Uncle* and she has been dubbed *Aunt*."

"I did not encourage…" he began.

"Come now, brother! You know Richard. He needed no enticing but had good reason of his own for taking you both into this family. I do honor his decision. With the taking of our vows, we three have always been kin in God, but after all we have been through together since my coming to the priory, I believe we may claim a closer mortal relationship as well."

"My lady, you are kind…"

Eleanor waved her hand at him. "Go and see to the sick, brother. I will stay with the Lady Isabelle and the Lady Juliana."

As the door closed behind the priest, Eleanor shut her eyes so tightly they hurt, her body once more begging for a far closer bonding with the monk than that of brother and sister. Then, taking a deep breath, she faced the two women. "I share your grief over the loss of Sir Geoffrey, a good and honorable man who saved my own father's life."

"He was that, my lady, as well as a kind father to me," Juliana said. She tried to move but found it difficult to pry herself from Isabelle's grasp.

"Nay, Juliana, stay close to me." Isabelle looked up at her stepdaughter, revealing as she did a face ashen with fatigue and eyes red from so many tears. "Now that your father is dead, you cannot go to Tyndal. Surely you see that."

Juliana turned her head away from Isabelle and frowned, but Eleanor saw pain in the look, not anger.

Isabelle fumbled at her stepdaughter's hands. "You can pray all you like in the chapel at Lavenham. There is no need for a more distant cloistering." The corners of her mouth turned vaguely upward, but the smile was feeble. "You must stay with me. Think of how much I need your comfort and companionship now. My oldest friend. My dearest sister." She pulled Juliana's hands to her breast and looked at Eleanor. "Sir Geoffrey may have murdered Henry, but he was a good husband to me as he was a good father to Juliana. I shall not marry another but will remain a widow for the rest of my days." She reached out to touch Juliana's face. "Hear me, my sweet friend, for I share your desire to remain unmarried! I swear to take mantle and ring in front of the bishop with a vow of chastity for the remainder of my life. Thus you need not marry either, don't you see? You can stay and give me consolation. We can give each other succor in our prayers, two sisters bound in grief." Isabelle tugged at Juliana's robe and laughed, but the sound held little mirth.

As gently as she could, Juliana pushed her hands away, walked to Eleanor and knelt in front of her. "I still beg admission to Tyndal as an anchoress, my lady," she said, her voice muted but her words firmly spoken.

"No!" Isabelle screamed. "You cannot do this. There is no need!"

"Hush, Isabelle," Juliana said.

Isabelle threw herself down on the rush-covered floor and crawled to the kneeling woman. She wrapped her arms around her stepdaughter's legs and pressed her head into the back of Juliana's thighs. "Don't you see that God has answered both our prayers?" Her voice was muffled and hoarse. "When I married your father, I knew he was an old man and must soon die. His death now, however, is surely a sign from God! As a widow, I have enough income from my lands for both of us to live in peace and comfort. George will not force you to marry Robert nor anyone you do not fancy. God surely means for the two of us to live, as we have…"

Tears began to flow down Juliana's cheeks. "It is you who does not understand, Isabelle. I do not want to share a life with you. My calling to become an anchoress is a true one."

"You cannot leave me! I will not be left alone again!" As Isabelle struggled to her knees, she grabbed the front of her robe, ripping the fabric of her dress from neck to waist and clawing deep ridges into her chest. Blood quickly filled the wounds and flowed down her body in crooked rivulets.

Eleanor and Juliana stared at her in shock.

"See how you have slashed my heart!" the widow screamed as she smeared the blood across her breasts. "You say that I am the one who does not understand, but you are the one who is blind! You have lost one mother to the tomb, but God has torn two mothers from my arms. *Two*! Then He cut the sweet babe from my womb, a child who might have had my mother's eyes to look on me again with love. Indeed, God has stolen from me everything that I have dearly loved. Now, surely, He can leave me one sister for warm and loving comfort?"

Juliana paled, then jumped to her feet and stepped away from the bleeding woman.

Isabelle stared at her stepdaughter with mute despair. Then she began tearing at her own face.

Eleanor rushed forward and grabbed her hands as the woman tried to claw her eyes. "Juliana," she cried as she wrestled with Isabelle. "Bring Sister Anne. Quickly!"

Chapter Thirty-Four

Eleanor sat in silence, unable to form thoughts. The memory of the writhing, screaming widow flooded all words from her mind. Perhaps it had taken only a short while to restrain Isabelle so Sister Anne could force a drink of sleep-inducing poppy juice down her throat, but it had seemed to take forever.

"I pity her, my lady. Few among us have been faced as often as she with the choice between two equally evil paths and no other."

Eleanor looked at Juliana, but she was still seeing the whimpering Isabelle with her exposed flesh and raw soul bleeding from more wounds than she could count. She had felt inadequate to deal with such pain and knew how thoroughly she had failed in comforting the woman. Perhaps Isabelle had been right about her. Perhaps she had fled from the world because she was unable to face its harshest realities. "Aye," she said wearily. "She has suffered much."

"I knew of the rape." Juliana's eyes were moist with unwept tears.

"As did I, but only after your brother's murder."

"She told me that she was pregnant by Henry."

"And that she told me as well."

Despite the chill air, drops of sweat began to glisten on Juliana's forehead. "It was then she told me she would marry my father, not my brother."

"A sin to have intercourse with both son and father, however unwilling her sexual act with the former. Even if God were to forgive that, man's law would still find any marriage with your father invalid as a consequence of the rape." Eleanor inwardly cringed at the sound of her own voice. Her words were so cold, so pale, against the bloody backdrop of Isabelle's searing agony. "How did you reply to what she told you?"

"I told her she must marry Henry, that there was no other choice. If she did marry him there would be no shame in a birth soon after the vows for we had all long expected them to marry. To bed my father, however, would not only make him an unwitting sinner and she a witting one, but it would be a cruelty to so use and deceive a man who had been as kind to her as if she had been his own daughter."

"To be abused by Henry and then marry him, knowing that she now owed him the marriage debt for the rest of their lives together? Could you have so willingly shared a bed with the man who had raped you, then borne his children and supported him as a wife must do?"

Juliana sharply turned her face away. "What choice had she? Common wisdom tells us that she could not have been raped because she quickened with child and thus she must have taken pleasure in the act." Returning her gaze to meet Eleanor's, her brown eyes turned as dark as a moonless night. "I may not concur with common wisdom, my lady, but I repeat: What choice had she in fact? A man may make as many bastards as he wishes and take them all to his wife to rear, but a woman is a whore who has but one, unless she marries the father."

"From the anger I hear in your voice, Juliana, I wonder that you advised her to do something you found as abhorrent as she."

Juliana walked over to the pitcher and poured some wine into her cup but stared at the contents without drinking. The sweat on her forehead was now running down her cheeks like tears. "You are most observant to detect the serpent wrapped around my heart. In truth, I did tell Isabelle that she had no choice, but did not do so until after I told her that there were ways of getting rid of the child and that I would help her find a safe remedy."

Eleanor hesitated, then replied in a quiet voice. "A sin for cert."

The weak smile on Juliana's lips was at odds with the terror Eleanor could see in her eyes.

"And her response to your suggestion?"

"She refused."

Eleanor nodded and sipped at her own wine, more to gain time to think than from any wish for it. "Then you are innocent of a graver act," she said at last. Juliana's head was bowed and she could learn nothing from her look. "Did she say why she refused?"

Juliana's laugh sounded brittle, but the terror had receded from her eyes. "She hated the father but love quickened for the babe."

This matched what Isabelle had told her before. "Did she tell Henry about the child?"

"No, but when Sir Geoffrey claimed he was the father of Isabelle's baby, Henry suspected the truth. My brother may have suffered from many faults, but simple he was not. He was quite able to count both days and months."

Faults he had indeed, but Juliana's words reminded Eleanor that there was another issue that troubled. "I must say I was surprised," she said softly, "that Henry took her with such force. He had every reason to believe they would wed in good time, although no formal betrothal had taken place. Did she tell you why Henry had attacked her?"

Some men might rape a whore they had bought or some other man's woman as an act of humiliation, but she did not believe they would ever ravish the one they cherished. Although Henry had been thoughtless, a willful and often selfish man, Eleanor did not remember him as a brutal youth. She could certainly imagine him beseeching Isabelle, like the whining puppy of her father's description, but Eleanor had always thought that Henry wanted Isabelle as his companion in life as well as a playfellow in bed.

"I asked. She replied with a laugh." Juliana rubbed her cup as if to polish it, then took a deep drink of the wine. "In the summer we all spent together, did you ever see her behave as she did the night my father mocked my brother?"

The change in direction with that question surprised Eleanor, but she had been quite taken aback at Isabelle's wantonness during that dinner. Running a hand so shamelessly up Robert's thigh was not the gesture of a faithful or happy wife, nor was it something Isabelle would have done that innocent summer so many years ago. She shook her head.

"After she lost the babe, her manner with other men became quite immodest, and I warned her that her actions promised more than she might be willing to give to the men who watched her. She told me what she told my father, that she meant nothing by it. I fear I doubted that sometimes, although not as much as did my father."

Eleanor did not like the thought that just came to mind. Could Isabelle have used Henry? Was such a thing possible? Yet if it were, why? Why would any woman encourage a sexual attack? "Did she perhaps explain the choice of your father as her husband?"

"Out of gratitude, she said. She owed her lands to our family for the comfort we had given her. She had only entered her fourth winter when her parents died. The day she came to us, my mother told me that I must treat her with the gentleness and affection any sister owes another for she was a most solemn child. Indeed, my task was a happy one because I quickly learned to love her, and she soon gained a merrier manner. Our family became her own. She had little choice if she wished to stay with us. If she would not marry Henry, she must marry my father."

"What of George? Surely she could have married him."

"He was already betrothed to a woman who died after Isabelle married my father."

Were all the Lavenhams so cursed with such ill fortune, Eleanor wondered. "Yet this marriage dishonored your father and caused him to sin most deeply, however unwittingly. You were grieved, yet you did not tell him that his own son was the father of the babe Isabelle carried?"

Juliana fell to her knees and began to weep, her sobs so sharp and gasping that Eleanor ran to her friend. Juliana pushed her back with one hand.

"Stay back, my lady! There is a snake that lies in my breast, its fangs dripping with a venom that will send you to Hell should it bite you."

Eleanor stepped back, making the sign of the cross as she did. "Shall I bring Brother Thomas to you, my child?"

"Nay, my lady. Nay." Then the sobbing slowed and Juliana rose, wiping the tears from her swollen face. Turning her back on the prioress, she walked over to the window and looked down into the open ward. The sun was shining with winter pallor. In the background, there was the sound of the slow dripping of melting ice. It punctuated the long silence between them.

Eleanor waited.

"Do you love your father, my lady?"

"Aye."

"If you had a sister, would you not love her as well?"

"Such love is precious in God's sight."

Juliana turned, and her eyes narrowed with pain as she looked at the prioress. "Is it?"

"Teach me your meaning."

"I have not yet confessed this, but you must hear it from me first for it is at Tyndal where I long to entomb myself." She took a deep breath. "When I offered to help Isabelle destroy the child within her, I first heard the hiss of Eden's snake. When I failed to tell my father that he was committing a sin by marrying the woman I called *sister*, I saw the snake approach."

"God is merciful to the penitent, and both these sins He will forgive. Isabelle did not take your advice about the child, and your father would probably have refused to believe you just as he did when Henry tried to tell him enough of the truth. But you asked about love? What do you mean?"

"When Adam and Eve were in Eden, they were at peace with God in their innocence. Satan rejoiced with the closing of those garden gates, for man became corruptible, sinful, and cruel. That I understood, yet in my willful ignorance, I believed I could remain pure because I wished no man ill but felt only love for those around me. Even when I wrestled Henry to the ground and cuffed his ears, I injured only his pride. Indeed, I loved my brother, although I despised his petty meanness."

"In childhood fights, there is little sin. Again, God has surely forgiven…"

"God has shown me that no mortal love is without its corruption. When I told Isabelle that she could rid herself of the child, I did so out of love because I did not want her to suffer further for a violent act she had already endured. Do you not see? Out of the love I bore her, I urged her to sin." Juliana stopped, her eyes growing wide.

"Yet she did not do so. Thus you sinned only in making the suggestion. Once she told you that she cherished the child, you did not urge her further."

"Out of love, I failed to tell my father about the sin he would commit. Oh, I gave him reasons he should not marry her, but they were weak and he mocked them readily enough." Juliana's voice began to rise, her tone pleading. "He had suffered so after the death of my mother, my lady. How could I take that little joy from his eyes by telling him the real reason he could not marry Isabelle?"

"Juliana, these are not faults that a loving God would not forgive…"

"Will He forgive me for murdering my brother?"

Eleanor blinked in horror. Had she been wrong after all? Had she been so misguided by a proud and frail logic that she had forced an innocent man to wrongly confess, even die, to protect a daughter he loved? "Your father admitted…"

"My lord father did kill my brother, my lady, but it was I that sent Henry to his death."

Chapter Thirty-Five

As Eleanor held the weeping woman, she raised her eyes, looked out the window encased by dark stone at the lighter gray of God's heaven, and prayed for the wisdom she lacked. "Tell me the tale. In doing so, we will both wrest the serpent from your heart."

For just an instant, Juliana pulled the prioress closer, then released her and moved away from the comfort of a friend's arms. "It will take more than the telling to kill Satan's beast, my lady."

"It is a beginning."

Juliana's smile resembled the look of one in extreme pain who had just realized she would soon die. "As you heard, my father and Isabelle did not share a bed when she had her monthly courses. He found such womanly things distasteful, but he began to fear that his wife would use such absence to invite other men into their barren bed."

"Did he have reason or were his fears born only of jealousy?"

"I have much to tell, my lady."

Eleanor nodded and fell silent.

"While we were out on that tragic morning ride, Isabelle told me that although her courses had come early, they had been quite light, ceasing much before their time. Indeed, she suggested that her womb might have quickened. When I asked if she had told my lord father the happy news, she laughed and said she would in good time. She wished to wait until certain, but made me promise to say nothing until she gave permission. In the meantime, she said, she would enjoy a night or two quite alone since he believed her to be bleeding still."

"Then your father was not as impotent as she claimed?"

"I found her quickening quite miraculous."

"Such has happened."

Juliana shook her head with a deep sadness. "Indeed I knew that my father sometimes did spend sleepless nights watching in the shadows to see if other men came to their marital chamber. Isabelle had seen him once or twice and told me so. Thus I tried to assure him of her innocence, claiming that I often came early and stayed with her on such nights to keep her company. Nonetheless, I began to share my father's fear. She displayed her charms more, and much more than was seemly."

"Did she truly do so often?" Eleanor asked, thinking of the young woman who had ordered suitors to sing of their passions in the tradition of courtly love and the girl who, with the innocence of youth, had chosen only to dance with her sister, Juliana.

"In the early days of their marriage, she had done no more than play at it, my lady. Indeed, she spent much time weeping in my arms over her lost babe. Oft we prayed together to bring her husband virility just once so she could have a child. I do believe she longed less for pleasure in the marital bed than for a baby girl with her mother's eyes. Yet as her prayers continued to go unanswered, I began to suspect that she would lure some man into her bed so she might conceive once again. Her humors were growing quite unbalanced with her sorrow."

Eleanor shuddered with a sudden chill of suspicion. "The night Henry died..."

Juliana struck her fist on the bench. "I was enraged! He had treated Isabelle cruelly that day, and I longed to see him punished. I suspected my father believed she had lied about her courses, as did I, and would be waiting in the corridor outside their chambers. It was then I decided how Henry should suffer for his actions." She stared at her clenched fist with horror, then peeled it open with her other hand as if it had frozen in place. "I asked him to meet me in the chapel, and I told him that Isabelle had succumbed to his pleas and would be waiting for him. He thought my father was sleeping in the barracks."

Eleanor felt almost dizzy from her racing thoughts. Once again, she felt utterly inadequate to the task. If only her Aunt Beatrice were here to advise her, but she was not. "And thus you believe you sent him to his death?"

The groan that came from Juliana's lips was as hopeless as that of a soul facing the fires of Hell. "I meant only for my father to give him the beating he deserved, my lady! I did not mean him to die!"

Eleanor reached out and took her friend's arm. "Again I will say it! You did not kill your brother. Your father did and with him lies the ultimate guilt. Juliana, you need only confess…"

"Confess I shall, but I will no longer live in this world!"

"Give yourself to God and enter a convent then. Your soul will find peace."

"I must say more, my lady."

How could there be, Eleanor asked herself, but the chill that had run through her body now settled in her heart.

"Isabelle did seem to have hope that she might conceive, and my father could not have been the one to give her that joy."

The chill now froze Eleanor. "A man? She had seduced…"

"After what I saw at dinner that night, I did wonder if she expected your brother to share her bed that night, my lady."

⨳ ⨳ ⨳

Eleanor stood at the window and watched as a solitary bird flew past. In such a moment, she felt alone, so utterly alone. "And he did come, did he not?"

Juliana said nothing. Then she rose and walked over to the prioress, standing so close that Eleanor could smell the sweet scent of her body. "Your brother is a man like all other men, my lady, but I believe he meant no ill."

"The man who was to be your husband came to your step-mother's bed and you say he meant no ill?"

"And so she may have hoped, but I do not know with certainty that your brother was complicit in her sinful desire that night." She touched Eleanor gently on the arm. "Since Isabelle suspected when my father usually began his vigils, she would certainly have told Robert when to come and leave to avoid discovery. For this reason, I think his presence in the hall must have been by chance."

Or not, Eleanor thought sadly. She had tried so hard to believe her brother innocent of adultery, but she could no longer ignore the evidence suggesting otherwise. "But it was Henry who came first."

"When I heard the commotion in the hall, I waited, then left my room expecting to see my father with Henry. Instead, I saw the outline of another man and recognized the shape and size to be that of your brother. Coward that I am, I retreated to my room and prayed that my wicked plot would not bring my father's blows upon Robert."

"If he was coming to cuckold your father, he would have deserved such. How could you have borne such a thing, Juliana? He was to be your husband!"

Juliana shrugged. "In my heart, I believe him to be innocent for Robert is an honorable man, my lady." The light was stronger now and, with eyes shut, she stood in the middle of the sunbeam that poured into the room with a warmth they had all forgotten in the snow-filled days. She turned to the prioress, her eyes as sad as those of Mary Magdalene at the sepulchre. "Do you know how jealous Henry was of the sisterly closeness I had with Isabelle? That jealousy was the only reason he sided with me over my wish to leave the world and take holy vows. Then he tried to taint the love with slander. When our families decided your brother and I should marry, he told Robert that he would have no joy of me in the marital bed unless his tastes ran more to boys. Your brother was chivalrous and defended me."

"As he should, Juliana," Eleanor said. She might never know if her brother had lied about the reason he had been in that hall at such an inauspicious time. Indeed, the love she bore him demanded that she honor his private frailties; thus she would never ask him, although there was one person she might…

"For Robert's courtesy, he and Henry quarreled. For that decency, I honor your brother, and because of that integrity, I also realized I could not marry him. A good man deserves a wife who will take delight in his body and long to bear his children. In His grace, God cut from my heart any wish for a husband or children."

"Many share that feeling, but would it not be a kindness to stay in the world and give comfort to Isabelle?"

Juliana sadly shook her head. "It would be as much a lie as if I were to marry Robert. I cannot be a comfort to Isabelle who tried to sell her soul and that of my father. What love we might have borne for each other is now as sour as milk left in hot sun for me. There can be no joy for us together any longer."

"You might bring her to a greater peace with God."

"Could you bring serenity to one for whom you bore a flawed love?" Once again, Juliana's eyes turned black.

Eleanor realized that the groan she heard was her own. How often had she wished to brighten Brother Thomas' dark moods to no avail? "A hard question, but I confess it is a fair one," she replied.

There was silence between them.

"Why did you confess to Henry's murder?" Eleanor asked.

"I had led him to it, and I thought it would have been better for me to hang than my father."

Eleanor was outraged. "So you would not take your own life but would make use of the hangman to do the deed for you?"

"Nay! I confess to the desire for self-murder, but it was your priest that stopped me, my lady. As I stood on the parapet of your father's castle, I thought to throw myself from the stone walkway." Juliana's eyes grew glazed. "Do you understand? For an instant of pain, I might have destroyed a lifetime of anguish."

"For an instant of pain, you'd have gained an eternity of anguish."

Juliana leaned against the prioress as if all her strength had vanished. "Take me, my lady, for I am so very weary of the world. Sometimes I fear I am the greatest sinner on this earth. Sometimes I know I am not. I beg you to allow me the peace of a hut in the forest where God can give me the understanding and solace I need."

Eleanor hugged her. "If you seek to understand love, He will teach you," she said with a hopeful tone, for indeed she sought such understanding herself. "But why ask to be an anchoress? Why not come to Tyndal and join the community of nuns?"

"I long for a life so silent that even I will be able to hear whatever wisdom God may grant me. The voices of other nuns, no matter how sweet their prayers and songs, would be like a roar in my ears, preventing me from hearing His precious words." For a moment, she fell silent. "Do you fear that my calling is only for the moment, that my wish to leave the world is based only on sins God would forgive, as you rightly noted?"

"Not to question would be an injustice to you and to God."

"Never have I desired marriage, my lady. Once I was consumed with lust, then had it quenched."

"You might feel the same again, then wish for marriage."

Juliana smiled. "It was a youthful folly, my lady, a burning in the loins, quickly slaked and never to be repeated. Indeed, I have long wondered if God meant me for the chaste life, but I felt no calling. It was after Isabelle married my father that He began to send me signs pointing in that direction. Of course He would forgive those sins I have confessed to you, but He meant me to see how deeply corrupted my soul was. I thought my love for Isabelle and for my father was innocent. Innocent? It was befouled with sinful ignorance, and I began to realize I knew nothing of what love meant."

"But to turn away from all human comfort and support?"

"I spent more time in prayer, but the sound of other voices dragged my thoughts back down to earth. Isabelle called out to me, clinging, and needing my comfort. My father found solace in whatever silly distractions I provided for him."

"All this is good in God's eyes."

"I found no peace. Where was the silence I needed to hear God's wisdom? I longed to understand so much, but the wailing of the world kept me from my desire. Slowly God began to reveal to me that I must escape from all human kind. By the time we came to Wynethorpe Castle, I knew I should. When I led my brother to his death, I knew it without doubt. I must not remain in the world. It is God's will that I be entombed at Tyndal, my lady, and I must obey."

"Why Tyndal?"

Juliana looked up, her eyes darkly luminous. "Because God has directed me there. I had a dream. A light brighter than the sun at noon awakened me, and, from that light, a voice rang forth with the sweetness of church bells on a summer morning. It told me that I should find my abode where lived a young priest with red-gold hair. That very next day, I looked down into the inner ward of Wynethorpe and saw Brother Thomas. As I watched him walking from the chapel, his cowl slipped and I saw his hair. Then I knew the dream had been a sign. Tyndal was to be my home."

Eleanor flinched. For just a moment, she found herself wondering with unaccustomed spite if the dream might have come after seeing Brother Thomas rather than before. She shook the malice from her heart. Such jealousy was reprehensible. Hadn't her priest taken vows to reject worldly lust, as she had herself, and wasn't Juliana asking to do the same? Juliana could not be a rival for the monk's affections. Indeed, she was begging to separate herself from all men. Eleanor shut her eyes tightly. Ignoble thoughts, she said to herself.

"You have visions then?" Eleanor asked in a steady tone. The changing color of her friend's eyes from brown to coal black made her feel uneasy.

"Visions or dreams, my lady. Do they not both come from the soul and hopefully from God?"

"You know you must still ask your brother's permission. I cannot accept you without George's blessing."

"He will give it."

"If so and the bishop gives his approval, then shall I. You will have your sanctuary at Tyndal, Juliana. I pray it brings you peace."

Chapter Thirty-Six

Sister Anne bent over the shivering woman. "Do you need another blanket, my lady?" she asked gently.

Isabelle drew her knees up toward her chin and continued to stare. Her eyes did not blink.

"May I call Brother Thomas to bring you comfort?"

The woman's only response was a broken cackle.

Sister Anne stood up, beckoned to Isabelle's maid to keep watch over her mistress, and walked out of the room. Just outside the door, Brother Thomas was standing, head bowed in thought.

"She'll have none of you, brother."

"If not, perhaps she will see me?" Eleanor asked, as she emerged from the stairwell, then shook her head. "Indeed she will whether or not she wishes it," she said and walked into Isabelle's room, slamming the heavy door behind her. Thomas and Anne looked at each other and shuddered. There was something in the tone of their prioress' voice that neither of them had ever heard before.

❦ ❦ ❦

The maid having been dismissed, Eleanor sat next to Isabelle. The widow's eyes were closed. Her arms hugged her knees close to her body. Blood still stained her hands and fingernails.

"Isabelle?"

"Go away."

"I think not. You need to hear what I have to tell you."

"You? What could you possibly have to tell me?" The widow snorted. "Bloodless, unsexed thing that you are."

"Unsexed? Bloodless? Not long ago you were accusing me of everything but playing mare to George's stallion. I shall lay that aside, however. What I have to tell you has little to do with sex or love, yet all to do with fear and hate."

Isabelle blinked, her face grew mottled.

"You did not kill him you know."

Isabelle put one stained hand over her mouth.

"You wanted to, but the sin was in your heart, not in your deed."

"How did you know…"

"Henry's corpse spoke well enough. When you opened your door, you knew it was not your husband. He had been safely banished to the barracks and your maid sent off to sleep elsewhere as well. You had hoped that Robert would come to your room and thought it was he. Were you horrified to see Henry? Did he whisper at your door, disguising his voice?"

Isabelle lowered her hand and stared at Eleanor, then gave her an almost imperceptible nod.

"Tell me where I err. He grabbed you? You clawed at his face? Did you then twist away from him? Somehow you got that knife. A small woman's knife. And you stabbed him. All you could think about was the time he had raped you." Eleanor hesitated. Was she right in this or was she about to make a horrible situation worse? She swallowed and continued. "Or was it you who seduced him and drove him wild with lust until he took you and gave you the child you could use to marry his father? Did you stab him to protect your honor or did you want to silence him…"

Isabelle sat up, then spat at Eleanor. "How dare you say I willingly enticed Henry to couple with me! I loathed him more than any imp of Satan." A light now danced wildly in her eyes. "Yes, I thought it was your precious brother at the door. At dinner, my hand invited him and his cock most willingly accepted."

Eleanor felt the heat of rage flood her face but willed herself to say nothing.

Isabelle then shut her eyes and her color paled. "When I opened the door and saw Henry's face, his lust and anger twisting his piggish features, I drew back, but he grabbed me. I clawed at him, but he forced me against the wall. On the chest next to me was the knife I used at dinner. I grabbed it, then struck at his face, his neck, anything I could reach. He drew back at my assault, and it was then I struck him in the side."

Eleanor bent over and touched the trembling woman on her arm. "You believed you had killed him."

"He fell backwards. I must have fainted. When my eyes opened, my husband was standing over me. I was lying naked in my bed and he was wiping Henry's blood from my body. My husband then threw a robe at me and told me to go to the door, that I should scream but not until he had escaped back toward the tower."

"Henry's body was outside in the corridor."

"Aye, and then I heard a sound from the stairwell just as my husband disappeared into the shadows. I shut the door and, when I opened it again, Robert was bent over Henry's body, his hand upon the corpse to check for life and wound. For cert I knew not what to do. When your brother saw me, he stood, his hand red with Henry's blood, and gestured for the candle I held to light the hallway torch. I gave it to him, then screamed." Her voice rose hysterically. "My nightmare had come true. I would be accused of Henry's death. I knew I would be hanged…"

Eleanor shook her. "Your dream did not come true."

Isabelle blinked, then continued as if unaware of what she just said. "I screamed. I did as my husband had bidden me. I did not know otherwise. It was then the corridor filled and the guards came and Robert stood accused of the deed I had done."

"A deed your husband had done, Isabelle. You may have stabbed Henry in the side, but it was your husband who gave him the fatal blow in the back."

"If you know what I did, how many more…"

"I tell you that your husband did kill his own son to protect you, and you are still most worried about yourself?" Eleanor could not keep the contempt from her voice. "Fear not. As you heard, Sir Geoffrey took full blame for the murder. Indeed, he loved you very much to have done so. He remained silent about what you might have done, and anything said in confession is cast into eternal silence. It is the corpse that suggested what you did, a corpse soon to be buried."

"And my guilt?"

"Is between you and God. Your act might be construed as defense of your honor…"

Isabelle snorted and grabbed Eleanor's hand. Her eyes were dry as sand. "Honor? What honor had I when I showed myself naked at my chamber door in hopes of enticing Robert into my bed? What honor have I left when I whored after your brother to gain a child I will now never have?"

"I meant the rape."

"Rape? What about the rape of my heart, the ripping away of each meager tenderness I have had from this world?" Tears over-flowed down Isabelle's cheeks like a flooding stream. "Mother, babe, and now sister have abandoned me!"

"And your husband, Isabelle? Sir Geoffrey gave you the ten-derness of a father when he took you into his household. Then he married you, as you wished, even though it was a sin. How could you wish to cuckold him, and do you not grieve his loss? I do not understand…"

"Grieve? One can only weep so long over a corpse. He died when his first wife did! And all I wanted was to give my husband the child he could never father himself. Wasn't that a kindness? He had my lands. He could share *my* child." She howled with pain. "But what can you understand about love? When I spoke of you and George, I was mocking you, Prioress. There were no such tales about the two of you. You would never play such lusty games. You are a leech that bled yourself of life and longs only to bleed others, like George who may have loved you. Had Juliana married Robert, she might have kept her womanly nature and remained near to warm me with it, but she chose to follow your example and become just as bloodless as you." Then she wailed, "Where is the sin in wanting a mother's love, a child's smile, a sister's comfort? Where?"

Eleanor looked down at the long scratch on her hand where Isabelle's nails had dug into her. The white welt was beginning to fill with blood. What more could she say to this woman who was going mad with grief over loves she had lost and would never find again? The prioress wanted to weep for the woman but found she had no tears left. There was much more she wanted to know but found herself bereft of the words to ask the questions. She shut her eyes as if in prayer, but knew that this was one time she had no idea what to say to God.

Chapter Thirty-Seven

"I owe you my life, brother." Robert stood by as Thomas mounted his horse.

"Nay, Robert. Thank your nephew and your sister instead. Richard had the courage to speak the truth about a grown man who was his grandfather's dear friend. Not many children could do that. And it was your sister's idea that I announce, in front of Sir Geoffrey, that Father Anselm had seen the Lady Isabelle kill Henry. Sir Geoffrey was not the sort of man who could let an innocent person take the blame for a murder he had himself committed. Your father and sister agreed on that. Indeed it seems it was always Sir Geoffrey's hope that no one would ever be accused of the crime."

"I was and might have hanged for it."

"Had you faced the hangman's noose, your own obstinacy might have been more to blame than any other reason, my friend."

"How could you say that any Wynethorpe was stubborn?" Robert grinned up at the monk. "I cannot imagine how you came to that conclusion."

Thomas bent down and loudly whispered, "Your sister is my prioress."

Robert laughed, then grew silent as he stroked the horse's neck and glanced at Eleanor, who sat easily on her gray donkey, apart from the rest of them, in close conversation with their father.

Thomas waited for him to say more but realized that any secrets this man had been willing to die to keep would not be willingly spoken now. Finally, he put his hand on Robert's shoulder and quietly asked: "It is of no moment, my friend, but humor me and explain why you thought your betrothed had killed her brother?"

"Why do you think I did?"

Thomas smiled as he patted Robert' shoulder, then withdrew his hand. "You were protecting someone. The story of the voices did not ring true. You first said that you thought they might have belonged to two lovers, then claimed you did not know if one voice was that of a woman. Or, indeed, whether you had heard any voices at all. The failure to see anyone in the corridor, although you may have just heard the voices was a little strange, especially for a man who is sharp enough of sight to be out safely hunting when the sun is but a promise in the sky. Still, the most telling sign to me was your failure to look either of us in the eye when you told untruths. You are not a practiced liar, Robert."

"Clever, you are, Thomas, and quite right. After I got to the top of the stairs, I saw Juliana further down in the passageway. As you remembered, my eyes are keener than most in the dark. I saw the body on the floor. I did not stumble, as I told you, but got blood on my hands from touching Henry's corpse to see if he was alive. And the dagger I found was not a man's weapon. It was small, a woman's knife."

"The Lady Isabelle…"

"…came out as I said, with candle in hand. By then, Juliana had disappeared. At the time, I did not think it strange that the Lady Isabelle was so calm as she let me light the rushes, only to scream when she saw me bend over the body and pick up the knife. My only concern was to protect Juliana. George had told me how Henry had tormented her in recent months. Indeed, he had made crude remarks to me about her as well." Robert shrugged. "The precise reason I know not. Perhaps he was jealous. I do think their father had greater love for Juliana, and you heard yourself how he spoke to Henry. Whatever the cause, I thought Henry had met his sister in the dark hall, attacked her, and perhaps she had stabbed him in the struggle."

"And allowed her stepmother to call forth witnesses while you held the dagger with your hands stained with Henry's blood? Did you not wonder why she did not quickly come to your defense?"

Robert shrugged. "I did doubt my conclusions for a time, then wondered if perhaps her stepmother had heard their argument and had done the deed to save her. Not knowing what had happened, I still felt honor bound to stay silent for the protection of both women." His face flushed with embarrassment. "In truth, Thomas, I do not always understand the minds of women. I deal better with oxen, sheep, and the occasional goat."

Thomas smiled. "Juliana did claim she had killed her brother later, but it was Isabelle who seemed to deflect the evidence of guilt on to you in the beginning." He nodded toward where Isabelle stood. "You could hate her for that."

"Why, brother? Are we not to forgive those who trespass against us? I am not swinging with cracked neck from a hangman's noose, and the Lady Isabelle has lost a good husband. I think she will suffer greater pain than I and has certainly lost far more."

Indeed, Thomas thought, Robert would have made a fine monk, had the man chosen such a calling. Such he had not, however, and the monastic life did not tempt him. Briefly Thomas wondered if Robert had been in the hall the night of Henry's murder on his way to seek his father's counsel, as he claimed, or had succumbed to the temptation of Isabelle's bed. Just as quickly he dismissed the question. The answer no longer mattered. "You are a better man than I," he said aloud, "and one who deserves a fine wife. Will you now grieve over your lost love?"

"As I said to you some days ago," Robert said, his voice sad, "Juliana and I were suited, but neither of us, it seems, felt any passion for the union. I told her she was free to pursue her vocation and wished her well in it. My father agreed." Robert laughed. "Although he did grind his teeth over the loss of lands."

"I will miss your wit."

"And I yours. I have not forgotten, however, that you owe me for your insults against my former betrothed. Do not think that you will escape the payment in wine and good tales of your past that you promised as amends."

"I promise you wine and to tell you tales, Robert," Thomas said, choosing his words with care.

"Until then, fare thee well, brother, and keep my sister safe. Violence seems to have more fondness for her company than is proper for anyone of either sex." Robert reached up and briefly took Thomas' hand, his grasp gentle but his hand rough to the touch.

Robert was a countryman, Thomas thought, hard on the outside but loyal and loving in his heart. Perhaps he was himself finally growing more tolerant of the country himself, as well as becoming a more docile priest. He looked up at the high, gray sky. Docile indeed. Had he not, after all, gone along with the lie his prioress wished him to tell to bring forth the truth of the murder? Had he not remained silent when he suspected the baron of…? Nay, he said to himself, now was not the time to ponder all that. He'd save such thoughts for the long ride back to Tyndal.

Thomas looked back down at the brother of his prioress and grinned. "I promise to do so to the best of my ability, Robert, but she does follow her own mind about what she does and where she goes."

⟨≈⟩ ⟨≈⟩ ⟨≈⟩

As Robert walked away, Sister Anne, not quite as comfortably settled on her donkey as Thomas was on his horse, looked up at the monk. "You look sad, brother," she said, nodding at the retreating figure. "Will you miss his company so much?"

He smiled, but his eyes now glistened with imminent tears. "I will miss Robert as a friend, sister, but the one I shall regret leaving most is Richard."

Anne reached over and patted Thomas' horse, which was the closest thing to the monk she could touch with any ease.

"And he shall miss you, your fine tales, and your great skills in the breeding of hobbyhorses. But grieve not. I have heard our prioress invite the boy to Tyndal for a visit after the weather warms."

"I look forward to seeing him chase monsters down the halls of the priory." Thomas looked over at the boy, who was standing with his hobbyhorse and talking to a tall soldier who stood next to him. Richard and Thomas had already said their good-byes, and the monk had felt as much reluctance on the boy's part as his to end the hug. "Indeed, it may seem strange for a monk to say this, but I quite love the lad as if he were my own son."

"Not strange at all, brother. His nature is sweet and he has quite won my heart too." For a moment a deep and inexplicable sadness slipped across her face, then she brightened as she continued. "As to exercising his dragon hunting prowess in the halls of Tyndal," she smiled as she pointed to Thomas' head, "he may find you make a fine dragon with all that red hair of yours, although your skills at making hobbyhorses may save your life. The boy will not be parted from the one you gave him, and I am sure he will bring Gringolet with him on his visit. By then, the boy should have many tales of their brave exploits together in the hunting of fantastical beasts."

"Richard is hero enough at Wynethorpe Castle. His fame for exposing a murderer and saving his Uncle Robert has spread from stone wall to wooden gate. He needn't tell tales, only the truth."

"You do sound like a proud father! Nay, blush not, brother. Such a feeling is nothing to feel shame over."

Thomas smiled down at the nun. "I am only a doting uncle, but I have heard how the Lord Hugh does love him and how he brought his son into his family with joy; therefore, I know his real father will feel much pride in his son when he hears of his deeds this winter."

Anne watched as he turned his gaze to the south and, not for the first time, caught herself thinking on what his past had been. She was fond of Thomas and had never pried into the life he'd led before coming to Tyndal, but she worried when dark clouds drifted across his eyes as they did now. If she knew more about him, she thought, perhaps she could offer a comfort she had been unable to give heretofore.

"I cannot help wondering how he could have borne separation from the boy, even knowing he'd be well cared for," he continued.

"I suspect in much the same way you do as you leave him, brother. You must return to your duties to God at Tyndal. The Lord Hugh's duty took him with Prince Edward on crusade. I doubt either of you grieves less at leaving this dear lad."

"Do you not think it odd that a monk should love a child so? I swear I have no desire for one of my own…"

"Are you telling me that you did not beget any children before you came to us?" Anne asked, giving him a teasing but openly appraising look.

"I did not, sister, but I confess it was not for lack of trying." Thomas returned frankness with frankness, then grinned. How grateful he was for the friendship of this forthright nun.

"That, I never doubted!"

"But now…" His eyes turned sad.

"One does not doff love with the donning of a monkish cowl, brother. Sometimes we enter the contemplative life to better understand the many manifestations of that emotion." Anne nodded at the figure of Juliana standing far behind Baron Adam and well apart from everyone with her head bowed. "There stands such a seeker."

"Do you think she will find the object of her search?"

"May we all find what we desire," Anne replied, her pensive gaze resting on the monk.

Thomas looked at the Lady Juliana. As he did, she raised her head and smiled at him. He was startled. Her expression was kind enough, but her eyes were as dark as they had been that day on the parapet when he thought her mad.

Was she? He shifted uneasily in his saddle. Assuming all the secular and religious parties agreed, this woman would be coming to Tyndal, and he would be her confessor as part of his duties to the priory. As he thought about it, he knew that likelihood should have made him more apprehensive than it did. Instead, the prospect was oddly comforting. So Thomas smiled back at Juliana, then continued to study her as she lowered her head and became, once again, a solitary figure standing apart as if waiting patiently for something to happen.

⌘ ⌘ ⌘

As they, too, said their farewells, the baron bent close to his daughter's ear.

"You shock me, daughter," Adam said, his voice low and hoarse.

"I do not condemn, father."

He stood back, arms folded. "You are dedicated to God. How can you not?"

"My vocation does not mean I am less a sinner. As such, I have no right to cast stones."

"You might as well have. You suggest I have committed a very grave sin. Whether or not you condemn me, the Church would surely judge me harshly for it," he retorted. "Thus your accusation is as cruel as the wound of any stone cast."

"Father, I intend no cruelty, and the Church's judgment is what your confessor deems proper penance." Eleanor glanced briefly at the auburn-haired Brother Thomas some distance behind. A sigh escaped her. God might condemn her passion for the monk, but for the loyalty he had shown her family and the love he had given so freely to her nephew, she loved him more. Why was she so cursed? She shook her head and turned back to the baron. "Since I am still in my youth, there are many sins I have not yet been tempted to commit. Others, I have. None of us may say what we will or will not do until we are faced with the choice. If we make hard choices with a good heart, God may perhaps deal more gently with us."

"Something your Aunt Beatrice would say."

"Perhaps, but do you still deny what I have suggested?"

"A hungry dog with a bone, you are!"

"Why is that? Do I not remind you of someone, father?"

"Your mother."

"If you will," Eleanor said, thinking somewhat otherwise. "And how often was she right to pursue a steady course?"

"Often." He looked down, avoiding his daughter's eyes. "Usually."

"Then I am right, am I not? After Sir Geoffrey confessed to Brother Thomas, you came to your old friend, and, in a gesture of mercy, reopened the wound so he would bleed to death. He had neither to face the hangman nor condemn his soul by the taking of his own life. A reopening of the wound would not be uncommon with so grievous an injury. Who would even question such a thing, especially after the distress he suffered when his wife and daughter each confessed to the crime he had committed?"

"Knowing such could happen, why accuse me, or anyone, of deliberately reopening it?"

"Because the rewrapping of the bandages did not quite match Sister Anne's careful work. She knew from the way they were redone that he could not have tied them so with only one hand and it was certainly not how she had done it. You were the last to see Sir Geoffrey and the one who forbade anyone from entering his room, until he would have died." She gazed at her father for a long minute. "Father, remember that I am her prioress to whom she owes allegiance. In truth, she is a loyal friend as well. She spoke only to me about this, and, as you should know, I would never betray you."

Adam turned his face away and said nothing.

"Sir Geoffrey was not an evil man," Eleanor said quietly. "In Satan's quest for souls, he had bound a cloth of green about your dear friend's eyes. All he could see was tinged with jealousy, yet even in his blinded state, he struggled to do the right thing. He tried to save Robert's life at the cost not only of his own life but that of his soul. Perhaps as Sir Geoffrey struck the killing blow at his son, he did so less out of jealousy than out of love for his wife. He may well have deserved punishment for the killing of his son, but your way of sending him to God's judgment may have been the kinder act than the hanging and humiliation he would surely have faced. Who is to say that your way was less just? Men, convicted of crimes, are sent from this world to face God by equally mortal and imperfect men who may err in both judgment and punishment. The only perfect judgment is God's, and, as we speak, Sir Geoffrey is facing both that judgment and His mercy."

Adam looked at his daughter. "I had heard tales at court of your talented leadership of Tyndal, daughter, but I confess I discounted some as exaggerated for the sake of flattery. Now I must say that, had you been born male, your wits might well have found a welcome in the courts of kings. For a woman, your view of justice is quite practical, yet," he said with gentle tone, "it is tinged with a woman's kindness."

"At Amesbury I did learn that God's justice may not always be the same as Man's. I shall not take credit for the wisdom of others."

"If I did commit the act you suggest, what do you think I will suffer for my crime?"

"That is between you and your confessor."

"As you have mentioned confessors, I must tell you that since Father Anselm has been so gravely ill and will not recover for some time…"

"…you found another priest when you felt the need to cleanse your soul of whatever sins were oppressing you. Indeed, Brother Thomas was a good choice for, like all of us who love you, he will take any secrets far from Wynethorpe Castle and bury them at the altar in the priory of Tyndal."

"I appreciate your kindness in allowing me to use him as confessor while he was here. Indeed, I found the compassion of your handsome Brother Thomas formed much in same mold as that of his prioress."

Eleanor felt her face flush. "He has proven himself to be invaluable at Tyndal. I could not replace him."

"So I see, my child," her father retorted, raising one eyebrow.

"Father!"

"I would not dream of casting a stone, my daughter. What I think will be kept hidden away in my heart, buried deep into the profound love and respect I bear you," Baron Adam replied, then he reached over, clasped his daughter's hand in his, and kissed it.

Chapter Thirty-Eight

In good time, Father Anselm did recover, gaining sufficient strength to return to his duties as priest to the soldiers and residents of Wynethorpe Castle, where, it is said, he continued to counsel all and sundry against the eating of meat and the sins of excess bathing. Never again did he chase young boys riding hobbyhorses down dark corridors, although he did mention from time to time that he might have had just the smallest part in solving the mystery of Lord Henry's murder.

Juliana and Isabelle remained as Baron Adam's guests until the road to the Lavenham estates was passable. When the women did at last return to their home, Juliana immediately petitioned the bishop to allow her admission to Tyndal as an anchoress. At the same time she begged her brother, now Sir George of Lavenham, to give both his blessing and financial support so that she might enter Tyndal with honor.

Despite his reluctance to lose a much loved sister to such an austere life, he granted both pleas, and, when his sister was given approval to enter the priory from both Eleanor and the bishop, Sir George sent her off with tears and a generous dowry. Included with his gifts was a letter in which he sent most courteous and quite brotherly affection to Juliana's new prioress, although Eleanor detected just a hint of wistfulness in his words.

Of the Lady Isabelle, little more is recorded, although the bishop's register does show that she, shortly after Juliana left for

Tyndal, formally took the mantle and ring of a vowess, never to marry again.

There was kept amongst the miscellaneous papers of Tyndal, however, a letter from Sir George of Lavenham to the Prioress Eleanor which was written many years after Isabelle took that vow. In it, he told the prioress that Isabelle did indeed still live. After the young widow had taken her vow of chastity, she locked herself into self-imposed imprisonment in a tower room in Sir George's castle. She had since aged much, he wrote with apparent sadness, and was seen only rarely except by the woman who served her. On those occasions when she allowed him to visit her, he noted how bent her back had grown and how her eyes had dulled to a milky blue. She said little when he came, refusing to sit or allow him to do so, and silently gazed out the only window in her room, a window that faced toward Tyndal Priory.

Author's Notes

From the distance of over seven hundred years, we know that 1271 was a relatively tranquil time in England, but for those living through it, peace was not a certainty. The Welsh had agreed to an uneasy truce, but many on the borders were wary about the continuation of that when the prime summer fighting season arrived. The Scots were only temporarily quiescent, and the cause once headed by the long-dead Simon de Montfort was very much alive in the minds of many ranging from the laboring classes to the ruling ones. Minor firefights, internally and on the English borders, always threatened to flare into major conflagrations. At best, any calm was a nervous one.

King Henry III was probably growing senile in the year 1271 and would die late in the following year. His heir was in Acre on a very expensive crusade that almost cost the prince his life. Nonetheless, he would survive the assassination attempt and eventually return to England as King Edward I.

Edward at this time was very much an unknown quantity. He had jumped from one side to the other on the issue of baronial reforms championed by de Montfort with amazing agility. He had demonstrated rather questionable judgment, and his behavior was sometimes irresponsible. Many questioned how competent he would be as king. Whether he would prove able or not, however, everyone knew that the ways and preferences of the new king would not be the same as those of the long-reigning Henry.

In an era of transition, the powerful and ambitious firmly plant one foot on the old path while keeping the other poised to step into whatever fork the new will take. Such times may present the aura of tranquillity, but the lull is often a prelude to chaos. Barons loyal to the monarchial line in these waning years of the old king's reign kept the fragile peace while begging Edward to return home to keep the borders peaceful and avoid any wars of succession or the renewal of the less than civil ones.

The castle in this book may be fictitious, but Wynethorpe is intended to resemble those outposts of secondary note used by the English in their less than successful attempts to gain complete control over the Welsh after the Norman Conquest. With some notable exceptions, the post-Conquest forts were not magnificent structures and cannot be equated to Caernarfon or Harlech that Edward I built with his brilliant architect, Master James of St. George.

These older castles started out in the simpler motte and bailey, timber and earthen style. At some point their wooden walls were replaced with stone, and other modernizations were sporadically attempted over the two hundred years before this story takes place. In addition, some fortifications, especially in the north of Wales, changed hands between the English and the Welsh with some frequency, each group altering the walls and other structures to suit their own needs and tastes. Thus the architecture of some pre-Edwardian forts was a hodgepodge of projects begun, then changed in mid-plan, or never completed.

One role of any castle was military, of course, but that was not always the primary one. Keeping an armed force at the ready was expensive, then as now; thus the number of troops in residence at any given time could be quite small. Castles were also administrative centers where trade was conducted, pleas brought, justice dispensed, and plans made for running a district. They were also family homes.

As grim and formidable as these places may look today, those who grew up within their walls often thought of their castles with much fondness. Gerald of Wales in the twelfth century waxed almost poetic in his descriptions of the orchards and vineyards at Manorbier in Pembrokeshire where he had spent his youth. We might understand this affection with the later and more elaborate castles. They have survived in fair shape with evidence remaining of quite sophisticated comforts such as separated latrines and urinals. Many smaller castles, however, not only suffered the expected destruction of time, they were often dismantled for their stone after their usefulness passed. What remains often looks bleak and crude.

Part of the difficulty in visualizing life within such stark walls lies with the lack of evidence about the internal structures. Buildings inside these smaller castles, such as kitchens, stables or housing for the troops and noble family, were often made of wood and either burned or disintegrated. Few traces are now extant. Nonetheless, there is evidence that attempts were made to provide some creature comfort, at least for those longest in residence.

Although the fictional Baron Adam seems not to have installed such at Wynethorpe, glass windows were fairly cheap and often used at the time of Henry III. (They apparently had a greenish tint.) Castle walls were not just bare, rough stone. They were whitewashed and sometimes painted in colors, both internally and externally. (Henry III showed a fondness for green paint as well as star designs; his wife favored a rose color.) Painted wall hangings served to ameliorate the severity of rooms and kept drafts at bay. Rushes, strewn with scented herbs or flowers and changed with passable frequency, covered the floors of the dining hall.

Since the affluent changed residence often, in part so the castle could get a major cleaning, furnishings were few and designed for ease of transportation. Although simple in overall design, details such as the clasps on chests were often crafted with intricate and stunning workmanship. Just as we take pleasure in our homes, adding a splash of color to brighten a room or a particularly beautiful object to give us special pleasure, those of the medieval period did the same.

Indeed, our ancestors did as we do in so many ways. People of all classes and conditions have always argued with their parents, grieved over the death of a loved one, had marital spats, gossiped, told jokes to a friend and sung while washing up—or simply looked outside on a beautiful day and sighed with unspoken contentment. Records of such mundane things have survived, but these tend not to be studied with the same emphasis as power struggles, major battles, and significant documents. Perhaps this is why we forget that our ancestors were having babies, struggling to make ends meet, getting sick, and falling in love, all while trying to cope with the impact of whatever decisions those in power made—just as we do today. This lost sense of commonality may be one reason we have formed some erroneous assumptions about the way our distant kin behaved or thought.

One such assumption is that medieval children were badly treated, ignored, or, at best, considered nothing more than small adults. In fact, medieval law was very concerned about protecting children, especially orphans, and believed childhood to extend to the age of fourteen. Abuses did occur, of course, and legal protections were often ineffective, especially amongst the poor who have always suffered most from lack of equity under all legal systems.

It is true that a person was deemed capable of what we would call adult behavior (getting married, taking on a business, or being found guilty of a capital crime) at an age we might think rather young. Interestingly enough, many teens coped quite well. For those who did not, the debate about how to handle the sentencing of young felons was as fierce then as now. Although the law allowed fifteen-year-olds to be hanged or burned at the stake, the recorded instances of same are few despite the perceived brutality of the era.

Although we have made significant progress over the last few decades in how we treat children born to parents without a license to have them, those in the medieval period were also quite advanced compared to, say, the Victorians. Illegitimacy was a barrier to some inheritances but not to all, and it did not carry quite the stigmas or limitations which society has sometimes imposed for whatever variety of reasons. In his own time, for instance, William the Conqueror was commonly called William the Bastard, the term having no pejorative intent and nothing whatsoever to do with what others thought of his personality.

A loving and joyful welcome by the family to a son's illegitimate child was not unusual in the thirteenth century. Men could even bring their offspring from extramarital relationships to their wives for rearing, although wives and daughters did not have quite the same right or expectation of cheerful reception. When the inclusion was successful, both sets of children received equal respect and care. Although we could reasonably argue that this practice was unfair both to the innocent spouse and to the birth mother, the practice was an attempt to encourage paternal responsibility.

From the records we have of the elite in particular, these offspring were not only loved but also provided with honorable positions and were respected by others. King John, as one example, may not have been the best of rulers or husbands, but he seems to have been a rather good father. When he gave his illegitimate daughter, Joan, to Prince Llywelyn of Wales as a wife, the Welsh ruler not only seemed rather fond of her, he also considered her quite the marital prize. Some illegitimate sons of kings became bishops, such as Geoffrey Plantagenet, Archbishop of York and son of Henry II, or wealthy and titled, such as Robert, first Earl of Gloucester and son of Henry I.

Of course there were parents who battered or molested their children, but there were just as many that would have done anything for the benefit of their offspring, regardless of gender or disability. Henry III and his wife, Eleanor of Provence, adored their mute three-year-old daughter. When the little girl died, they both fell seriously ill as a consequence of their deep mourning. Serious illnesses, the death of a child, or a miscarriage have always been painful things. No matter how common death or the threat of it might have been, it could never have hurt less to see your child die.

Nor was it less painful then for a child when a mother or father died. With the high mortality of women in childbirth, of men in wars, and everyone due to disease, the luxury of having birth parents throughout childhood was a rare one prior to the medical advances and relatively peaceful period, at least in the West, of the late twentieth century. The most common parental relationship for a child throughout history has been that of step-parent, sometimes a succession of them of both genders. Thus our assumption that children were better off in the good old days before divorce was so easily obtained is an illusion. Such dulcet times are largely mythological. If the two adults handle the situation with maturity, modern day divorce may actually be kinder. At least both parents are alive and often available to the child. Death is never that considerate.

The misconception that medieval children were seen as mini-adults is more amusing than accurate. The impression probably does derive from the few pictorial images we have in which they are dressed in fashions similar to their parents. In fact, dress was very functional in the thirteenth century. Clothing was not cheap nor was it easily kept clean (many did care about this) or repaired. In the late thirteenth century, everyone, including children, wore comparable, practical attire. The nuances of style, appropriate to a gender or age, were minor, sometimes only a matter of robe length, collar width, or who wore the linen drawers. (And all differences were viewed with as much passion and nervousness as they are now.) In fact, we dress our own children much the same way: practically for daily activities and in miniature versions of adult styles for the obligatory family photo. These photographs, which will last longer than the memory of what children wore to playgrounds, do not reflect our view that children are tiny adults any more than it did with our medieval ancestors.

As a final note on medieval children, a favorite plaything for boys was the hobbyhorse. Even Alfred the Great mentioned one. It did not apparently get that name until the mid-1500s, presumably from "hoby" meaning "a small horse." Prior to the 1500s, it was called a stick-horse or just a wooden horse, but I have used the term "hobbyhorse" because that brings an accurate picture to a modern reader's mind more quickly.

Other assumptions about the medieval period involve the status of women. Indeed, the assumption that women were treated as property in the period, especially amongst the upper classes, has some justification in medieval law, although women of all classes exercised much more freedom in the rough and tumble of daily life. Women have rarely had an easy time in any period of history, but practicality has always demanded the reverse of common or legal assumptions in eras with a less than stellar grasp of the wide range of feminine competence. Such was the case during the First and Second World Wars when women took on "men's" civilian jobs. Such was the case in 1271.

The frequently expressed view of medieval women at this time, especially by religious leaders, was that they were "weaker vessels" and incapable of logic or rational thought. Whenever men were called away for commercial reasons or during the frequent wars, however, wives or mothers were quickly put in charge of farms, businesses, castles, and nations. Even contemporary sources noted that they did rather well. Fortunately, most of us are surprised that anyone would think otherwise.

Nonetheless, it is true that medieval law could be hard on a woman. Followers of Galen's medical theories, for instance, believed that a woman must ejaculate "seed," much as a man did, if she was to conceive. (Pregnancy resulted from the union of male and female "seeds.") If she became pregnant, she was presumed to have ejaculated and thus experienced the same kind of orgasmic pleasure as a man. This assumption of pleasure in the act made it very difficult for a woman to claim in a court of law that she had been raped if she conceived as a result of sexual assault. If the rapist was unmarried, she did have the option of marrying him. This was certainly not a happy choice and a woman had the right to reject such a marriage; however, refusal was often not a practical choice in the face of family pressure because of the damage done to the woman's character.

All this may seem both boorish and ignorant to us in the West; however, we shouldn't be too smug about how much wiser we have become. The rate of conviction for rape has changed little in seven hundred years; many continue to question whether a woman didn't really "lead him on" or somehow "ask for it"; and the concept of date or marital rape is beyond the grasp of others to understand. Even modern societies have failed to comprehend what rape means to a woman or to develop adequate measures to prevent it.

Not all medieval laws were harsh for women, however. There is an interesting little clause in the Magna Carta, a document touted as a precursor of modern democracy in some circles. One of the tiny provisions in that charter of 1215 is the prohibition against the king extracting fines from widows who wanted to stay single or remarry someone of their own choosing.

During the reign of King John, upper class widows paid dearly for the privilege of doing either after the death of a husband. The crown grew quite rich with the fines they paid; therefore, the barons probably added this paragraph, not to give women any real choice, but to stop the drain on the baronial wallet. In practice, widows often had few options about what they did with their lives after the death of a spouse either before or after 1215. Nonetheless, this clause did open the door to freer marital choice by widows, a concept that was even respected on occasion.

Since many widows must have been put under pressure to make another marriage lucrative to the family, there was one fairly certain way a widow could retain her independence. This was through the practice called "taking the ring and mantle as a vowess." By taking this single monastic vow of celibacy, a woman gained God as an ally in her decision to remain single and thus comparatively independent, financially as well as legally. This ceremony and vow were not taken lightly in medieval society and took place in front of a bishop. When Henry III's widowed sister, Eleanor, remarried after taking such a vow herself, the question of the validity of that second marriage was brought before the Pope for a decision. The fact that she had conceived de Montfort's child prior to the wedding was of lesser concern in this instance.

Becoming a nun was a common career choice for a medieval woman, either because she had a calling to the religious life or her family decided she would. Not all nuns were strictly sequestered, however, and they were often called back to their secular homes whenever someone in the family fell ill or their services were otherwise needed. In some instances, prioresses also spent much time at court. Just as charities do today, monasteries of all kinds needed money and the court was a good place to get donations of land or other valuable items. Many women, especially those trained in running large households or holdings, opted for the religious life as one way to exercise considerable administrative talent. Despite the general belief that Adam should not be ruled by Eve, there were even a few double houses, with monks and nuns living and working in close proximity, where both genders were overseen by a prioress or abbess. Such an order was the one to which the religious in this story belong, the Order of Fontevraud.

The calling to become an anchoress is less well known. An anchoress (men were called anchorites) was a woman who took a special vow, in addition to the other monastic ones, to remain in one limited locale, apart from the rest of the world. In the earlier years of Christianity, remaining in place meant that a woman, or a man, could live in a specific hut or cave. Later, it often, but not always, meant spending their lives in one room, frequently next to the chapel where they could observe Mass and take Communion through a small hole in the wall. Since an anchoress wished to practice an even more reclusive and austere life than most nuns of the period, her request had to be accepted by the local bishop and the head of the convent to which she was attached. When approved, her reception into her new vocation was called "entombing" to signify her death to the world.

Although they may have wished for a more solitary life, many anchoresses were not, in fact, "dead to the world." Some parents gave daughters as an *oblate* (meaning a gift) to a convent to be raised and educated by an anchoress, who was considered especially wise and holy because of her severe vows. One such *oblate* was Hildegard von Bingen, who was educated and brought up by Jutta, an anchoress at the Benedictine convent of Disibodenberg. Hildegard later left the enclosed cell to become the head of her own convent as well as advisor to both spiritual and secular notables. Many anchoresses did weaving and similar commercial crafts to raise money for their convent. Still others had visitors who came to the open but curtained window in their cells to seek their advice. Julian of Norwich is one example and is mentioned in the autobiography of Margery Kempe, who sought the anchoress' opinion on the verity of her own visions. (Julian's response was quite kind.) Thus an anchoress was not exactly lonely, and servants were usually assigned to take care of her mundane and earthly needs such as the bringing of meals, the washing of clothes, and the removal of the nightly slops.

Bibliography

For those who would like to know more about the life and period involved in this particular book, the following are some of the sources I consulted which may be of interest. As always, I blame any and all errors of fact or interpretation to the demands of fiction, at best, and to my ignorance, at worst.

Ancrene Wisse: Guide for Anchoresses, trans. Hugh White, Penguin, 1993.

John Cummins, *The Hound and the Hawk: The Art of Medieval Hunting*, Phoenix Press, 1988.

Brian K. Davidson, *The Observer's Book of Castles*, Frederick Warne, 1979.

Joseph & Frances Gies, *Life in a Medieval Castle*, Harper & Row, 1974.

P. W. Hammond, *Food and Feast in Medieval England*, Alan Sutton Publishing, 1995.

Julian of Norwich, *Revelations of Divine Love*, trans. by Elizabeth Spearing, Penguin, 1998.

Margaret Wade Labarge, *A Baronial Household of the Thirteenth Century*, Barnes & Noble, 1965.

Henrietta Leyser, *Medieval Women: A Social History of Women in England 450-1500*, St. Martin's Press, 1995.

Nicholas Orme, *Medieval Children*, Yale University Press, 2001.

Sir Maurice Powicke, *The Thirteenth Century: 1216-1307*, Oxford University Press, 1962.

Michael Prestwich, *Edward I*, Yale University Press, 1997.

To receive a free catalog of Poisoned Pen Press titles, please contact us in one of the following ways:

Phone: 1-800-421-3976
Facsimile: 1-480-949-1707
Email: info@poisonedpenpress.com
Website: www.poisonedpenpress.com

Poisoned Pen Press
6962 E. First Ave. Ste 103
Scottsdale, AZ 85251